The House with a Sunken Courtyard

LIBRARY OF KOREAN LITERATURE
6

The House with a Sunken Courtyard

Kim Won-il

Translated by
Suh Ji-moon

DALKEY ARCHIVE PRESS
CHAMPAIGN / LONDON / DUBLIN

Originally published in Korean as *Madang kip'ŭp chin* by Munhak kwa Chisŏngsa, Seoul, 1988

Library of Congress Cataloging-in-Publication Data

Kim, Won-il, 1942-
[Madang kip'un chip. English]
The house with a sunken courtyard / by Kim Won-il ; translated by Suh Ji-moon. -- First edition.
pages cm
"Originally published in Korean as Madang kip'up chin by Munhak kwa Chisongsa, Seoul, 1988"-- Verso title page.
"Published in collaboration with Korea Literature Translation Institute."
ISBN 978-1-56478-913-6 (alk. paper)
1. Families--Fiction. 2. Korean War, 1950-1953--Fiction. 3. War and family--Fiction.. 4. War and society--Fiction. 5. War victims--Fiction. 6. Taegu (Korea)--Fiction.
I. So, Chi-mun, translator. II. Title.
PL992.415.W65M3313 2013
895.7'34--dc23
2013027137

Partially funded by a grant from the Illinois Arts Council, a state agency

Library of Korean Literature
Published in collaboration with the Literature Translation Institute of Korea

LTI Korea
Literature Translation Institute of Korea

www.dalkeyarchive.com

Cover: design and composition by Mikhail Iliatov

Printed on permanent/durable acid-free paper

1

When I finished primary school—with great difficulty because I was also working as a kitchen boy in a pub on the market street of my hometown Jinyeong—my sister Seonrye came to fetch me. Holding on to her skirt, I boarded the train bound for Daegu. What with the severe motion sickness suffered on the train and lack of confidence about facing the life that lay ahead, my figure was exactly that of a pony on the way to market to be sold. I had only bleak visions of the life with Mother that was to unfold from that day. It was late in April, 1954, the year after the armistice was signed following three years of war. As I had been separated from my family since the winter of the year war broke out, it was after more than three years that I was going to live together with my family. Daegu was a strange city to me. When I came to Daegu with my sister, it was already after the middle school entrance exams were over.

Our house was located in Janggwan-dong, bordered on one side by the Medicine Lane in the center of Daegu City and the Jongro Street heavily inhabited by the Chinese population. Well, I suppose I shouldn't say "our house," as it was not owned by my family—we were just renting a very small room in the middle quarter of that residence. Janggwan-dong was a small district of about two hundred and fifty houses, and the street, that stretched for only three hundred meters, was narrow and winding, too narrow for automobile traffic and only wide enough for hand-drawn carts, and was bordered by other administrative districts on either side. Along both sides of the street ran open sewers, so it stank except during the winter, and in the summer pink mosquito larvae swarmed in them. Janggwan-dong was sliced into a diamond shape by the newly paved artery roads of Daegu City. The house that my family was living in as tenants was located halfway down the long road that cuts across Janggwan-dong from north to south, the road that connects the Medicine Lane and the Jongro area. Houses in Janggwan-dong were mostly around 100 square meters with a main wing and two side wings. The house that my family was living in was one of the few exceptionally large and imposing residences in the area and belonged to a wealthy family of old.

From the time I rejoined my family in 1954 after finishing primary school until I finished military service in the mid-1960s at the northernmost post in Yanggu, Gangwon Province, my family continued to live in one rented room after another in and around Janggwan-dong area. We lived in no less than nine rented rooms until my mother was finally able to purchase a house of our own next to the Sangseo Girls' Commercial School, which at the time I came to Daegu was being used as a temporary campus by the Gyeongbuk Boys' High School, whose own campus had been requisitioned by the armed forces for headquarters. In some of the rented rooms we lived for less than a year, and in one we lived for almost three years. So, to distinguish the house we were living in when I rejoined my family in Daegu from the other rented rooms we lived in, we called it "the house with the sunken courtyard." Our reminiscences about that most poverty-stricken and squalid period of our lives were often prefaced by "When we were living in the house with the sunken courtyard . . ."

It seems that we were able to rent a room in that house, even though at that time finding a room for rent was a feat comparable to catching a star, thanks to the acquaintanceship my aunt had with the lady of the house. It was very lucky for us that a family who came for refuge from Seoul early in the war vacated the room and returned to Seoul when the armistice was signed.

Even though the armistice was signed and another year had commenced, there were the headquarters of the Second Corps, the integrated military hospital, the U. S. Eighth Army headquarters, and so forth still stationed in Daegu. Consequently a great many military supply factories were in operation in Daegu, so the town was busy. The main streets of the city were traversed by many men in Western suits and also many young women in Western outfits and high-heeled shoes. Korean and American soldiers in military uniform were common sights as well. On the other hand, one could bump into refugees, bums, street vendors, porters, beggars, or shoeshine boys just as easily as one could kick away a stray stone while walking on an unpaved road. The saying back then went that those with money and 'pull' spent money like water and ate, dressed, and slept like royalty, but those with neither money nor 'pull' could hardly put their stomachs to work once a day. In what was originally Kyodong Market, now dubbed the 'Yankee Market' since the war began and whose scale was now more than a dozen times its original size, many luxurious commodities were traded, but in such street markets as the Chilseong Market, which had commoners for customers, desperate haggling over pennies went on in many dialects.

At such precarious times, there always appear to be extreme social divisions, such that, in hostess-served banqueting houses lined up along the Jongro and Doksandong alleys, lights shone late into the night and songs and live music spilled over into the street. When I joined my family in Daegu, my mother's main source of income was making party outfits for the entertaining women of such establishments. Those houses were so successful that my mother was able to feed her family from the work.

At the time I joined my family in Daegu, my sister Seonrye

was in her third year of middle school, and my younger brother Giljung, who had big blinking eyes that made him look scared and stupid, had just entered primary school. My youngest brother Gilsu, who was born in April of the year the war broke out, and was therefore undernourished when he needed nutrients most, was four years old and had a constantly runny nose. My mother, when she came to our hometown to see me once in a while, complained that it looked like her youngest would end up handicapped. It appeared to me also that Gilsu had a very slim chance of growing up normal. His eyes still could not focus, his limbs were mere skin-and-bone, and he tottered when walking. He was awkward of speech, and that seemed to reflect the slowness of his thinking.

"It's because I can now feed you all that I called you up to Daegu. If I'd left you in Jinyong, you wouldn't have starved but you'd have grown up a servant or a peddler. You are the eldest son of this family. So, how can you become the pillar of our family with only primary school education? And you're not very strong physically, either. You couldn't support yourself by becoming a construction worker or something like that. So you need to get an education. But look, Gilnam, the school year has already begun, so you'll have to just help around the house this year. I'm sorry. I'd have liked to call you up a month earlier and put you in a middle school, but as a matter of fact, I can't afford to pay your tuition this year. So, you'll just have to study hard at home and pass the entrance exam for a good middle school next year. I promise you if you study hard I will give you all the education I can, even if I have to sew until my fingers fall off."

This was what my mother said after she related to me the anecdote about how Mencius's mother moved their abode three times to give her son the best environment for study.

Before the war, while my family was living in Seoul, my mother used to sew not only her own garments but all my and my siblings' garments as well. She was so skillful with her sewing and had such excellent sense of style that when she went out attired in a Korean dress she'd sewed herself, the whole neighborhood complimented her on her craftsmanship. So, even though my father was earning enough money for our livelihood, my mother sometimes gave in to the importuning of her neighbors and sewed Korean traditional garments for them, which served her as a hobby and earned her a little pocket money as well. At that time we had a Singer sewing machine at home. It was a gift from my father to my mother when she was inconsolable after losing her first son, who lived barely a month. At that time, my father, who was a graduate of Masan Commercial High School, was an official of the financial co-op in our hometown Jinyong, so we were rather well-off.

There is a saying in Korea which goes, "women whose fingers are nimble will live by using the thimble." As if to prove the truth of the saying, my family was separated from my father just prior to the recapture of Seoul by the South Korean military. My father defected to the North alone because he had lost contact with us. That turned out to be a permanent separation.

All that autumn we waited and waited for word from my father, watching the war situation anxiously, but had to board the flatcar of the refugee train for the south early in November. We left Seoul almost empty-handed, after living there for two years. After parting from Father, we sold off our household goods one after another to keep ourselves fed, and at last had to sell off that sewing machine, to my mother's unbounded grief. It was with the money from that sewing machine that we could eat rice dumplings on the uncovered refugee train. Taking refuge in our hometown of Jinyong, my mother managed for a while to feed us, but as we had sold off our house and fields and paddies there before moving to Seoul, we had no means of support. On top of that, the police station dispatched detectives to interrogate us about my Communist father's activities in Seoul during the three-month Communist occupation of Seoul and to find out if he'd contacted us after his defection. So my mother left me to work as an errand boy in a tavern in the market street of our hometown and moved to Daegu, where some of her relatives were living, taking all my siblings with her.

After coming to Daegu, Mother had entrusted my siblings to the care of my aunt and worked as a live-in maid for almost two years. At the time she could hardly feed herself and my siblings two meals a day of gruel. Mother always recalled those two years as the hungriest and most miserable time of her life. But she managed to scrape together the money to buy a used sewing machine, and started taking in sewing from the spring of the year before I joined her. Janggwan-dong, located in the middle of the city, was a good spot for attracting such business, and once her skill was known, customers began to queue up. My mother worked at the sewing machine from dawn to midnight, "till her back felt it was breaking in two," as she put it herself, to feed us and send us to school.

For a few days after joining my family in Daegu, I had nothing to do but saunter around the city, leading my youngest sibling by the hand, after my elder sister Seonrye and my younger brother Giljung went to school. I thus familiarized myself with the streets. The Medicine Lane was called an "alley" by tradition, but it was a paved thoroughfare much traversed by cars. Lined up on both sides of the alley were tiled-roof houses with glass doors that were either medicine wholesalers or herbal clinics, and in the houses and under the eaves were piles of innumerable medicinal herbs stacked up like hay. The alley was an interesting and pleasant place, where you could see the medicinal twigs and herbs sliced with slicers, and smell the pungent and fragrant smell of herbs.

If you made a right angle turn from Medicine Lane onto Jongro Street, you ran into "Gumbanggak," the largest Chinese restaurant in Daegu. On the days large banquets were held there, we could see buses and sedans lined up in front of the entrance. It was there that I again beheld a handsome jet-black sedan for the first time since leaving Seoul four years before. Opposite the Chinese restaurant was a school for Chinese children, from which strange yells in funny syllables erupted at break times, making me wonder if I were in a foreign land.

The cityscape was strange and exciting, and also a little scary. One day, I followed Sunhwa, a fellow tenant in the same house and a few years my senior, to Bangcheon Creek, with my brother Gilsu in tow. Sunhwa went to Bangcheon Creek every day to wash the old military uniforms that her mother took in for mending and cleaning. Bangcheon was the only major creek flowing through Daegu, and its banks thronged with more people than any marketplace. The people gathering there were mostly women. Because the city water supply was very, very poor, most inhabitants of the city used Bangcheon to do their laundry. Because so many people did their laundry there, there were some who earned money by letting people boil their laundry in makeshift furnaces of used oil drums suspended over log fires. At the creek you could hear heavy northern dialects, and meet "sandwichmen," who had advertisement boards suspended on both their front and back. Most of the advertisement boards had such lines as these written on them: "Looking for Jeonghun, Jeonghun's mother and Malsuk from Jangjin, Hamgyeong Namdo. Parted at the Heungnam Port. Jeonghun's mother has a mole under her ear . . ." and so on. Three decades later I was to watch similar advertisements on KBS television when the station ran the campaign in 1983 for reuniting sundered families. I'd already had a very good preview of that in Daegu in 1954.

For a while my mother left me alone to spend my days roaming the streets. As a matter of fact, it was extremely uncomfortable to stay in the room all day with Mother. To be more exact, it was my mother's customers who made me uncomfortable. My mother's customers were mostly entertaining women in the peak of their youth and beauty. They came by with fabrics to place orders, to urge the completion of their dresses in good time, and to take away the finished apparel. They took off their blouses and outer skirts to try on the new garments, stealing furtive glances at me, an adolescent. At those times their fair bosoms and smooth shoulders were apt to be exposed. Some of the more innocent of them would relate to my mother what went on between them and their patrons, prompting my mother to steal uneasy glances at me. When my mother's eyes seemed to indicate that I shouldn't stay to listen, I left the room quietly.

More than thirty years have elapsed since then. As for my family, of the five of us living together then, two have passed away. So, I suppose most of the elderly among those who were tenants in that house have passed away as well. But I can still recall all their faces, even though they may have changed a lot over the three decades and I may not be able to recognize them if I happened to run into them today. Yes, I can recall their faces very distinctly. I imagine it is because we crossed the turbulent waters of those hard times together. I suppose it is also because it was in that house that I began my long sojourn in Daegu.

I guess I had better explain the structure of that house first. You entered it through a very imposing gateway. The gate, which faced east, was a high structure with a lofty roof, but at the time we lived there the eaves sagged on one side. And from between the tiles of the roof, weeds grew in the summer. Because the old lady of the house always told the tenants to be sure to lock the gate, it stayed barred all day. If it hadn't been barred, petty salesmen and beggars would have pushed it open many times a day. Even though it was obviously impossible for anyone to shout something and be heard through the massive gate, in the mornings and evenings beggars cried for alms and then pasted their ears to the gap for a while, only to wend on their path with disappointed steps. Some beggars kicked the gate in anger before turning away.

According to the old lady of the house, when she first came to the house as a young bride, her father-in-law was a high official in the Orient Settlement Company, the Japanese government outfit for controlling and exploiting Korea's agricultural resources and produce. Inside the imposing gate was a small thatched house for the the servants. The thatched house was torn down at some point, and the site was then left alone to be covered by weeds, and was later converted to a vegetable patch. Then, in the autumn of 1945, the year of liberation from Japanese colonial rule, a tin-roof building was built on the site to accommodate some of the landlady's kinfolk who had returned to Korea from Japan. Afterwards, in the summer of the year the Korean war broke out, that family suddenly left, and a new family came to inhabit that tin-roof house. They were called the Gimcheon family because they were from Gimcheon originally. The mother of the family tore down the clay wall to the left of the main gate, built a small shop, and sold candies, crackers, and rolls to children. She was a heavily freckled woman who looked out at the world from small frightened eyes. She had a son who was a preschooler.

All the tenants of the house entered and left the house through that store rather than pass through the imposing gate. Only the landlord and the landlady went in and out through the high gate, making a great creaking noise as they opened the two panels wide. The woman with the shop was responsible for keeping the gate locked, so you might say she was the gatekeeper of the residence.

Between the outer yard and the main courtyard was a middle gate, whose sky-blue paint had peeled off in many places. The sliding panels of the middle gate were always open during the day, until the landlord, who returned home latest of all the inhabitants, or Miseon, another teenaged tenant girl who went to commercial night school, came home and closed them.

If you stepped inside through the middle gate, which was a great disappointment after the imposing, ancient main gate, you descended about five steps into a sunken courtyard of about one hundred and sixty cubic meters. When I first stepped into the courtyard with timid steps, following Seonrye and clutching my clothes bundle, weeds were already growing on the edge of the open sewer that ran along the wall separating that house and the next house. The sewer started from the improvised toilet built at the foot of the steps descending into the courtyard from the middle gate and always emitted a stale, sour stench. In the middle of the courtyard was a small pond, and around the pond was a lovely flowerbed edged with moss-grown rocks. The trees and tall flowering plants of the flowerbed screened most of the rooms of the middle quarters and the inner quarters from one another's view.

The inner quarters, which faced south, had a living room in the center and on one side of it the living quarters consisting of four rooms and on the other side a drawing room. The traditional Korean-style inner quarters was a handsome ribbed-tile roof structure positioned atop a platform raised by five stone steps. Grass grew on mossy roofs, and wind chimes were suspended from the curving eaves. There was an elegant traditional-style balustrade girding the verandah attached to the drawing room, but the living quarters, which had been repaired during the Japanese occupation days, sported glass doors and a Western-style sofa set in the living room, so that the house was neither Korean style nor Western style as a whole. On the living room floor next to the rice chest stood a large stereo console which greeted me with a noisy popular song in English that Sunday afternoon as I first stepped into that house.

The middle quarters, which were built at right angles to the inner quarters and had the city water bin between them and the inner quarters, faced East. When the family was wealthy and powerful, the middle quarters, which had a low plain-tile roof structure, must have been occupied by servants. In the earlier days the inhabitants of the middle quarters must have looked up at the inner quarters and its inhabitants straightening up and tilting their heads backward, as they were on a level lower by five imposing steps. That must be how houses were designed in those days of class distinction—the lower classes to occupy physically lower terrain.

The middle quarters had four rooms of identical size, which were occupied by four families. But between the rooms of the middle quarters and the side wall of the house there was barely space enough for chimneys and certainly not enough space to build kitchens. So, each family had constructed an improvised kitchen outside their doors on the edge of the verandah, a small cupboard of tin roofing over a small stove. The rooms had no storage closets, so the families installed shelves to store their motley paraphernalia of life. For most refugee families in those days, all of their kitchen utensils and tableware could be stored in an apple crate, and cooking consisted of boiling rice and making one side dish per meal. Pretty much all the houses in the Janggwan-dong area had one or two refugee families renting rooms, so all four rooms in the middle quarters of the big house being occupied by refugee families was nothing very extraordinary.

The room our family occupied, which was only about thirteen cubic meters—the size of a powder compact was how my mother put it—was located at the end of the middle quarters farthest from the inner quarters, and the smell of the sewer wafted in through the window all day long. As a matter of fact, there were originally only two rooms in the middle quarters, but to accommodate more families and collect more rent, the landlords divided each of the two rooms in half, so when the five of us lay down to sleep, the space was full and we could hear the conversation in the next room without straining our ears in the least. But, compared with the plank huts or straw matting huts which the refugees built along the outlying hills of Daegu, which you could only enter bending double and which had no facilities of any kind, our room was a decent and dignified nest.

Now, to enumerate the inhabitants of that house is no small task. They were legion. But I remember every one of them as distinctly as if they were items in my pocket.

The room right next to the city water bin was occupied by the Gyeonggi family, who fled the war from Yeonbaek, Gyeonggi Province. There were three people in the family. The mother of the family was in her early fifties, and she was a graduate of a high school in Gaesong, which means that she was exceptionally well-educated for a woman of her generation. Her son Heunggyu, a tall and thin bachelor, was a dental technician working at a dental clinic on the outskirts of the city. Like most tall and thin men, he was always smiling good-naturedly. His sister Miseon flaunted a buxom and sinewy figure and dressed stylishly. She was always chewing gum, and was constantly making small clacking noises from popping the bubbles against her teeth.

The room next to that was inhabited by a retired military officer who was a wounded veteran. That family also had three members. The veteran, who had two steel hooks attached to a rubber arm for his right hand, stared at people with hostility, as if he were looking at an enemy on a battlefield, and was a man of few words. His wife was in an advanced stage of pregnancy when I joined the house, so that her belly was greatly swollen. Their only child till then, Junho, was five years old, about the same age as Boksul, the son of the Gimcheon woman who ran the snack store, so the two constantly quarrelled and made up. My youngest sibling Gilsu tottered after them all day long and exhibited his mental retardation. This wounded veteran's family was from Pyeonggang, Gangwon Province, and joined the house the latest of all the tenants, moving in during the spring of the year I came to live in the house.

The room next to that was occupied by a family from Pyongyang. There were four in the family. The mother of the family, who was in her late forties, mended and sold old military uniforms on the black market. She had a daughter and two sons. The daughter, Sunhwa, had an oval face and attractive double-lidded eyes, and was of marriageable age. The eldest son Jeongtae, who was gaunt and always looked like he was seething with fury, was loafing at home because of a poor lung condition. The pimply second son, unlike the eldest, was stocky and was a senior at Gyeongbuk High School located not far from the house.

So, the four families occupying the middle quarters knew each other's circumstances just as if they were one family. Each family knew what the other families were having for a side dish at each meal, and what ratio of Vietnamese rice and barley the other families mixed with white rice for their staple diets. When dividing up the electricity and water bills there were disputes as to what was the fair division, but we were all families doing our best to make an honest living. There was gossiping, inevitably, and a little hypocrisy, but we all understood what hard work it was for refugees to keep alive, and did not withhold emotional support from one another.

The landlords were a family of prestige originating from the Euiseong area of the Gyeongsang Bukdo Province. The great-grandfather of the present owner was a high-ranking official of the city of Daegu in the last years of the Joseon Dynasty. It was this dignitary who built the house in Janggwan-dong. The gentleman retired to his hometown after serving in the office, but the house in the city was used by his son who was an important officer in the Orient Settlement Company, and by his grandchildren who went to school in Daegu. The present landlord, who was the grandson of the officer of the Orient Settlement Company, was the lucky inheritor of the house. It was in the year of liberation that he became the owner of the house, and he was already a businessman of note by then.

The landlord's family consisted of eight members. The head of the family was a very busy person, so we only caught glimpses of him when he went out in the morning or returned home in the evening. He often slept out, and when he returned home at night he was usually very drunk. He ran a textile factory in Chimsandong, on the outskirts of Daegu. His wife, our landlady, had a fair and glowing face and was well-built. She seemed to have no aptitude or taste for housewifery, and her arena of activity was outside the house. With the help of her businessman husband she was able to open a jewellery shop in the Songjuk Cinema building, and she also managed private credit unions. As she added to the household income but neglected household management, her mother-in-law ran the house. The mother-in-law was in her seventies, but she was erect in stature and mentally alert, so that when going to the market she took the helper with her but made the purchases herself. The mother-in-law roundly abused her daughter-in-law behind her back for neglecting the household and paying scanty respect to her mother-in-law. The Gyeonggi woman, who did not have to work because her son and daughter earned their living, was her conversation companion. Owing to her educational background, the Gyeonggi woman was able to give the old lady appropriate cues and sympathetic responses.

The landlord and landlady had three sons. The eldest was a college sophomore, and the youngest was in the second year of middle school. Seongjun, who was rumored to have been admitted to the law department of a private university because his parents made a hefty donation, went to school in formal suit and tie, hair slicked back with pomade oil. He was never seen to study, and when staying home he always played the stereo at full volume and practiced dancing on the living room floor, so that we tenants of the middle quarters nicknamed him "playboy." The second and third sons of the house, a junior in high school and an eighth grader in middle school, were tutored by Jeongmin, the younger son of the Pyongyang woman, for two hours every day of the week. Of course, Jeongmin thereby earned money. There was also a highschool girl in the family, a niece of the landlord, who came from Euiseong to attend high school in Daegu and was in her senior year. Lastly there was the helper, Mrs. An, who originated from Goryeong, Gyeongsang Bukdo. Although she had her hair done in a bun like a matron, she was a young widow in her mid-twenties, and was diligent and kind-hearted.

So, this, in thumbnail, is the make-up of the inhabitants of that house—sixteen in the middle quarters after the baby was born to the military veteran and his wife, and eight in the inner quarters. Besides these, there were the two members of the Gimcheon family in the outer quarters. Twenty-six people preparing for the day every morning created a bustling scene, just like a marketplace in the morning.

As there was some distance between the inner quarters and the middle quarters, of what went on in the inner quarters we only heard the old lady waking up her grandchildren in the morning, but we could hear every small exchange going on in any of the rooms in the middle quarters. I can still vividly recall the mornings in the sunken courtyard. When the day began to brighten, the four households made fires in their portable stoves first of all. Then smoke veiled the front of the rooms, and the whir of fans working at fires resounded in the courtyard. My sister Seonrye, who was in her final year of middle school, woke up early and began studying for the high school entrance exam, so I was the one who made the fire in my family. The Gyeonggi family was the latest to rise, so Miseon, their daughter, often went around the other rooms to exchange three or four pieces of unused charcoal for two lit ones. Miseon sometimes gave me a piece of American chewing gum as a bribe when she asked for a live coal from my stove, smiling prettily and showing her dimples. I liked the chewing gum, but mostly for profit in charcoal exchange I was anxious for Miseon to buy live charcoal from me, so I sometimes made the offer on my part, saying "Miseon, my stove is lit." Unlike Sunhwa, Miseon was sophisticated and always emitted a whiff of fragrance.

The most remarkable feature of the morning scene involved the use of the toilet. In front of the improvised toilet near the middle gate, built with pieces of planks stuck together, there was always a queue. The toilet was built for the tenants of the four rooms in the middle quarters and the family in the outer quarter, but some busy mornings the students of the inner quarters came across the courtyard to use it, too. Therefore, in the early morning there were always one or two people fidgeting in front of the toilet. Of course, the inner quarters had a clean, tiled indoor toilet, but it was not available to the tenants. So, the families in the middle quarters had chamber pots and used them in emergencies.

The one most often seen fidgeting in front of the toilet was the Gyeonggi woman. Her sallow and puffy face indicated that she had digestive problems, and sure enough, she was the first to use the toilet in the morning. Then, within half an hour she had to use the toilet again. By then the toilet was sure to be occupied by someone or other, so she had to wait. At those times she would smoke, squatting in front of the toilet till the cigarette almost burned her finger, and complain about people who could stay so long in the toilet inhaling the stench of feces. She claimed to have begun smoking after she had her first child because she suffered severe stomach pain. She must have had grave digestive problems, because she not only used the toilet frequently but also broke wind very often.

My mother was none too happy about the Gyeonggi woman

occupying the toilet so often. She muttered to herself that the Gyeonggi woman ought to pay a double portion of the sanitation fees. But ironically, the Gyeonggi woman insisted, at those times when the sanitation bill was divided up, that it was unfair for her family to bear an equal portion, as her son and daughter were absent from home all day, so it was only she herself who used the toilet during the daytime. She insisted that her family and the wounded veteran's family should count as half households, since her children and the war veteran couple were away from the house from morning till evening.

After breakfast was cooked and eaten, the students were the first to leave the house. There were four students in the inner quarters, and in the middle quarters Jeongmin, son of the Pyongyang woman, and Seonrye, my sister. Giljung, my younger brother who had just entered primary school, alternated between school in the morning and in the afternoon from week to week.

Of the grown-ups, the earliest to leave the house were the son and daughter of the Gyeonggi family. As the mother of the family had to spend a good part of the morning inside or in front of the toilet, it was always her daughter Miseon who made breakfast. Heunggyu, her brother, was good at whistling, and when leaving the house in the morning swinging his lunch-box, often gave melodious whistling recitations of such popular tunes as "Parting at the Pusan Terminal" and "Serenade at the Frontline." He is said to have picked up dental skills in the army working as a medical aid at a dental clinic in Gaesong during the war. The woman from Gyeonggi always referred to her son as "my dentist son." Miseon left the house attired in Western clothes, a purse slung on her arm and silky hair streaming in the breeze, making staccato sounds with her chewing gum. When she crossed the courtyard swinging her hips to the beat of her high-heeled shoes, all the young men of the house furtively eyed her figure. Miseon worked as a sales clerk at the Command Post Exchange of the Eighth U.S. Army during the day, and in the evenings she changed into a student uniform and went to night school to finish her schooling the war had interrupted.

After the young people left, the head of the house and the wounded veteran left for work at about the same time. When the master of the house left for work, his wife came out only as far as the edge of the living room to see him off, but his mother followed him to the main gate to bid him good-bye. And she always saw him off saying "My dear, don't go to a drinking party tonight but come home early. Have mercy on your stomach." Then the middle-aged son would try to placate his mother by saying, "You know business is just beginning to pick up after a long slump. Demand for textile is not constant. One must make money while the boom lasts." That his business was thriving could be seen from his expanding girth and his sleek face. The landlord's textile company, "Oseong Textiles" had stopped operating for a long time due to low demand and the difficulty purchasing thread. I suppose it was during that time that they took in tenants, to earn tuition for their children and help with the household expenses, even though, having paddies and fields in their hometown, they had no difficulty keeping themselves in grain. But when the war entered the armistice phase, production of thread increased, so the thread supply could be secured, and with refugees shaking off poverty and beginning to look after their appearance, demands for fabric soared. The landlord's factory produced textile night and day. True to the belief that at the end of a war, food and garment industries thrive, the master of the house was raking in money. He was expanding his factory, and it was rumored that from having relatives in the government and the armed forces, he was having no difficulty cutting through red tape and winning contracts.

Junho's father, the wounded veteran, went out clad in military uniform and an officer's cap without the insignia, and carrying a small military duffle bag containing his lunch-box. He was always neatly clad, as his wife laundered his garments frequently and ironed them neatly. "He'd better be neatly clad. Nobody would defer to a handicapped veteran in squalid clothes," his wife would say. According to his wife, the veteran worked at the Veterans' Relief Section of the Second Army Headquarters, but nobody in the house believed her. His wife always came out as far as the main gate and saw her husband off deferentially, then did the dishes, prepared a lunch for Junho, and afterwards went out to sell fruit. Her haggard face was tanned copper and her neck and arms were emaciated. I don't think I ever saw a smile on her face, which always looked fatigued.

How she came to be a tenant in this house was well known to the rest of us. When she showed up to rent a room, she was accompanied only by the real estate agent. She told the old lady of the house that she had only one child and that her husband had been a teacher in a primary school in her hometown in the North but joined the army as an officer when the war erupted and was now demobilized and working as a civilian in the Second Army Headquarters. The old lady liked her quiet demeanour and good-natured eyes, and decided to take the family in. As rooms were scarce, landlords could have their pick of tenants. But as most tenants had multiple children and no source of stable income, it didn't seem a bad choice at all. When, ten days later, the family moved in, the father of the family had steel hooks for his right hand. Everyone in the house winced to see the hooks. Junho's father had some bedding bundled on his back and a worn leather suitcase slung from his shoulders, and was carrying an urn in his arms. Junho's mother was carrying upon her head a big wooden tray with pots and pans stacked on it and a portable table in her hand. Little Junho was carrying a winnowing basket draped over his head. Those comprised all their belongings. Seeing their poverty, the old lady of the house regretted her decision to take them in, but it was too late.

A while after Junho's mother went out with the fruit basin on her head, the Pyongyang woman and her daughter Sunhwa left to do their business. The Pyongyang woman, who lost her husband to American bombing while fleeing from the Communist Chinese intervention in the war, wore bloomers made from a military uniform and a loose military jacket. And she had a money pouch strapped to her waist. Like most women from the north with thick, husky voices and stocky figures, she was also very diligent and aggressive. She went out of the house carrying about fifty sets of military uniforms bundled on her head and with a portable stool in one hand. She sold the uniform in the black market till sunset. She had no stall of her own, so she spread out her wares on the ground. Sunhwa went out with her mother carrying old military uniforms in a big laundry basin. She washed the uniforms in the Bangcheon Creek and came home around lunchtime. On reaching home, she hung the washed uniforms on a laundry line and spent the afternoon mending the uniforms. Then she cooked dinner and afterwards went to the market to help her mother carry her merchandise home. Most of the time, the mother and daughter came back with an additional bundle, which contained soiled and worn military uniforms to be washed and mended for sale.

The lady of the house was the last to go out. After eating breakfast she put on elaborate make-up, donned a classy Korean dress, and went out with brisk steps. When she passed by, wearing a gold necklace and bracelet and carrying a bead bag, the women in the neighborhood whispered, "There goes *our lady*."

When all those who had work to do or business to look after went out, the house sank into deep silence. Only the old lady of the house and the young helper remained in the inner quarters, and in the middle quarters only the Gyeonggi woman and Jeongtae the consumptive patient and my mother and myself remained. Junho, the war veteran's son, and my younger brother Gilsu played in the alley or made expeditions to the wide thoroughfares with Boksul, the Gimcheon woman's son.

2

It was one spring day in early May, when azaleas adorned the courtyard in profusion. My mother, myself, my younger brother Giljung, whose class met in the morning that week and was back from school, and the youngest Gilsu had just finished lunch. My mother, sitting at her sewing machine, bade me come close to her and took some notes out of the drawer of the sewing machine and handed them to me.

"See how much there is."

When I counted the money there were eighty *hwan*, which was the value of four packs of the "peacock" cigarettes. I thought my mother was going to send me on an errand. But she eyed me keenly and said, "Listen, Gilnam. You are the eldest son in this family with no father. You have seen how the world treats people whose only crime is their poverty. I'm sure that, young as you were, you have experienced through grinding hunger what sorrow and bitterness poverty causes. As you know, those who have nothing but their brawn to rely on must work twice as hard just to put food in their mouths. You must realize you are very differently situated than our landlords' sons. Those boys have wealthy parents, an imposing house, and plenty to eat. So, they can go to college if they study hard, and can get good jobs after graduating from college. And they can get on in the world easily. It's true that even if you study twice as hard as those boys until you come of age there may still be exactly the same gap between you and them. But you can't just stand by and leave everything to fate. That'd be like a farmer doing nothing but pray in a severe drought. Rice doesn't grow of its own accord. It's true that even ten years later we may still have to look up at landlords from down below. But you must try as best you can to improve your lot. As for me, my mission in life is to support the four of you until you can become independent. I have no life of my own apart from raising you."

Mother's voice had become tearful. I raised my head and looked at her. Her eyelashes were wet. She was not forty yet, but she was talking like an old woman. As a matter of fact, she had changed—from a vigorous, blooming woman in her thirties in the days before the war to a dry-skinned and tired woman, as if she had become twice her former age. She blew her nose into her handkerchief and continued her speech:

"Gilnam, you have your whole life before you. So, you must make up your mind very firmly to get out of this poverty. As I see it, there are only two options for you. One is for you to study very hard and become twice as able as the others. Look at Jeongmin. He has no father, either, and his mother sells repurposed military uniforms, but because he is an excellent student, he earns money by tutoring the landlord's two younger sons, and he does his own studies until midnight. So, he is the best student in his class and the class president year after year. I am sure he is going to be a judge or a prosecutor or a university professor."

"Another option for you to make headway in this life is for you to master the ways of this world by plunging right into it. If you're not very bright and you have no aptitude for study, you must work hard. Look at Junho's father. He has only one arm, but he goes out every morning to make a living. A man has to go out as soon as he finishes breakfast if he's to fulfill his duties as the head of a family. So even though you're still a teenager, you shouldn't be loafing at home all day every day. That's why I'm giving you this money."

"What do you want me to do with this money?" I asked, completely at a loss as to what Mother might have in mind.

"Gilnam, why don't you try buying newspapers with that money and selling them in the street? It doesn't matter how much money you can make. The important thing is for you to realize the value of earning money. That will give you a good sense of the hardships of making your way in the world. And that will be a valuable asset for getting on in this world. You know the proverb, 'Invest in hardship early, whatever the cost,' don't you?"

I dared not disobey such an earnest command from Mother.

In retrospect, I think it is certain that my mother meant to make me earn money when she called me up from our hometown. She left me alone to roam the streets for about ten days, to let me familiarize myself with the ways of the city, so that I could earn my tuition engaging in some trade. She must have thought ten days would give me sufficient time to get a good sense of the city's layout and its ways.

I left the house with the money in my pocket, but with no plan in my head. As I was leaving, my mother said, "If you don't think you can sell newspapers, you can use that money to go back to Jinyeong and become a servant in a tavern or a vendor in the market." That was an ultimatum that spurred me to buck up with desperate courage. If I returned home in the evening after just roaming the streets, my mother was quite capable of making me skip dinner and even throwing me out of the house. She was a very stern and harsh parent.

At the time, there were three newspapers published in Daegu. *The Daegu Mail Chronicle*, *The Youngnam Daily*, and *The Daegu Daily*. All three were evening papers. My mother had already gathered that basic information. Walking with uncertain steps, I was wondering how I could find the newspaper offices. By luck, I ran into a mailman. I asked him the location of the three newspaper buildings. *The Youngnam Daily* happened to be nearest my house, being located between the Daegu Police Headquarters and the Seomun Market.

When I hesitantly stepped into the backyard of the newspaper building, I saw about twenty teenage boys with shaven heads. Some of them eyed me suspiciously, but as I was standing a little apart from them, none of them accosted me. When it was two o'clock in the afternoon, a young man wearing a round cap stepped out of the building with a sheaf of just-printed newspapers. The teenagers quickly purchased newspapers from the young man and dashed out into the streets. I bought ten copies after all the boys made their purchases and dispersed, and went out to the street. I had no courage to hawk my wares, so I walked on with my eyes fixed on the ground.

"This evening's *Yeongnam Daily*, hot off the press," I muttered, but the words were indistinct even to my ears. I traversed the Jungang Street and the black market area, the busiest sections of the city. Other newspaper boys must have had the same ideas as myself, for I ran into many other vendors. The other boys were good at catching people's attention and selling newspapers. Spotting someone who looked like he might be interested in the latest news, they blocked his way and, waving the newspapers in his face, cried out the top headlines. I lacked the guts to follow their example.

That first day, I sold six copies. Two were to men in Western suits having their shoes shined sitting in a shoeshine boy's chair. When someone called, "Hey there, newsboy!" I was so happy that my heart turned somersaults in my chest. I wasn't even thinking of how much profit I could gain from selling a copy. The sheer fact of being able to make a sale was ecstasy itself. But again and again some other newspaper boy beat me to the customer. Some of them were not even selling the *Yeongnam Daily* but one of the other papers.

I returned home that evening with four leftover newspapers but having made a profit of five *hwan*. My mother was very pleased, and said that thanks to her eldest son she was now a newspaper reader. I was also very happy, so that even though our dinner had its usual pickled cabbage and bean paste soup as side dishes, it tasted just delicious.

A week later, I was buying and selling fifteen copies. In that short time, I had discovered that if you carried the newspapers half wrapped in cement bags, you could prevent ink smearing on the nethermost copy and becoming soiled through contact with your fingers or your jacket. I also discovered that the best places to sell newspapers are train stations and tearooms, where people are waiting for someone or something. One day, I went to the Army Hospital and sold as many as five copies in the visitors' room there.

The Army Hospital used to be Gyeongbuk University Medical School until it was requisitioned by the army, so it had a spacious campus and landscaped woods. On benches sparsely strewn throughout the campus, there were many convalescent patients and their kin.

One day, coming out of the waiting room of the hospital, I caught sight of Junho's father sitting on a bench under a maple tree and eating lunch out of his lunch-box using his chopsticks awkwardly with his left hand. There was a small military duffle bag on the ground beside him. I wondered why he was eating his lunch on a bench in the open air rather than in his office, but I hastened away because I was ashamed of selling newspapers. But while stealing one last glance at him, I caught his eye.

"Good afternoon," I called out, bowing. Junho's father returned an awkward smile.

"I heard you were selling newspapers. It must be hard, at your age."

"You're having lunch rather late, aren't you?" I said, so as to say something.

"Yes, I came to see a former comrade of mine. He's a long-term patient here. I was hoping I could get some news of my other former comrades."

Junho's father closed his lunch-box. It was a barley-and-millet meal, with no side dish except for some red bean paste. Junho's father looked visibly embarrassed at my having seen the contents of his lunch-box, and was very unlike his usual austere and rigid self.

"Well, excuse me, sir. I have to sell these copies before nightfall," I said and hurried toward the gate.

About a fortnight after I began selling newspapers I was able to muster enough impudence to hawk my wares. "*Yeongnam Daily News! Yeongnam Daily News! Yeongnam Daily News* with special feature stories!" I shouted, running with the speed of the wind. Soon, it was not at all hard to sell fifteen copies in one afternoon. I had my route established, so that every day I visited the tearooms on Jungang Road and around the Songjuk Cinema, the black market, the Daegu Station, and the Army Hospital. There were days when shoeshine boys or hoodlums snatched away my newspapers and robbed my money so that I returned home in tears. On such days, my mother patted me on the shoulder and said, "That experience will help you avoid ruffians in the future. Don't worry. I'm happy you came home unhurt. Have courage. If you lose courage now, you'll never be able to weather bigger crises." By and by I got the hang of how to win regular customers, and secured three customers in the black market. I owed two of them to the good offices of the Pyongyang woman who plied her business of selling second-hand military uniforms in the black market and was very gregarious. Both of them were black market merchants from the North, and as they opened the newspaper, they always said, "Let's see if there's any news of my hometown folks."

On days that I sold all fifteen copies early, I roamed the downtown area instead of going straight back home. I had nothing to interest me at home, and was only apt to be lectured at by my mother or have to leave the room when her young female customers called. So, I roamed the streets until it was about time Seonrye was back from school and cooking dinner. Sauntering through the black market, I was likely to run into the Pyongyang woman a couple of times a day, and she sometimes gave me leftover rice cake or steamed potatoes that she had bought for a snack. If you crossed the Dongseong Road from the black market, you came to where the Songjuk Cinema and Liberty Cinema stood facing each other obliquely across the street. Along that street were the most expensive shops in Daegu, such as designer boutiques, jewellery shops, timepiece shops, tailor shops, and electric appliance shops, and the street always bustled with well-clad passersby. I loved to look into the shop windows. Our landlady's jewellery shop, "Bogeum-dang," was a fascinating place. There was Mr. Jeong, a goldsmith in his mid-thirties, who was carving the Chinese characters for "longevity" and "happiness" on silver spoons and chopsticks by tapping the tip of an iron gimlet into the handle of the spoon or chopsticks with a small hammer. The characters had many strokes and sophisticated structures, but the goldsmith went about carving those characters just as if it were a pastime to him. He had short, crew-cut hair, small eyes, and a pointed chin, so he reminded me of a hedgehog. My landlady, who had fair skin and red lips, was often smiling friendly smiles to her customers.

One Saturday afternoon, I ran into Donghi, the high school senior niece of my landlord. She was not wearing her school uniform but was in a one-piece dress of red flower print on white background, and had her hair just hanging loose, instead of having it in two braids as usual, so I almost passed her without recognizing her.

"Oh, is that you, miss? What are you doing here?" I made

the mistake of accosting her instead of passing her by pretending not to have seen her. I realized my mistake when I caught the glance of a tall shaven-headed youth whose face was covered with pimples and who, like Donghi, was wearing a plaid shirt instead of his school uniform.

"Oh, it's you, Gilnam," Donghi said, blushing scarlet.

"Oh, I didn't know you had company. Well, please excuse me," I said and prepared to move away.

Donghi took out two candies wrapped in cellophane paper and put them in my hand.

"Please don't tell anyone you saw me here. He is a distant relative from my hometown. I just ran into him by chance over there," she said.

As I looked back while wending my way toward Jungang Street, Donghi and the lad were walking toward the ticket booth of the Songjuk Cinema, stealing glances right and left. At the cinema, a Hollywood movie with the title *History is Made at Night* was playing. I thought it sounded very provocative. On the advertisement board was painted the scene of a Western man and woman just about to kiss. I hadn't thought anything amiss when I saw the university student Seongjun walking the Jungang Street with a stylishly dressed woman who looked a good ten years his senior, but I thought it was a very serious matter that Donghi was on a date with a boy. Being a high school student, she was sure to run into trouble if her teacher caught her walking with a young man. I suppose the boy who was dating Donghi must have thought it odd that Donghi, who was well-to-do, had a newspaper boy among her acquaintance.

Although newspaper selling was turning out to be manageable and profitable, I couldn't help being depressed when I saw boys of my age in school uniforms carrying school bags. At those times, I went to the train station. There were many beggars and jobless vagabonds loitering around the station. I took solace at the sight of children in tattered clothes clinging to travelers asking for alms, or those unemployed people wearing soiled military uniforms sauntering the station square and smoking the cigarette butts they picked up from the ground. The sight of them made me realize how hard life is for many people, and the thought consoled me. The sight of A-frame carriers running up to train passengers with heavy luggage and offering to carry it for a small fee or those vendors selling fruit and rice cakes on a wooden tray under the blazing sun, chasing away flies, also gave me solace. It made me feel that I was not the only one who had been dealt with unfairly by life.

It was one day in mid-June, when the heat was beginning to be really uncomfortable and the foliage on the roadside trees was thick. I was running at full speed with newspapers tucked under my arm when I caught sight of Junho's father in front of the Bank of Korea building on Jungang Street. He was clad in an officer's combat gear minus the insignia. As it was around 3:00 PM, the hottest hour of the day, his uniform was wet with sweat and his two hooks peeped out of his right sleeve. He was just emerging from the stairwell of the three-story building and hadn't seen me. In fact, he had his military cap worn low on the forehead, had his eyes fixed on the ground before him, and was not paying any attention to who might be passing on the street. He was carrying his military duffle bag in his left hand.

Junho's father turned into the stairwell of a two-story building right next to the building he'd just emerged from. I followed him up the creaky stairway a few steps behind. The tearoom on the second floor was my favorite place to do business. When Junho's father stepped into the tearoom, I followed swiftly behind. Inside the tearoom, I went the other way from him and made the round of corner tables. The tearoom was very crowded. In those days, almost all the tearooms in the downtown area were crowded, even though half the patrons didn't give the establishments any business and were chided by the waitresses for not ordering beverages. Most of the 'patrons' were jobless people or people with insecure jobs who were seeking news and employment or trade opportunities from similarly situated people. The general election for the lower house had taken place on the twentieth of May, so it was almost a month old, but the patrons of the tearoom were repeating stale political gossip and analysis.

By that point I wasn't so interested in selling my newspapers. I was much more interested in guessing what had brought Junho's father into the tearoom. Was he trying to sell what was in the duffle bag, or was he there to meet someone? I eyed the cashier. The comely proprietress in beautiful traditional dress was sitting in front of the cash register and was changing the record on the phonograph. Junho's father stationed himself in front of the cashier's desk and tapped the counter with the hooks of his right arm. Wounded veterans plying their petty sales could be identified at once, as there was an unmistakable aura of shabbiness common to most of them, so waitresses were anxious to chase them out of their establishments. Junho's father, however, was wearing well-starched and ironed military garments albeit sweat-stained around the shoulderblades, and was clean-shaven, so he didn't look like a petty vendor. The proprietress visibly started at the sight of the iron hooks. Junho's father stared at the proprietress just as if he was a creditor, and began taking out his merchandise from the duffle bag and putting them on the counter. There were pencils, notebooks, combs, toothbrush and other everyday commodities. He didn't speak a word until he put them all on the counter.

I had long suspected that Junho's father might be doing something of the kind. In fact I was tipped by the Gyeonggi woman, who said that she had once inadvertently opened the door of Junho's family's room and saw Junho's father counting small coins strewn on the floor. She added her guess that he must be selling things like chewing gum and pencils making the rounds of tearooms and business offices. All the inhabitants of the house agreed with her, saying that he couldn't be doing clerical work as his wife had claimed, being without his right hand. So, I had a secret wish to run into Junho's father and watch him doing his business. As I had never run into him all that while, I thought the Gyeonggi woman might have guessed wrong. If he wasn't plying his trade downtown, then there was nowhere petty vendors could find any customers. It is true that some disabled veterans knocked on the gates of residences and made coercive sales, but I didn't think Junho's father, a former officer, would do such a dishonorable thing. Besides, earnings from such unpleasant practices amounted to very little.

"Oh, my! We've had dozens like you today already. You know, we bought enough of this trash from the likes of you to last us a whole month," the proprietress spat out. Junho's father stood there immobile and stared at the proprietress with hostile eyes. The woman took out a paper note from the till and put it on the counter. "Here. We don't want any of these things so please put them away," she said, and averted her face, fanning herself with a fan.

Junho's father picked up his wares and put them back in his duffle bag. Then he walked out of the tearoom without saying a word.

"He must be a deaf-mute," the woman muttered to herself, looking at the door closed after him. I came out of the tearoom after Junho's father. As I passed the cashier I could see that the paper note the woman had placed there for Junho's father was still on the counter. I didn't think Junho's father forgot to pick it up by mistake, and his pride despite his poverty was a considerable shock to me.

I followed him at about thirty yards' distance. For the moment I had forgotten that I had my own wares to sell. I had expected Junho's father to go into another tearoom or any of the shops, but he kept walking along the Jungang Street in the direction of the train station. I wanted to see Junho's father trying to sell his wares one more time, so I had my eyes riveted on the back of his uniform and followed him. But Junho's father turned eastward at the station and kept walking, past the red-light district and Dongin Roundabout. Was he perhaps looking for a good place to eat his lunch? But I couldn't just retrace my steps, as I'd invested a considerable amount of time following him. Junho's father was now walking toward the Chilseong Market, through the tunnel under the railroad. At last, he halted at the entrance of the vegetable market thronging with sellers and buyers. Opposite the regular stalls were women selling vegetables on trays. Among them was Junho's mother. She spotted her husband looking around for her, and stood up. She was carrying a newborn baby strapped to her back. I hid myself among the crowd and went behind them.

"I just can't do this any more," he said to his wife gruffly.

"I know. It's too much for you. One has to have a designated territory to have any kind of tolerable business. Like a station building or a few schools."

"The authorities are growing more strict about forbidding former officers from petty vending."

"But it's not as if you're forcing people to buy your things," his wife said.

"They say that former officers must maintain their dignity. And they're right, too. I went to the intercity bus terminal this morning and saw military police checking up on wounded veteran vendors. So, I had to go downtown, but met only humiliation."

"Why don't you rest at home and wait for the veterans' relief office to find you a job? I'll work harder in the meantime," the wife said and wiped the sweat from her husband's face with the towel she had wrapped around her head.

"It might take forever for them to find a job for the likes of me. I have to earn my rice."

"I can earn enough to feed our small family," she said.

"But we must both work and save for the future."

Just then, a shrill whistle sounded, and the illegal vendors all snatched up their vegetable trays. Junho's mother also hurriedly put her tray of half-ripe apples on her head and ran in the direction opposite the whistle. The head of the baby strapped to her back shook like a gourd on a vine.

Junho's mother had given birth to a baby about two weeks after I began selling newspapers. She didn't go out to ply her trade but stayed home on the day she gave birth. From around noon, moaning sounds came from that family's room. My mother went to look in on her, and when she came back she clucked her tongue in pity and muttered to herself, "How does she figure to do it all by herself?" When I came back after selling my newspapers, the moaning had changed to screams at frequent intervals. "Why doesn't one of you give her a helping hand?" the old lady of the house said in front of the tenants' rooms, to no one in particular.

The Gyeonggi woman pretended not to hear, and the Pyongyang woman hadn't returned from the market. So my mother went over to Junho's room. Junho's mother told my mother not to worry, saying that her husband would return shortly and help with the delivery. It was past midnight when Junho's mother finally delivered her baby. My mother and the Pyongyang woman helped with the birthing, and Junho's father paced the courtyard while it was going on. The baby was a daughter. Junho's mother rested at home for two days and then went out to ply her trade again on the third day. The tenants of the middle quarters told her that she must rest at least seven days, but she didn't pay any heed. She said, as she stepped out of the middle gate with her bloodless face, that she must work harder as there was one more mouth to feed. My mother said to me, "Take note of that, Gilnam. That's how people can overcome poverty. That family will some day be rich. They will be looking back fondly on their days in this house."

3

The rainy season in the summer of 1954 was a long and tedious one. The flooding caused by the heavy downpour was severe as well. It was as if God meant to sweep away all three years' debris of war with a flood. So, poor refugees who were just beginning to find their footing were staggered again. The rainy season began on the twenty-ninth of June and went on until the twenty-fifth of July and, according to newspaper reports, claimed forty-four lives and caused four hundred and fifty million *hwan* worth of damage in the southern provinces alone.

Throughout the rainy season rain poured down hard almost every day, as if the bottom had fallen out of the clouds. The sky was constantly hidden by black clouds, enough to make us forget what the sun looked like. It was dark even during the day, and the whole city was drenched. Food distribution was growing irregular, and grain prices had doubled in a month. There were frequent blackouts. And, even though water was everywhere, the city water supply had stopped, so we had to rely on water carriers to bring us water. The city water came on from time to time in the middle of the night, so the families in the middle quarters often stayed up on the short summer nights to get water.

My trade volume had increased to twenty copies before the rainy season began, but on rainy days I had a hard time selling even ten. So if the rain thickened around the time I headed toward the newspaper company, I bought only eight to ten copies and wended my way downtown. Holding up a torn paper umbrella with one hand and carrying newspapers in a cement bag in the other, I hawked my wares at the top of my voice, but no one stopped me to buy a newspaper. As it was hard to tell the time of the day from the cloud-covered sky, I peeped into the windows of clock shops to catch the time and headed home around dinner time. On the days sales were low, my legs, whose calves inside my breeches were wet through and through, shook severely as I trudged heavily home in the evening. Not only was I shivering inside my rain-soaked garments, but my stomach growled just as loudly as the water gurgling in my rubber shoes. When I reached the Gimcheon woman's stall beside the main gate of my house, the smell of rolls being cooked in the tin drum made my mouth water. My most ardent wish in those days was to eat my fill of white rice and broiled beef. My mother mixed rice and barley in the ratio of three to seven and didn't give us enough of even that, saying that overeating makes us dull in the head and lazy. I always finished the meal yearning for more. But as we always cooked the same amount of rice, it wasn't as if there were any more in the pot.

"Gilnam, you have leftover copies today, too? My poor lad, and you're wet through, too. Take care not to catch cold," the Gimcheon woman said, patting me on the back, on those days I returned home limply with heavy steps.

It was on another of those rainy days. I was coming home with two leftover copies out of the ten I started with. Approaching the Gimcheon woman's shop, I saw a sharp-jawed man in his thirties asking something very urgently of the Gimcheon woman. The man was wearing a short-sleeved shirt.

"It's no use pretending you don't know. We know you are in touch with him. Just tell us where his base is in this area." The man stopped speaking when he caught sight of me.

The Gimcheon woman made no response to his query and

just turned her fear-strained face toward me. I shut my umbrella and crossed the woman's shop into the house. As I was walking toward the middle gate, I heard the man calling, "Hey, you there." I opened my umbrella again and halted. The man, emerging into the courtyard from the Gimcheon woman's shop, stepped under my umbrella.

"Oh, you're a working student. I have a question to ask. I bet you've seen a man coming to see Boksul's mother from time to time. A man of roughly my age, and who has a scar on his cheek. I'm sure you saw that man," the man said, eyeing me keenly from head to foot.

"No, I've never seen a man like that," I said uncertainly, but I knew exactly who he meant. I had seen such a man a couple of times. The first was soon after I began selling newspapers. One afternoon, as I was going out of the house to head for the newspaper company, I saw the man stepping out of the Gimcheon woman's room into her kitchen. He was of sallow complexion and had a long scar running from his cheek to his jaw. Because of that scar, I remembered his face vividly. Like many people in those days, regardless of whether they'd done service in the army or not, he was wearing a military uniform dyed black. The other time was about a month ago. By chance, I was walking the long Janggwan-dong Street a few steps behind him. He looked back from time to time, and when our eyes met, had smiled at me a little sheepishly.

"You look like a middle school student. What grade are you in?" my interrogator asked.

"I'm not a student," I said.

"Then you are a newspaper boy?"

"Yes," I said, realizing that he made a distinction between a student who sold newspapers to earn his tuition and a boy who just sold newspapers.

"Look here," he said, but hearing some stirring inside the

middle gate, he halted. Jeongtae, the Pyongyang woman's elder son, was coming out of the house without an umbrella and coughing. His sunken eyes looked feverish as he eyed the man and myself.

"Well, good-bye. I'll be seeing you," the man said hastily and ducked into the Gimcheon woman's kitchen to avoid the rain.

Going into the courtyard through the middle gate, I thought it was lucky I told the man that I had never seen the man with the big scar. In October of the year the war broke out, my mother told Seonrye and me that we must simply must say that our father had been killed in an air raid if anyone were to ask about him. Also that if anyone were to ask about anything that had happened during the three-month communist occupation of Seoul, we were to say we didn't know anything. So, I believed, until I reached my mid-twenties, that my father, who was never seen again from around the time of the Communists' retreat, had died in an air raid. Now, I am not certain if my father died in an air raid as Mother had said, or was abducted North, or defected to the North of his own will, or met his death in the chaos and confusion of war. In any case, he was "missing," like so many other fathers of the children of my generation.

My mother later told me, shortly before my marriage, how we lost contact with my father. "I don't think your father was a Communist before the war. But after the war broke out, it must have been hard for a man to stay away from Communism, if only to keep alive. I didn't think he was leaning toward Communism even when he cursed Syngman Rhee for deceiving the people into thinking that the Communist invasion would be contained and for fleeing to the south in the middle of the night with the high officials, leaving the poor people trapped in Seoul. But from mid-July, he came home only once in a long while. And he didn't tell me what he was doing outside even when he did come home. I didn't like to ask questions. Anyway, he usually came home with sacks of rice, for which I could only be grateful. I did ask once or twice, 'How did you get this precious rice in this hell?' but he never told me anything. It's not a woman's place to ply her man with questions . . ." That was Mother's account of the last days of Father. When I was about to be married, nearly two decades had passed since Father's disappearance, so there was no hope of seeing him appear before us alive. That must be why she let me know that my father had not passed away during the war but had been missing since then.

When I stepped into the yard, I saw Mother sitting on the narrow verandah in front of our room looking vacantly up at the sky. Anxiety lay heavy on her brow. Seonrye was squatting in front of the stove fanning the fire under the pot with one hand and looking at her English vocabulary notebook held in the other. When she saw me, she said, "Oh, you're back," by way of greeting. My brother Giljung, who rarely smiled or played like the other children, was doing his homework, with his belly pasted on the floor, sucking the lead of his pencil. My youngest brother Gilsu was sniffling and looking at his elder brother working on math problems. As on most days, the mood of my family was cloudy and dark.

Mother's sewing work had dwindled since the rainy season began, so she didn't try to comfort me when I came home dripping wet and with unsold newspaper copies. Even if Mother had said "Gilnam, why don't you take a rest on some rainy days? It's too hard for you, and there's little or no profit, I know," I would have said, "It's all right, Ma'am, I'll just do the best I can," and gone out. But Mother didn't say a word to me even though she saw me coming home shivering like a rat fished out of a ditch. She didn't even say "I'm sorry you're not going to school like other kids your age, or like your sister and brother. I wish you were." Feeling my mother's heartlessness, my eyes watered and my throat felt hot.

At the dinner table, Mother said, how can there be patrons at high-class restaurants when there are flood victims everywhere? She went on to say that if this flood continued, we'd soon run out of rice. Mother had lost her appetite completely, so she put down her spoon after only half-emptying her rice bowl. Seeing the rice left in Mother's bowl, I ate my rice very quickly, in the hope that Mother would let me eat the rest of her rice.

"Gilnam, you eat the rest of my rice," Mother said, going out to the verandah. I quickly transferred the rice in Mother's bowl into my bean paste soup.

"I guess summer is a low season for the food and drinks business, even without the rain. Street tavern hostesses all say their business is slow," I ventured to say to Mother, fortified by the extra rice I had eaten.

"So you're beginning to have some *savoir-faire*. It was worth going around busy streets and shops selling newspapers, wasn't it?" Mother asked weakly.

The electric bulb blinked a few times but didn't come on. The rain-soaked courtyard was growing darker. Even while eating dinner, I was wondering why the Gimcheon woman didn't seek me out, and I often turned my eyes toward the middle gate. I was sure the Gimcheon woman would seek me out to ask what the sharp-jawed man had asked me.

After finishing dinner I went to the outer quarters. The Gimcheon woman's shop was closed early and there was a sound of sobbing coming out of her dark room.

"Mother, Mother!" Boksul, the Gimcheon Woman's son, was sobbing and crying.

"Hush, Boksul," I said, sliding open the door of their room.

"Is that you, Gilnam?" a husky male voice asked from inside the dark room, making me almost topple over the doorsill. I never thought a grown-up male would be inside the room of a widow and her young son, so at first I couldn't even figure out whose voice it was.

"Who, who are you?" I stammered.

"It's me, Jeongtae. Come in," the voice said in the dark.

"It's so dark. Why don't you light a lamp?"

"There's no need," the voice countered.

I crept into the room and slid the door shut. I could dimly make out Jeongtae's face with the sunken, bloodshot eyes and high cheekbones. Jeongtae was exempted from military service on account of his bad lungs, and was taking tuberculosis medicine that his mother got for him with great difficulty. The medicine, called Nidrazid, was bead-like tablets pirated from the U.S. Military Post Exchange. I saw Jeongtae taking those tablets from time to time.

"Boksul, where's your mother?" I asked.

"The man took Mother away. Mother didn't give me supper and went away with him," Boksul said, between sniffles.

"I gave him the leftover rolls from the shop but he's still hungry," Jeongtae said and asked me, "Gilnam, what did the son of a bitch ask you?"

"He asked if I saw a man with a knife scar on his face coming to see Boksul's mother," I answered hesitantly.

Of all the tenants of the house, Jeongtae was on closest terms with Boksul's family.

"The son of a bitch. Trying to worm information out of kids," Jeongtae said.

"Who is he?" I asked.

"A bloodhound, what else?"

"A bloodhound . . . ?"

"A police detective," Jeongtae explained.

"What did Boksul's mother do wrong?"

"You needn't worry about that yet. You have to be older to know such things. Or the country has to be unified."

His words struck terror into me. I felt scared of sitting there in the dark room with him, so I said my mother might be looking for me and left. As I came out of the room, Boksul started to cry again. I heard Jeongtae coughing and trying to soothe Boksul.

Jeongtae stayed in his room in the mornings and read. In the afternoons, he sometimes went out—perhaps to take a walk or to meet someone, but mostly he sat on the doorsill of the Gimcheon woman's shop and talked with her. Jeongtae was only a degree less unsociable than Junho's father and, other than his own family, talked with almost no one except the Gimcheon woman. He rarely if ever exchanged friendly conversation with any of the tenants of the house. Through the thin partition between his room and ours, I heard his mother, the Pyongyang woman, chiding him with, "I wish you wouldn't hang around the Gimcheon woman's shop so much. Because you talk with her so often in plain sight of passersby, people gossip about you and that woman. You don't want neighbors to think you're trying to seduce a widow, do you?"

But Jeongtae didn't seem to mind his mother's anxiety in the least. So in the afternoons, either Jeongtae or the Gyeonggi woman could be seen in the Gimcheon woman's shop. Sometimes they were both there at the same time. When the talkative Gyeonggi woman was there, Jeongtae had his mouth firmly closed and eyed the passersby through his hollow eyes.

The next morning, when I woke up, the sky was still heavily overcast, though it wasn't raining. But it didn't look as if it would brighten up. Passing by the Gyeonggi woman who was smoking her cigarette squatting in front of the toilet, I went outside. The Gimcheon woman had apparently come back during the night. She was making fire for breakfast in her stove.

"Oh, you're back, ma'am. Boksul cried so last night."

"I got back only a little while ago. Jeongtae kindly watched over Boksul last night."

The Gimcheon woman had bloodshot eyes and her face was puffy. Her hair was a mess, too.

"Where have you been?" I asked boldly, even though I had my guess.

"Oh, I . . . well, I went to a relative's. I borrowed some rice," she said, flustered. As I was coming away, she called to my back, as if she just recalled something, "By the way, Gilnam, how did your father pass away?"

"He was hit by a bomb in Seoul."

"Did you see his corpse?" she asked.

"No, but that's how he died."

"Well, I don't know what crimes we all committed to deserve this kind of life," she said, sighing. She fanned the stove with her torn fan. Blue smoke rose from the stove.

"Ma'am, I heard that Boksul's father is still alive. Is that true?" I brought out the question that had long been a matter for discussion among the tenants of the middle quarters. At the end of the discussion, people always speculated whether the landlady, who was said to be a relative of the Gimcheon woman, was taking her under her wing.

"Well, I wish I knew for certain," she mumbled and wiped her eyes with a corner of her apron. I felt it was not just because the blue smoke from the wet twigs stung her eyes.

When I went back to the middle quarters, I could hear the Pyongyang woman scolding her son in a shrill voice. She was berating him for having slept in the Gimcheon woman's room.

During the rainy season of 1954, the house with the sunken courtyard and its inhabitants had to suffer flooding three times. The third and the last time, which took place in late July, was really terrible.

That day, the rain poured all day long. According to the broadcast news that I picked up from the loudspeaker outside the radio shop, it had rained more than one hundred and ten millimeters that day in the Daegu area by six o'clock in the afternoon.

There was no electricity that day, either. So the five of us in my family ate our dinner in a darkening room. Mother said that we would have to skip lunch from the next day, as she'd had no business for so long. From the next room, I could also hear the Pyongyang woman saying that business was so slow that she could not afford her elder son's medicine or her younger son's tuition fees.

After finishing dinner, we lit the kerosene lamp, under whose light Seonrye and Giljung studied. Mother, having no work to do, went to sleep early. My little brother and I sat on the verandah and watched the streaks of rain.

The rain noisily struck the tin roofs of the tenants' improvised kitchens. And the water in the sewer flowed noisily as well, as if the sewer were a creek. It was as if the whole world were under the sway of rain.

"Gilnam, go and take a look at the ditch. Surely, it must be overflowing." The Gyeonggi woman, who had been smoking a cigarette sitting on the verandah of her room, shouted to me.

I put on my rubber shoes and went outside. Muddy water was whirling in the ditch and wasn't draining properly. The house to the rear of ours was on terrain raised about two steps above ours, and the ditch was draining into a gap under the wooden fence of that house. It was good that the filthy ditch, which was covered with weeds and emitted a dank odor all the time, was being swept clean by the heavy rain, but if this rain kept pouring and the ditch continued draining poorly, it was a sure thing that our courtyard would be flooded. I picked up the rod that stood against the wall and poked the ditch all along the wall of our house. But because the sewer in the house to the rear was not draining, there was a pool in the ditch. I poked the ditch with the rod a few more times and then came back in. My undershirt and breeches were soaked through.

"Oh, what hateful rain. It looks like the floodgates of Heaven were opened. Well, why isn't this girl home yet? How can she have classes at the institute in this blackout?" The Gyeonggi woman was muttering, casting her eyes toward the middle gate and throwing away the butt of the cigarette she had been smoking.

When the night school was out for summer vacation, Miseon attended the English language institute in the evening. She was a chic young lady, but also a hard-working and economical young woman, like most women from the Gaesong area. Her mother cooked their dinner, but Miseon cooked breakfast for the family, worked in the office during the day and studied at night school. On Sundays, she did all the laundry for her lazy mother after coming back from church. She washed her long hair every other day, and her office outfit and school uniform were always neat and clean. It must have taken a lot of maintenance to keep herself in such neat shape, but she never looked as if those things cost her an effort. Mother also commented on her admiringly, saying, "I guess she is asleep when she isn't making that smacking noise with the chewing gum, but really, it seems as if she never sleeps."

"If the rain continues to pour like this, our courtyard will be flooded again," the Gyeonggi woman muttered once more and cast her eyes towards our room.

"Gilnam, if she asks you to do anything again, don't do it. She has hands, too. And she has a grown-up son of her own. She shouldn't ask a mere lad to do such hard work," said my mother, who was lying on the floor in our room.

The Gyeonggi woman's son Heunggyu was in the room, as was obvious from the sound of whistling coming from there. My mother strongly disapproved of the Gyeonggi woman. So did the Pyongyang woman. So, the Gyeonggi woman talked mostly with Junho's mother, who was always polite to her elders, and the old lady of the house.

That night, it happened. My family had fallen asleep, listening to the noise of the hard rain.

"What's this noise?" Mother's words woke me up. I could only hear the sound of rain in the pitch darkness. We hadn't spread the mosquito net because it was raining, but our door was closed, as usual. My mother never went to bed without closing the door fast and locking it, even in the sweltering heat of summer. The only thing worth stealing in our room was the sewing machine, but later on, it dawned on me that it was a widow's instinctive caution against intruders.

Somebody was shouting in drunken anger. "Isn't anybody home? Is it all right for all of you if this house gets swept away by the flood? Even though you're only tenants, how could you be so indifferent to what might happen to the house you're living in?" A streak of lightning lit up the door and then all was dark again. The drunken shouting must be the landlord's. It was impossible to tell what time it was. The landlord had a night pass, so he often came home after the midnight curfew.

My mother hastily put on her clothes. And she lit the kerosene lamp, which she never lighted unless she had an urgent sewing to do or so Seonrye could study.

The landlord's drunken shouting came again. "Is it fine with you if the courtyard becomes a lake? You think the water won't flow into your rooms?"

It was only then that there was stirring in all of the rooms in the middle quarters. Only my two younger brothers kept on sleeping. Seonrye also got up and put on her clothes. Mother unlocked the door and opened it. The courtyard, dimly lit up by the lamp in our room, was a horrible sight. It was flooded, and the water was almost lapping onto the narrow verandahs of our rooms. The flowerbed in the middle of the yard had become an island. When lightning flashed again, we could see the landlord walking toward the inner quarters with shaky steps, wading in almost knee-deep water, holding an umbrella. Streaks of rain hit the water hard, swelling it. Laundry boards and rubber shoes were floating on the water.

"Oh, our stove and our rice must have become soaked. So has our charcoal. How are we going to make breakfast?" Mother sighed.

"Oh, what rain! Our yard must have become a river!" shouted someone.

"Good God! All our shoes must have been swept away," cried another.

"Water will be flowing into the room in no time," fretted someone else.

Two oil lamps lit in the living room of the inner quarters illuminated the courtyard. All the inhabitants of the middle quarters had poured out onto the verandahs of their rooms. Unable to step into the flood, they stood there fidgeting.

The inner quarters being five steps higher than the courtyard, water had reached only their third step. Members of the landlord's family, standing along the edge of their living room, looked down on the flooded courtyard and the fretful inhabitants of the middle quarters like spectators, some of them yawning and stretching. They seemed to be thinking that even if the flood poured into the rooms in the middle quarters, it couldn't rise high enough to flow into the inner quarters. In truth, the flood couldn't invade the inner quarters until the whole of Janggwan-dong, Jongro Street, and Medicine Lane were inundated.

"My God, what should we do? The middle quarters might wash away," the old lady of the house shouted, but seemed to lack the courage to step down into the flooded courtyard for a closer look at the middle quarters. Of course even if she did come down, there was no way she could stem the flood.

"I suppose the drainage pipe in the courtyard water bin is blocked. I don't hear any draining noise," Mrs. An, the landlords' housekeeper, said, stepping out of her back room next to the kitchen.

"Is our kitchen all right?" the old lady asked the housekeeper.

"Water hasn't come into the kitchen, ma'am," Mrs. An said, and stepped into the flood to pick up the kitchen utensils piled up along the edge of the water bin. Junho's mother and my mother also stepped into the water to go to their respective makeshift kitchens to pick pots and pans and dishes out of the water and put them on the verandah.

"We could float a boat in the courtyard," commented Seongjun, the eldest son of the landlord.

"My fish must have all gotten swept away," lamented the landlord's youngest son. The lad often went to Chimsan-dong to visit his father's factory and fished up baby trout and tadpoles from the branch of the Geumho River nearby and put them in the pond in the courtyard.

The landlord, whose trousers were soaked through, stepped up to the raised platform of the inner quarters. The landlady, who had come out to the balustrade of the guest room in her pyjamas, scolded her husband for staying out late drinking so much in such weather.

"The factory is working even in the rainy season. How could I stay cooped in the house even if it's raining? My clients are clamoring for our products. If I'm to get a high price, I have to drink with them and explain how hard it is to run the factory," the landlord said in his defence.

"Oh, so it's hard work for you to let yourself be treated to banquets," somebody in the middle quarters sneered, but in a voice too low to carry to the landlord. It was Jeongtae.

It looked to be only a matter of time before the water in the courtyard would pour into the rooms, if the rain didn't let up immediately. When the inhabitants of the middle quarters were busy fishing up dishes and pans to put on the verandah, Junho's father forded the flooded courtyard and approached our rooms. He was carrying a shovel in his left hand. I stepped down into the flooded yard, and followed Junho's father to the backyard. We couldn't see the drainage hole in the wall, and a flash of lightning showed that the narrow backyard was also flooded. Beyond the wooden fence, people next door were also talking and scooping up water and throwing it over the fence.

"How are things over there?" Junho's father asked, tapping the plank wall with his shovel, trying to clear the drainage hole.

"Water got into the yard and the kitchen. The sewer must have gotten blocked. We can't drain the yard," the man next door replied.

Junho's father stopped trying to clear the drainage hole and came back to the courtyard. "There's no other way. I think all of you have to take a bucket each, scoop up water and throw it over to the outer yard," he said to the tenants of the middle quarters. But all of the tenants were busy saving their own things and paid no heed to Junho's father. Everyone put their belongings on to shelves, and Heunggyu and Miseon were carrying a big suitcase stuffed with their household goods toward the inner quarters. The Pyongyang woman and Sunhwa followed them with big bundles of military uniforms on their heads.

"What if our room was to get flooded? We must move the sewing machine somewhere safe," Mother said, hoisting up the heavy sewing machine and placing it on our shelf. Seonrye came out carrying our beddings wrapped in cloth. My younger brother Giljung gathered up his books and notebooks, and the youngest also had woken up in the bustle and was shivering inside the door.

"It's raining. Raining much. Soup is falling from the sky," the youngest said, clapping his hands toward the sky.

Junho's father stripped off his military jacket. "How can you think only of saving your things when the whole house is going to be flooded! Hey, you boy, follow me with a bucket," he said to Jeongmin, the Pyongyang woman's second son who was coming out with a small desk. All the inhabitants of the middle quarters looked at Junho's father in surprise, as he hardly ever spoke in the house, to say nothing of ordering people about.

"That's right. Everybody do what the veteran says. This house has a sunken courtyard, so water's bound to collect in it. There's no way except to scoop water. The ditch in the alley seemed to be draining all right," the landlord said, wiping his face and hair with a towel.

Heunggyu and Jeongmin, who had been taken aback by Junho's father's sharp reprimand, walked behind him toward the middle gate. Junho's mother, who had a towel wrapped round her head, went up to the inner quarters carrying the newborn baby in her arms. I picked up a bucket and followed Heunggyu and Jeongmin.

"It's like draining the Han River with a scoop. How can we stave off the flood with measly buckets when the sky is loosing all its waters on us?" muttered the Gyeonggi woman on her way to the inner quarters with a wooden hamper containing pots and pans.

Junho's father, who could not work the shovel very well with his left hand, turned it over to Heunggyu, telling him to scoop up earth and raise the sill of the middle gate. He then instructed Jeongmin to remove the sliding doors from the middle gate. Then he went to the tool shed beside the storage dais and brought out two straw sacks. When Heunggyu raised the sill of the middle gate with the earth dug from the outer yard, Junho's father put the sacks on top of it and trod on them to make the mound firm.

"You women there, you have to help, too. There's no time to dawdle," Junho's father thundered. Jeongtae and his family stepped forward. My mother, Seonrye and Miseon also followed.

"Jeongtae, you shouldn't get wet. Think of your illness," the

Pyongyang woman pleaded to her son, but Jeongtae paid her no heed.

"Everybody must help. We must divide into teams of three. One person must scoop up water, the next must hand it over to the person on the step, and the last should dump the water into the outer yard. You men must line up in the courtyard at the bottom of the steps."

Junho's father was a commander now. His undershirt was pasted to his body, and the rubber arm and the iron hook at its tip, exposed in plain sight for the first time, shone eerily in the lamplight from the inner quarters. The rubber arm seemed to make people bow to his authority without demur.

"Now, team up with those nearest you. Hurry up. All ready? Now begin. If you don't hurry, water's going to get into the rooms in no time." Junho's father barked the orders. The tenants of the middle quarters formed teams without a murmur. The hardest work, scooping up water in the bucket, was done by the young men, and the older teenage girls took up relay work. My mother, the Pyongyang woman, and Junho's mother dumped the water from the bucket into the outer yard. I did the work of carrying the emptied buckets back to the young men. Junho's father dug a canal from the middle gate to the main gate with his awkward shovelling, so that the water would drain out into the alley.

The work began and everybody worked hard, getting drenched in the pouring rain. Because it was teamwork, no one could take even a short rest. While we tenants were working so hard, a couple of the members of the landlord's family who had come out to watch went back to their rooms, while the rest of the family, including the old lady of the house, looked on from their verandah. Mrs. An, the housekeeper, came to help, as did the Gimcheon woman. The two women made a team with Junho's father. Only the Gyeonggi woman didn't join in. While everybody was busy at work, the lightning and thunder grew more distant and the rain grew lighter as well.

"You're so slow! Is that all the strength you can muster?" Sunhwa complained to her teammate Heunggyu.

"Do you think dentists pull teeth with brute force? I'm not a gangster," Heunggyu retorted.

"Young man, young lady, you two keep your minds off each other and concentrate on the work. Don't let your hands touch when you hand over the bucket," Mrs. An joked, and everybody laughed.

"Miseon, please exchange places with me," Sunhwa asked Miseon.

"I think you two make a good team. I don't see why we should change places," Miseon countered.

"I don't like it. You team up with your brother," Sunhwa insisted.

Miseon changed places with Sunhwa, shaking raindrops from her face. Her blouse was soaked through, and her breasts and erect nipples could be discerned underneath it.

"Oh, I am a poor deserted castaway," Heunggyu intoned with exaggerated sadness and whistled the tune of the "Rain Tango."

That moment, Junho's father shouted sternly toward the inner quarters. "You young men of this house. You come help, too. This is your house. What did your school teach you to do at a time like this?"

"Well said," Jeongtae remarked.

"Yes, we were about to come," said the second son of the landlord, coming down with his trouser legs rolled up. The youngest, a middle schooler, also came down.

"Come back, children. Don't you know that's all sewage? The toilet in the courtyard is flooded!" The landlady shouted, but the two ignored her and stepped into the flood. The eldest son, Seongjun, who was rolling up his trousers, said "Oh, right," and retreated into the inner quarters.

"Oh, what stupid kids. Come back! Stay away from the dung water!" the landlady repeated.

"We're not asking anyone to drink this foul water. If this water is dung water, we must all scoop it away together if we're to get rid of it," Jeongtae shouted toward the inner quarters.

"That's right. My husband didn't fight in the war to save his own life. We must all work together at a time like this," Junho's mother ventured, but her voice was too small to reach the inner quarters.

The landlady, perhaps fearing that Junho's father or Jeongtae would break into the inner quarters in indignation, went inside, supporting her drunken husband. Seongjun, the eldest son, also slunk away to his room. Only the old lady remained in the living room.

"Oh, those stupid kids! They're going to catch cold! And they'll be caned tomorrow if they doze off at school," warned the old lady of the house, complaining about her grandsons exerting themselves side by side with the lowly tenants.

Among the tenants of the middle quarters, only the Gyeonggi woman took no part in the concerted effort and kept on moving her household things to the inner quarters.

The landlord's two younger sons and I formed a team, bringing the number of teams up to five, which made the steps descending from the middle gate crowded. Even after the rain grew thinner the five teams worked hard scooping up water and throwing it away. Everyone worked diligently without saying a word, perhaps thinking that by scooping up and dumping as much water as possible, they could prevent it from flowing into the rooms. If the dung-tainted water flooded the rooms, they would stink like a toilet for a long, long time.

"Back in the summer of fifty-one, when we confronted the Communist Chinese in Keumseong, it rained in torrents like tonight. The night was pitch black, and the strains of Chinese flutes came from everywhere, so we couldn't tell the north from the south," Junho's father began, recounting his war experience as if reminiscing to himself. Nobody heeded or responded to his story. Even though only a couple of years had elapsed since the war, it seemed that nobody wanted to recall the war or talk about it.

"Look! We can see the top step. We've bailed out that much water!" Sunhwa exclaimed, as if she'd made an important discovery.

Everyone halted their movements momentarily and looked at the steps. To me also it seemed that the water level had sunk by about ten centimeters. Some of the water must have drained through the drain pipe and drainage hole, but it was thanks mostly to our combined efforts that a crisis was averted.

"Well, let's work harder," Junho's father said. As if on cue, the work gathered speed and momentum.

The rainy season was followed by broiling heat. I dashed about the streets, trying to sell newspapers. Some boys my age sold popsicles, carrying them in a wooden box insulated with tin casing, and cried "popsicles, cool, delicious popsicles!" I yearned to eat a popsicle, but I couldn't spend my hard-earned money on that. When I considered how the shoe repairmen, tinmen, A-frame porters, and vegetable or fruit vendors managed to feed their family with the money earned by their trade, I realized that buying a popsicle is a luxury I couldn't afford. When the yearning for a popsicle became unbearable, I vowed to myself that someday I would eat fifty popsicles in one sitting and make my innards freeze. In those days, the sweet-smelling popsicles and a dish of Chinese noodles were the greatest delicacy I could think of.

Because the middle quarters were situated in the sunken courtyard, even when there was an occasional breeze, it just passed over our heads, so even if we sat on the verandah after dinner for a whiff of wind, sweat still streamed down our torsos. As mosquitoes were thriving after the rainy season, I suffered several mosquito bites every day before creeping under the mosquito net to sleep. When I went out to Jongro Street or Medicine Lane, I was always passing grown-ups hurrying toward their homes carrying a big watermelon in one hand and dangling a block of ice tied to a straw rope in the other. The thought of scooping the flesh of the watermelon out into a big aluminum bowl and putting shredded ice and sugar in it to share with my family sent an icy tingle down my spine. My neighbors, the families from Pyongyang and Gyeonggi-do, often had such watermelon parties. At such times, even Giljung, who pretended not to mind what our neighbors ate, would go out onto to the verandah and swallow hard, eyeing the room in which the party was going on. My family never had such a watermelon party even once during that summer. It was only several years afterwards that we could have a watermelon party. That summer, we ate only two meals a day, so watermelon was something we couldn't even dream of. I still groan when I recall those long hungry days of that summer.

My youngest brother Gilsu seemed to run out of the strength to follow after Boksul and Junho by lunchtime, and just hovered around the verandah of the inner quarters, moving about with his tottering gait. When the old lady of the house and the housekeeper ate lunch in the living room, Gilsu watched them with his crossed eyes, squatting under the verandah like a hungry puppy. One day, the old lady of the house took pity on Gilsu and called him up to the living room and shared her own rice with him. That night, Mother didn't feed him supper. She said coldly, that as he had received alms like a beggar, he would have to go without supper. Gilsu didn't seem to understand my mother's reasoning, so he kept sobbing in a corner. Even after we all got under our bedding, Gilsu sobbed like an ailing puppy, moaning that he was hungry. Mother paid him no heed and only continued to scold him for receiving alms like a beggar. There was only one way to make him stop crying, but there was no rice for him. Gilsu sobbed and cried until I fell asleep. Just before falling asleep I heard Gilsu mumbling between sobs that he will never eat what other people gave him. Although only five years old, Gilsu must have understood his "crime," as he never went near the inner quarters again after that. The war and its hardships had turned my mother into such a pitiless woman.

That summer was hell for me as well. I hated that life as a succession of hunger, gloom, and boredom. I yearned to go back to my life as a kitchen boy in the tavern of my hometown, and had a hard time enduring each day. I was always thinking about leaving home. In my dreams, I was always eating in a hurry or starving to death, and all my limbs were scrawny. Hunger made the whole world look yellow. I drifted through the city streets as if I'd turned into a mollusk, carrying newspapers. But I couldn't muster enough courage to leave my family, and managed to survive without collapsing on the street from hunger. I had daydreams of collapsing on the street and being found by a rich lady who had pity on me and took me to her house to make me an errand boy. I didn't care what happened to me if only I could eat three full meals a day. Giljung, my younger brother who had scrawny legs, often fell on the street that summer. He had no friends, so he never went out to play. He had the look of a much older person, and rarely spoke. When in the room, he helped Mother do her sewing, but he often sat on the verandah looking vacantly up at the sky, sunk deep in thought. He always got 100 points on his exam papers, but he often fell and scraped his knees, even though he never ran. "Are your legs made of rubber? Why can't you even stand up straight?" Mother scolded him, but Giljung just blinked his fearful eyes and made no response. Like Giljung, Seonrye was also a good student. As if to block out the fact that she was starving, she studied even harder. Her dream was to pass the entrance exam to a teacher training school and become a primary school teacher in a village where peach blossoms bloomed. "I'd like to teach children and play the organ in a peaceful village," she often said. Seonrye had been a fifth grader the year the Korean War broke out. I suppose because she was frightened by the cruelty and confusion of the war, she was fond of using the word "peace" in her speech, like for example "a peaceful home," "a peaceful time," and "doves are symbols of peace."

One shameful deed I committed that summer remained a blot in my memory for a long time. I still blush for shame when I recall that incident.

One night, even though I had had my supper of barley gruel, I was so hungry that I stole into the kitchen of the inner quarters. Waking up in the middle of the night with a growling stomach, I decided to search the landlord's kitchen and eat their leftover rice. I had noted earlier where Mrs. An the housekeeper kept the family's leftover rice. I stole out of my room after putting on my breeches and stepped into the courtyard. There was no telling what time it was, but it was quiet all around. I first went to the toilet. Because I had eaten so little, I had very little to pass on. Anyway, pretending to use the toilet, I strained my ears towards the inner quarters. Every room was dark. Approaching the kitchen like a wild cat, I pushed open the kitchen door. The small cubicle adjoining the kitchen, which was Mrs. An's room, was dark. I went into the kitchen and groped the kitchen rack. My hand touched a basket. Mrs. An kept leftover rice covered with a basket instead of a lid, to prevent spoilage. There was about half a bowl of rice in the copper rice pot. I took out a lump of rice and put it in my mouth in a hurry. I came back to my room after finishing the rice in the pot and went back to sleep. The next morning, as I was making fire in the stove, I heard Mrs. An saying from the inner quarters that a rat must have knocked off the basket and stolen the rice from the pot. I realized that I had forgotten to put the basket back on the pot, but I made no comment.

Two days later, I returned to that kitchen again. I became bolder, so I not only ate the rice but took down the bowl of kimchi from the cupboard and feasted myself. I also took down a small bowl that contained beef boiled in soy sauce with green peppers. It was the first time I had ever eaten such a delicacy. I said to myself, rich people make this kind of dish out of beef, too. Then, I skipped two days and went to the kitchen again on the third night after that.

The afternoon after my third venture, I was about to go out to sell newspapers when someone called me. It was Mrs. An.

"Did . . . did you call me?" I stammered. My cheeks were on fire, and my heart pounded.

"Gilnam, I know it's you who's been eating our leftover food in the kitchen," she said.

"How? Do you have any evidence?" I asked.

"Gilnam, I won't tell anyone, so don't do it again, ever. I know how hungry you must be, going without lunch. But a man must be able to withstand such hardships. Not only your Mother and your sister but your two younger brothers are all enduring that hunger. I won't tell anyone," Mrs. An said compassionately, and patted me on the shoulder.

"I'm sorry," I said faintly.

I remember even today that Mrs. An never used the word "stealing." My face, which had dropped low, was scarlet and tears were running down my cheeks. If Mrs. An had informed my mother, she would have whipped me until my whole body was a zigzag of birch marks, and I'd have had to skip many meals. And I would have been scolded by Mother for having disgraced my family as the eldest son. But Mrs. An was true to her promise, and from that day, I never touched anything belonging to someone else, even if it were a coin dropped on the floor of the classroom or a short pencil. I owe it all to Mrs. An's compassionate wisdom.

To round off this episode about food, I still can't put down my spoon until I am full, even though it has been a few decades since we were unable to afford three square meals. I agree with all the health guidelines that say "Fill your stomach only seventy per cent," "Overeating causes all age-related disease," and "Girth and your longevity are inversely proportional." But I don't feel I have eaten until I've eaten my fill, and in the back of my mind, I feel that instead of prolonging my life by stinting on food I'd rather shorten my life somewhat and enjoy my meals. Even today, I yearn to eat breakfast the minute I wake up in the morning. When I finish breakfast, I decide on what I'll have for lunch. After lunch, I imagine the delicacies I would like to eat for dinner. That is one of the most important "matters" of my life, and an indispensable joy. "Do you know your waist measurement? It's thirty-eight inches now. Aren't you ashamed when our children poke you in the belly and call you mountain-bellied? Please eat less. Many families are skipping breakfast. Why don't you eat less rice and more fresh vegetables and fruit?" my wife chides me every day, but I can't refrain from eating, although I can refrain from other things well enough. I know that it's good to eat more side dishes and less rice, but I don't feel I have eaten until I've had my fill of rice. And I can never substitute bread or noodles for rice. When, a few years ago, my wife changed my rice bowl for a smaller one, I became furious. It was an infringement of my authority that I could not tolerate, hung up on food as I am. My mother, who enjoyed eating meat after we escaped poverty, suffered from high blood pressure and died of it in her mid-sixties. But even that did not have a warning effect on me.

4

The terrible heat of summer abated its fury in the course of time. A cool breeze blew in the morning and evening, and the bladder cherries that grew among the weeds beside the sewage ditch began to ripen red. The dark clouds that blocked the view of the sky dispersed, revealing a high blue sky strewn with nearly transparent, feathery clouds.

When the cold wind began to blow, my mother's customers came back in droves. Mother sat at her sewing machine until after midnight. With the exception of the youngest, the three of us siblings had to sit with a book spread in front of us until Mother finished her work for the day. If any of us dozed, her birch ruler descended on our shoulders without mercy. Seventy percent of the blows fell on me. Once past nine o'clock, sleep overpowered me, so no matter how hard I tried to stay awake, it was no use.

One day, around midnight, Mother finished her work for the day and made this announcement. It shook me wide awake.

"It's all to feed the four of you that I am working like this day and night. Let's eat lunch from tomorrow. All summer long, when I had to see you fast from breakfast till dinner time, my heart just ached, as though riddled by sewing needles. I swallowed endless tears to see Giljung's scraped knees. He wouldn't have fallen so often if he could have eaten three meals a day. Oh, these dirty times! When am I going to be able to feed my children good, nutritious food?" Saying this, Mother buried her face in a towel and sobbed bitterly, her shoulders shaking wildly.

By the time I had been selling the *Yeongnam Daily* for three months, I became friends with the other boys selling the same newspaper. Many of the boys quarrelled with each other while waiting for the street edition to come out, but they also played games of marbles and territory invasion together. I was among the bystanders looking on as the other boys played. And I became friends with another boy who was also a spectator. He was about the same age as me.

Hanju was a refuge from Hwanghae-do, and like me he also wasn't going to school. He was selling chewing gum in addition to newspapers. So, he was treading the busy streets of downtown from early morning until evening. Although he had been doing street vending for two years, he was not a smart-ass, but a boy of few words.

"I'm going to middle school from next year, even if just an evening school. My mother said she's sending me," he told me, as if to reconfirm his resolve. Hanju's father was conscripted into the North Korean army when the war broke out, and died in battle soon after. When he told me that his two younger siblings had died of cold and hunger while fleeing south in the wake of Communist China's entry into the war, his voice was not shaky and tearful but was firm and resolute, as if he were inwardly vowing vengeance. At that time, he was living in a rented room in one of the plank huts on the slope of Sangyeok-dong with his mother and younger sister. That area was a shantytown of refugees, and had no city water or sewage canals.

"My mother is selling beef jerky, but she's making very little money. She earns about as much as I do. I'm working really hard. I've saved up a little money for middle school tuition, too."

Hearing that from Hanju, I thought that although my own future was uncertain, Hanju would surely realize his dream and become rich. He looked like a gentle kid, but he had iron willpower.

When September came, Hanju got employment as a delivery boy with the *Daegu Daily*, so I didn't see him any more. I was sad not to have his cheering words and encouraging smile as we prepared to dash through the streets with our newspaper bundles. But about ten days later, as I was waiting for the street edition to come out in the backyard of the *Yeongnam Daily*, Hanju rushed in breathlessly.

"Would you like to become a regular delivery boy, too? There's an opening. The best district, too. The delivery boy got hit by a jeep delivering the paper and broke his leg. So, they need someone now. You'll be really lucky if you get the job."

"You mean I can become a regular delivery boy, too?" I said. I was excited. I had envied Hanju very much when he got a regular delivery boy's job. Delivery boys were mostly middle or high school students. The salaries were small but enough to cover tuition. So, there were many students waiting for the job.

Hanju made an appointment with me to meet in front of the Songjuk Cinema around 5:30 P.M., the time his delivery ended.

I went to Songjuk Cinema before five-thirty. I had sold all twenty copies that day. At that time, in Daegu City, there was a serial killer, so many people bought newspapers to check for another murder in the last twenty-four hours. That day, too, the newspaper ran a report that a woman on her way to her church was found strangled to death in a quiet alley of a residential area in Bongsan-dong. That swelled the number of murder victims to four. The victims were not limited to one sex and were of diverse social status, but so far there were no children. And the time and place were also entirely unpredictable. One was killed in a paddy just outside the city, but some were killed in the back streets of residential areas. Three of the victims were killed during the night, but one was killed in broad daylight in a public toilet at the intercity bus depot. Two were stabbed to death, and two were strangled. The only thing common to the four victims was that none of them had any of their belongings robbed, and all of them were wearing pale green clothes. The newspaper article inferred that the murderer must be a madman with combat experience because the deaths were brutal and instantaneous, and the murder weapon seems to be a military bayonet. So, the police were searching for mentally ill people among the demobilized. At the murder of a Christian who was going to church carrying a Bible, a Christian minister was quoted in the *Yeongnam Daily* as saying that it was proof that the war had deprived us of reverence for life, and that therefore all men should repent before God. As I was selling the papers shouting "Another murder incident!" I noted interesting reactions in the people buying the newspapers. None of them looked really terrified. A middle-aged man bought a copy and opened it saying, "They haven't caught him, have they?" His face seemed to convey hope that the murders would go on. For my part, too, I was so bored with life that I also hoped the excitement would be prolonged. Of course the murder also helped my trade to no small degree.

Hanju didn't appear even after five-thirty. In the Songjuk Cinema, an American Western was playing. In front of the ticket booth was a long line of people waiting to buy tickets. I wondered how some people could afford to see movies and dance in dance halls when most other people could hardly afford to eat three meals a day. One morning, when I caught sight of Jeongtae looking at the cinema ads in a newspaper, I asked, "How can so many people go to see movies at a time like this?" Jeongtae's sarcastic answer was, "Those who go to cinemas in broad daylight are damned bourgeois post-war capitalists." I didn't understand what "bourgeois post-war capitalist" meant, but I didn't ask.

While waiting for Hanju to show up, I looked into the radio shop, the clothes shop, the tailor shop, the watch and clock shop, and also at the display cases of the jewellery shop run by my landlady. There, on shelves cushioned by soft black velvet padding, were displayed gold and silver rings, bracelets, necklaces, brooches and silver spoons, and chopsticks. Jewellery was displayed on one side of the store and on the other side were displayed wristwatches of many different designs. After getting an eyeful of the expensive jewellery, I looked further inside, past the glass partition. There, engineer Jeong was wearing a tube of magnifying lens on one eye and cleaning the inside of a wristwatch. He was competently putting a tiny sawtooth wheel back in place and was tightening a minuscule screw. I thought the delicate work well became his pointed face and protruding eyes.

My landlady was engaged in serious conversation with a man wearing a beret. A while later, the man who had been sitting with his back to the door got up from the chair and pushed his cap up in leave-taking. When he turned toward the door, I recognized him as the sharp-jawed police detective who had asked me about the man with a knife scar on the cheek. My landlady fumbled with her handbag and took out a few hundred *hwan* notes. The detective made a feint of refusing the money a couple of times, then accepted it as if compelled by politeness, pushed it down into one of in his back trouser pockets, and came outside. I quickly turned away from him.

Hanju came when it was past six o'clock. When he saw me, he said, "I've kept you waiting long, haven't I? I'm sorry. The delivery took longer than usual today." He must have been running, as he was panting and there were beads of perspiration on his nose.

I followed him to the *Daegu Daily* distribution center, which was next door to the scrivener's shop and across the street from the law court. Half the office was taken up by a long table, and three fee collectors were sitting on stools making tallies, with receipts and money scattered on the table. The chief of the office was not there. We were told that he had gone out to deliver newspapers in place of the delivery boy who had the unfortunate accident, and we had to wait for more than half an hour perched on stools. I felt guilty about taking up so much of Hanju's time when he should be selling chewing gum.

"So, you're not a student either?" The chief of the delivery office, having returned on his bicycle, surveyed me from head to foot. Mr. Son, in his forties, was gaunt with cheeks sunken like an old man's—perhaps his molars were missing.

"Gilnam is so good at selling newspapers. I'm sure he'll do an excellent job increasing subscriptions."

I blushed when Hanju recommended my sales instinct that way. Mr. Son asked many questions about my family members and about how we were faring. I had my eyes pasted on the ground—too shy to look at Mr. Son, whose eyes glittered like a rat's—and barely managed to answer his questions. It seems that Mr. Son was satisfied that I lived near both the newspaper company and the delivery beat to be taken over, that even though I was dressed in worn clothes, they were at least clean and neat, and that I didn't look like a smart-ass.

"As a matter of fact, students are too busy with their schoolwork to try to win new subscribers. But newspapers can't go on without expanding subscription. Well, though you're really much too young to be a delivery boy, maybe we can give you a try." To Hanju he then asked sharply, "So you guarantee this boy?"

"I sure do. Just trust me. You won't be disappointed," Hanju said confidently, even though he'd never seen any of my family and knew precious little about me except that I was relatively new to Daegu and that I'd come from the country. I don't know why he vouched as my guarantor without any hesitation, but his words warmed my heart.

"Well, since you don't have to go to school, come here early in the morning, as soon as you've had breakfast."

Mr. Son's words made my heart swell with pride and joy, as I realized that I was not a newspaper vendor any more but a regular delivery boy.

When I left the delivery office with Hanju, it was already dark, so that lights in the shops along the street were lit. When I got home, I told my mother that I was to become a delivery boy starting the next day, thanks to the good offices of a friend named Hanju.

"Oh, is that so? That's so lucky. It's wonderful. I will save all your salary and pay your tuition with it from next year." Mother smiled her first bright, happy smile since I had come to Daegu. She put down her sewing and stepped out to the verandah. "I know you must be hungry, but come with me to Yeommae Market," she said, and took me there and bought me a pair of black sneakers. They were my first pair of elegant footwear since my days with Father in Seoul. Mother said I could walk home in the new sneakers and carry my rubber shoes. As I walked the paved road wearing my new sneakers, I felt as if I were walking on a cloud.

The next morning, as I was coming out of my house to head toward the delivery center of the Daegu Daily, I ran into a policeman carrying a carbine gun.

"Which room is Mr. Park Jong-mo's?" he asked me.

"Mr. Park Jong-mo?" I asked, as I'd never heard the name before.

"He's a wounded veteran," the policeman said.

"Oh, Junho's father," I said, and pointed toward the second room in the middle quarters. Junho's father hadn't left for his daily work yet, as his sneakers were still underneath his verandah. I hadn't seen him again on the street after that early summer day, but he went out with his small military duffle bag every morning.

"Is Mr. Park Jong-mo in?" the policeman said in front of Junho's room. The door opened and Junho's father looked out.

The policeman asked Junho's father if he was Reserve Captain Park Jong-mo. Junho's father said yes, and stepped out onto the verandah.

"I must ask you to accompany me to the police station," the policeman said.

"Why? What about?" Junho's father said.

"I don't know myself. I was just ordered to fetch you. You'll find out when you get there," the policeman responded.

I wondered what the police could want Junho's father for, but I couldn't linger. I hurried to the delivery center. Mr. Son was waiting for me. Riding on his bicycle with me walking beside him, he pointed out the more than hundred households that I was to deliver the *Daegu Daily* to from that day on. Mr. Son collected the monthly subscription fees himself in that area, so I used a chalk to draw a "T" on the gate of every subscriber's house and noted down each address, numbering them serially in my notebook. But as there was no adequate wall to draw chalk marks for the fourteen subscribers inside Chilseong Market, I wrote down in my notebook the names of each store that had signboards. For those that didn't even have signboards, I could only make mental notes. On our way we happened to be passing the street stalls at the entrance to the vegetable alley, and I looked around for Junho's mother, but I couldn't see her. It could be that she had followed her husband to the police station and was anxiously awaiting him outside.

"On rainy days, take care to put the paper in from this side so that the paper won't get wet." "Take care, this house has a big dog." "You must deliver the paper to the room beside the kitchen, as there are several families living in this house." "You must always be friendly and obliging to this family. They're not too gracious when payment time comes. They may say they want to discontinue subscription. If you lose a current subscriber, it cancels out one hard-won new subscriber." Mr. Son thus tipped me on everything I needed to know about the subscribers.

After we had entered the 105th subscriber's address, Mr. Son and I returned to the delivery office. By then, it was lunchtime already. Back at the delivery center, I wrote down my address and family matters on the form Mr. Son gave me. I wasn't sure about the address of the house we were living in, so I drew a map. Mr. Son told me to come to the backyard of the *Daegu Daily* by 2:30 PM, and added, "We hire delivery boys not just to deliver our paper to subscribers but to gain more subscriptions. A delivery boy must win at least five new subscribers every month. So, you shouldn't just go home after delivering the papers; you must knock on those houses where people might be affluent enough or educated enough to want to read newspapers. You'll get a bonus for every new subscriber you win," he said, half to encourage me, and half to scare me.

When I heard the word "subscriber" and "subscription" from Hanju and Mr. Son the day before, I hadn't understood the meaning, so I had to ask Hanju afterwards. That day, I wondered what 'bonus' meant. But I didn't like to ask Mr. Son and expose my ignorance, so I just bade him good-bye and returned home. As I was stepping down into the low courtyard, I caught sight of Junho's father's sneakers in front of Junho's room. It seemed that Junho's father hadn't gone out to ply his trade after coming back from the police station. I could hear him teaching math to Junho.

"So, you now know all the houses you are to deliver the paper to?" Mother asked on seeing me.

"Yes ma'am. I have to go out to deliver the papers as soon as I've had lunch," I said and asked, "Why did the policeman take Junho's father to the police station?"

"Junho's mother, who went to the police station with him, said that it was because of the serial murders going on these days. The woman who was killed on her way to church service had a thread from a military uniform under her fingernail, so the police concluded that the culprit must be a man wearing a military uniform. They are investigating all men wearing military uniforms," Mother answered.

"But they let him go without giving him a hard time?" I asked.

"It looks like it. They came back early."

As my mother's customer Munja knocked on the door holding a bag of popcorn, our conversation about Junho's father ended. Munja was a hostess working at Hyangwon-jeong, a high-class restaurant. She was gorgeous, and gentle-hearted, too. A student at a woman's college before the war, she had lost all her family during the fighting and was now working as a hostess. She seemed to regard my mother as an elder sister, and even when she didn't have sewing to commission, she often came for a visit bringing snacks, just to chat with my mother. Sometimes she even brought notebooks and pencils for Seonrye or Giljung.

From that afternoon on, I was a delivery boy. Every afternoon at around two o'clock, I left my house and headed for the *Daegu Daily* building located next door to the City Hall in Samdeok-dong. Passing through the back gate, I came to a large backyard. Usually, several boys working for the Jungbu (central region) Delivery Office were waiting there. There were nine delivery boys in all working for the Jungbu Delivery Office, but a couple of them were students who always rushed in late because their schools ended late. The earliest print-runs, which were street editions, were carried off by street vendors. Then the provincial editions were carried off by trucks to be distributed to various counties in the province. After that, young men from the East, West, North and South Delivery Offices carried off the city editions piled up high on the back racks of their bicycles. The Jungbu Delivery Office was the last to get its copies because it covered the areas nearest the paper company and downtown.

The Jungbu Delivery Office, alone of all the delivery offices, gave out the papers to the delivery boys in the backyard of the newspaper company. When Mr. Son came out of the print room pushing a hand cart piled high with newspapers in bundles of one hundred copies, we delivery boys quickly gathered around the cart. Most of the delivery boys were in middle or high school uniforms, but there were four of us who weren't in school uniform. Hanju and I were the youngest of the group. Mr. Son distributed the copies to us quickly counting them out in units of five, and we left to carry out our assignments.

Before sending us off, Mr. Son often made warning remarks such as, "You gained no new subscribers last week. We expect you to do better than that. Don't you know how many boys out there are just dying to take over your job? Do you, or don't you?"

I hold that even today winning new newspaper subscribers is one of the hardest jobs mankind has ever tackled. The difficulty is matched by the difficulty on the part of consumers in refusing solicitation for subscription. Even these days soliciting a new subscription usually entails one month's or even two months' free offers. The potential subscribers try to stave off such unwanted gifts by pasting posters proclaiming "XXX Daily Not Wanted" on their gates, but the free trial copies keep coming in. When the fee collector appears at the end of the 'service' period, the harassed 'customer' loudly protests, but the collector says that he came to collect the fee because the person is on the list of subscribers provided by the delivery boy. He then says that if the customer would generously pay one month's fee, he'll see to it that he won't be bothered again. So the customer pays one month's subscription in the hope of being freed from unwanted favors, but the copies keep coming in. The customer sometimes lies in ambush for the delivery boy, but delivery boys are also on the lookout for such customers. If they catch sight of a householder standing before the gate waiting to catch them or sense someone standing inside an open gate, they walk away pretending nonchalance or tiptoe away and come back later stealthily to toss in a copy. So, the prospective subscriber has no recourse but to wait for the fee collector. But the fee collector has his part of the story, too. The latter says that both the delivery boy and he himself are students having to earn their way through school. He begs the customer to show generosity and pay up, in the spirit of helping poor students get needed education.

On my first day of delivery, I was told by three subscribers on the list to stop putting in papers, as they were not subscribers. Since I was frightened about losing subscribers on top of not winning new ones, I pleaded with them, saying that I took over because the former delivery boy had a traffic accident, so would they please read the paper at least for the remainder of that month? Two of the customers agreed, though reluctantly, but one customer was simply adamant, so that house had to be given up. When I told Hanju the next day how I'd pleaded with three and lost one customer, Hanju said he had to plead with seven customers on the first day.

"When you keep losing customers you lose your delivery job. So, we keep tossing in copies in stealth. Then, when there are too many such houses, the fee collector complains and the delivery office replaces you. If you take over such a beat, then you're in a sorry fix. And, to be frank, the *Daegu Daily* is the least popular of the three dailies published in the Yeongnam area," Hanju explained.

Following Hanju's advice, I told Mr. Son that afternoon that two houses on the list agreed to read the paper till the end of the month and one house refused flat, so I wouldn't be held responsible for losing them.

Every day, Mr. Son gave me three extra copies on top of the one hundred and four subscription copies. I was to use the extra copies to attract new subscribers. So, in the middle of delivery, I stopped at some of the affluent-looking houses to knock on the door and solicit subscription. Of course I offered them free trial copies for the rest of that month, assuring them that they can refuse subscription if the *Daegu Daily* didn't meet their standards. At those times, my neck and face flushed with shame, but recalling Mr. Son's glittering sunken eyes, I had to suppress that feeling of shame. If I saw a family moving into the area, I helped carrying in furniture and things and then solicited subscription.

"I'm working hard to earn money for my middle school tuition for next year. Please help a poor aspiring student," I would plead. Or I would say, "Please read this paper for just two months. If I don't gain new subscribers I lose this job." At such times my heart pounded as if I were telling a lie. But appeals to the heart were the most effective method for winning subscribers. It was not what I found by myself, but what I learned from Hanju.

"If you walk with a limp and plead with tears in your eyes, that'll be the most effective," Hanju had said. Perhaps that was how Hanju won new subscribers. He won Mr. Son's praise by successfully soliciting four new subscriptions. But increasing subscription is one of the hardest jobs on earth, as I said. Even when you won one or two new subscribers, there are bound to be old subscribers who want to discontinue their subscription, so the number of subscribers doesn't increase. The hardest part of a delivery boy's life is not delivering papers but soliciting new subscriptions and pleading for continued subscriptions. So even on Sundays, I sometimes went to visit all the houses on my route to solicit new or continued subscriptions.

On my delivery route there were two orphanages for war orphans. One of them was a subscriber, and I was able to win the other for a new subscriber. It was a lucky stroke. One day, it caught my notice that the orphans in the two orphanages were very different from each other. The children in one orphanage were neatly dressed, even though in mostly ill-fitting relief clothes, and had a well-scrubbed look and neat haircuts. So, they didn't look too much like orphans. They also looked well-nourished, their faces being smooth and on the plump side. That had to mean they were regularly and adequately fed.

But the children in the other orphanage, the one I persuaded to be a subscriber, were very different. Some of the children in that institution had protruding bellies with blue veins visible through the skin; some of them had boils all over their heads; and some had faces eaten up in patches by ringworm. All of them had unkempt, untrimmed hair and tattered garments, like street beggars. Orphanages in those days relied on aid and relief goods from foreign institutions for supplies, and there was obviously a big discrepancy between the aid the two orphanages received. I often went into the yard of the poor orphanage to sit on the swing for a few minutes to give my feet a rest. The house next door to the orphanage had a fierce dog, so I was always fearful when striking into that alley, and the orphanage was like a haven. The pitiful orphans were immersed in their games and play, seemingly oblivious to how pitiful their scrawny legs and boil-covered heads look. They reminded me of my youngest brother Gilsu. According to my mother, for two years after settling in Daegu, Gilsu had scrawny arms and legs due to undernourishment, and blue veins showed on his protruding belly. Resting my tired legs sitting in the yard of the miserable orphanage, I took comfort in the thought that I and my siblings were not undernourished and didn't have to live in orphanages because we had a mother, even though she was a very harsh mother and apt to punish us severely for even slight transgressions.

While delivering papers to shops in Chilseong Market, I often ran into another pitiful refuge like myself. It was Junho's mother, who was supposed to be selling fruit in the market but spent more time looking out for the cop and running this way and that with her basin of fruit to avoid being caught and paying a fine. Since the day Junho's father was summoned to the police station and gave up trying to earn money, Junho's mother had to earn twice as much what she had been earning before.

"Gilnam, delivering papers is hard work, isn't it? But how can any of us earn our keep easily? People are desperately trying to make a living everywhere, right? You should be grateful you survived the war," Junho's mother would say to me, with a wan smile.

While delivering papers, I was sometimes stopped by passersby who asked to buy a copy. Most of the time, it happened in the market. For more than a month my response to such requests was "I don't have copies for sale," because I was a delivery boy, not a vendor. But by and by, as most of the time the day ended with one of the three extra copies left over, I sold a copy on the sly, even though I knew it was not right. With the side income from that unauthorized sale, I bought a small bag of conches that old women sold on the streets. It was a big treat for me to eat the conches by breaking the pointed tip to create a vent and sucking at the other end. It was a great fun eating them one by one, speculating if I would have any left by the time I finished delivering the papers, or hitting with the empty conch shells the T marks I left on the gates for identification. It relieved the monotony of my work considerably.

Among the shops on Dongseong-ro that were my subscribers, there was a book rental shop dealing in children's stories, novels, and comic books. I made the acquaintance of the proprietor about two weeks after I started my delivery work. On seeing me casting glances at the titles of the books on the shelf, the gentleman said, "Looks like you're fond of books," and then told me I could borrow them to read for free. He must have thought me pitiful not to be going to school at my age. I borrowed *Little Lord Fauntleroy* on the spot. "Be careful not to soil the book, and return it by the day after tomorrow," the gentleman said. I read the book from cover to cover that night and returned it the next day. After reading all the children's literature in the shop—there were about a dozen—I was able to move on to novels. My mother had forbidden me to read comic books but she didn't object to novels, so I read many detective novels. That was how I became acquainted with the names of such thriller writers as Kim Naeseong and Bang Ingeun. And the fictional detectives such as Yu Bullan and Jang Biho are to me still the prototypes of masterful detectives who could solve all mysteries and riddles with their miraculous powers of ratiocination.

I was able to finish delivering papers by the time the sun prepared to set beyond Dalseong Park. When returning home through the Janggwan-dong Street, the smell of the cheap rolls the Gimcheon woman was baking tickled my nostrils.

It was about two weeks into my career as a delivery boy that I ran into the man with a knife scar on his face. That day, after finishing my delivery I had knocked on the doors of many houses and pleaded for subscriptions in vain, and was coming home with tired steps. Days had grown much shorter with the beginning of autumn, so dusk was falling. As I passed Dongin Roundabout and was walking toward the station, shops along the streets were already lit. In the shady areas at the entrance of the Taepyeong-ro thoroughfare there were young women who were heavily made up and had their lips painted red. Even though the days had grown rather chilly, they were scantily dressed in colorful shifts that revealed their shoulders. Some were smoking cigarettes and humming popular tunes. Some of them blocked the way of male pedestrians and suggested they take a short rest, and some even grabbed the arms of passersby and tried to lead them to somewhere. A train passed with a shrill whistle on the other end of the blind alley.

"You're Gilnam, aren't you?" Someone strode up to my side to ask this. It was the man in the dyed military jumper. He had a rectangular face with prominent cheekbones and bushy whiskers, and kept his hat pressed low on his forehead. Because of the dark and also because of his whiskers, the knife scar which ran from his left cheek to his jaw was not conspicuous. He grabbed my arm. It was a strong grip. I couldn't even scream, and could only look up at him.

"When you go home, tell the Gimcheon woman to come to meet me at the entrance of the tunnel bridge in Chilseong Market at ten o'clock tomorrow morning. You mustn't tell this to anyone else or let anyone else hear you say it. If you so much as tell even your mother, I'll break your legs and you won't be able to deliver papers any more," he said, then checking left and right to see if cars were coming, quickly crossed the road and disappeared into the narrow alley that led to the black market. At that very moment, for some reason his image overlapped the image of the serial killer who had not been caught. I felt gooseflesh bumps rise all over my body. I had no way of knowing how he knew my name, or from where he had been shadowing me. I felt as if I were under a spell.

When I reached home, I told the Gimcheon woman the message from the man with the knife scar.

"Oh, yes? I'd been wondering about him. Thank you very much," the Gimcheon woman said and checked the alley with fearful eyes. There was no one on the street. The Gimcheon woman gave me a piping-hot just-baked roll, saying, "Here. Eat this. And be sure never to tell anyone what you said to me just now."

"Who is he?" I asked.

"He's a relative of mine. He dodged military service, so he's wanted by the police. That's why policemen come looking for him," she said.

I couldn't take the roll into the house to eat. Not only did my mother never allow us to take a gift from anyone, even neighbors, and gave us a heavy thrashing if we accepted anything, anything at all, from anyone, I also couldn't eat the roll before my younger brothers. As I took a bite out of the roll coming out into the street and staying in the shadows of the house pillars, someone approached the house. It was our landlady. I quickly put the rest of the roll in my mouth and went into the Gimcheon woman's shop kitchen. I was choking on the just-swallowed roll. After a coughing fit, I scooped up water from the Gimcheon woman's water jar and gulped it to get the roll down. While doing that, I overheard some conversation.

"So, have you found a new room?" It was our landlady's voice.

"Please give me a little more time," replied the Gimcheon woman. "I'm looking for a room in the Chilseong-dong area. There is a suitable room, but it won't be vacant for about two weeks."

"I know I shouldn't be throwing you out, if only to honor my uncle's memory. But you know my situation. Detective Kang coming to see me at the shop almost every week and trying to draw out information gives me the chills. And it's embarrassing in front of my eldest son, who's grown-up. The only way I can get out of this hell is for you to leave this house. And I feel so guilty around my husband and mother-in-law, too."

"Oh, I know how it is for you. I am so sorry. I should have left here long ago."

"Do you know it's the fourth time you've said exactly the same thing to me? It pains me to say anything more to you. So, please do something very quickly. You know how we were harassed after what happened to our cousin who lived in this room, don't you? And now with this happening to you, it's like I'm sitting on pins and needles when I face my in-laws."

"I know. I will leave soon." The Gimcheon woman's voice as she made this vow was firm.

"Mr. Jeong keeps studying my face, too. I won't bring this up again. Please move out as soon as you can."

I walked toward the middle gate before the landlady came out of the Gimcheon woman's shop.

The next morning, when it was a little after nine o'clock, Jeongtae left the house with a book in his hand. At around ten o'clock, when I peeped into the Gimcheon woman's kitchen and her shop, she was baking rolls with her back toward me. I wondered why she hadn't gone to the tunnel bridge in Chilseong Market. But I couldn't ask her why she hadn't gone to keep her appointment. It occurred to me that maybe Jeongtae went in her stead. Jeongtae came back as I was having lunch with Mother and Gilsu.

5

The deciduous trees had all shed their leaves, and it was late autumn. The warmer months, from late spring to early fall, are easier on the penniless. When the trees all stand bare and shiver in the cold wind, poor people feel that they, too, are at the mercy of nature and worry how they can survive the freezing winter.

The mid-fifties were the days before homes used coal briquets, so as autumn progressed, fuel wood was first on the shopping list of all households. Well-to-do people bought two truckloads of firewood and had it piled up all along an entire wall. In those days, if you visited someone's house in late autumn, your eyes automatically turned to the pile of firewood inside the wall and you made a silent estimate of how well off the family was.

From spring to late autumn, almost all households made fire in their portable stove with charcoal to cook their meals. It was the same with my family. Most families like my own, living in single rented rooms, would use a sack of charcoal for about twenty-five days, if they guarded against waste. But in the case of my family, a sack of charcoal lasted only two weeks. It was before the days of electric irons, so for my mother's sewing work, we needed to have a portable warming stove lit and have a small smoothing iron stuck into it ready for use to shape up the collars or smooth out the seams. For real ironing jobs, Mother used a larger iron bowl with live charcoal in the belly. For lighting up a charcoal fire Mother used bush clover twigs or pieces of fuel log chopped into chopstick-thin strips. Because I had nothing particular to do until I went out for newspaper delivery, the task of making fire in the portable stove for cooking and making fire for ironing fell on me. Naturally, I often got dizzy from inhaling charcoal fumes, and even vomited several times. It was like the motion sickness experienced in the train on my way to Daegu from my hometown when Seonrye came to fetch me.

When the cold winter wind began to blow and the papered stone floor was too cold to sit on without heating, all the tenants bought up firewood and did the cooking in the stove that served as both a cooking stove and an *ondol* furnace for heating the floor through embedded vents. All through the 1950s, my family never fed firewood into the stove just for heating the floor, except on really freezing days. We only heated the floor with the breakfast and dinner cooking fuel.

That year, we cooked our meals on the portable burner with charcoal until mid-October. Only in late autumn when we could see thin ice covering the courtyard at dawn did my mother bring home firewood from the market. And she didn't have A-frame porters carry several bundles of wood, like the other housewives did. She herself carried home a single bundle on her head. The single bundle of ten sticks no thicker than a young man's arm lasted us only four days.

"I'm terribly scared of hunger but not so much of cold. I felt the claws of hunger too often during the war. When you're hungry you can't work. But if you eat properly, you can bear the cold and you don't freeze to death even in a winter storm if your belly's full and you have a roof over your head and walls to shield you." Perhaps because Mother thought food was all-important in fighting the cold and heating only secondary, she bought sacks of rice and barley at the proper season to ensure our grain supply, but she always bought fuel in single bundles.

It was one clear autumn morning with a gentle breeze. I was

lying on my belly on the sunny verandah of my room practicing writing English words with the hand-me-down seventh grade English textbook from Seonrye. The old lady of the house was turning over with a rake the red peppers she had been drying in the sun to use in their winter kimchi. Sunhwa hadn't gone to the creek as usual to wash old military uniforms but was mending the worn sleeves of some tattered uniforms while sitting on the verandah of her room.

"Because all my grandsons are grown up now, we need one more room. So, one of the families in the middle quarters must vacate their room before winter kimchi-making time," the old lady of the house said, as if to herself but also for anyone and everyone to hear.

"What did you say, ma'am? That one of the families must vacate their room?" Sunhwa asked in astonishment, her hands halting in mid-motion.

"That's right. My two younger grandsons are too grown-up now to share a room. We need to use one of the rooms in the middle quarters," the old lady of the house confirmed.

"Do you really mean it?" asked the Gyeonggi woman, stepping out onto the verandah of her room. She must have heard the conversation through her paper door.

"Of course. I don't say such things just to exercise my facial muscles," the old lady said.

"Why are you saying it so late in the year? How can any of us find a room to rent at this time of the year, with winter right on our doorstep? I don't think any of us can rent a room and move away this late in the year," the Gyeonggi woman protested. She broke wind once, then lit the half-smoked cigarette she had left on her doorsill. My mother's sewing machine noise also ceased. Mother drew open the sliding door of our room and stared at the old lady of the house. Heavy anxiety hung on Mother's face.

"My son mentioned it many days ago, but I didn't have the

heart to bring it up, so I've been putting off telling you till now. I know how hard you're faring, all of you, so I didn't know which of you to ask to vacate your room. As you know well, I have four grandchildren. My second grandson keeps asking for a room of his own, and it really is time we should oblige him."

"Ma'am, your family is using no less than five rooms, apart from Mrs. An's closet. So, how can you ask one of us to vacate our room, when you know we are living three to five to a room? How can you be so inhuman? It may be possible to find a room to rent next spring, but there won't be any rooms available for rent in this cold. It's just like telling one of our families to freeze to death on the street." The Gyeonggi woman's tone was rough as she went into her kitchen with her tobacco stuck in her mouth. We heard her breaking wind again.

Junho's father must have been in his room looking after the baby, but he didn't emerge to offer a protest or anything. Junho's father had not left the house for over a month now.

Because we had no clock or watch, I left for the newspaper company when the wall clock in the living room of the inner quarters struck two. As I was walking the lengthy back alley leading to Jongro Street, I saw Junho's father walking toward me pulling a worn handcart. He was wearing a military jacket dyed black. A rusty tin drum was on the cart and also Junho.

"Gilnam, this is our car. This is our car Father bought," Junho bragged.

"Stupid boy. This is not a car, only a cart," Junho's father said weakly, with a wan smile. Seeing that weak smile, it occurred to me that Junho's father may be a gentle and tenderhearted person, unlike the impression he usually gave.

"It's a car because it has wheels. Bicycles are cars, too," Junho protested.

"What are you going to do with this cart?" I asked Junho's father.

"I must do something for a living, mustn't I? Well, I guess you'd better be on your way," he said.

When I returned home after delivering the papers, Junho's father was scraping rust from the drum with a piece of metal. As there was a big hole in the middle of the drum, I could easily guess at its use. It looked very similar to the drum that the Gimcheon woman used for baking rolls in, so I guessed that Junho's father intended to sell baked sweet potatoes on the cart.

A well-made-up woman who worked as hostess came to collect her new outfit that she'd commissioned my mother to sew, so I went out into the yard. She was going to change into her new outfit and go to work at a restaurant. I thought I'd take a walk along Medicine Lane and stepped into the Gimcheon woman's kitchen to pass on into the street. There, the Gyeonggi woman was trying to engage the Gimcheon woman in conversation. Sensing that it was about the matter of one of the families needing to vacate their room, I stopped short.

"I tell you, the landlords wouldn't dare ask Junho's family to vacate their room. They'd be too scared of his hooks to say that. I get so frightened when Junho's father screams in one of his nightmares. Even though there are four men in the landlord's family, they wouldn't be a match for Junho's father if he picked up a knife and proposed a life-and-death match," said the Gyeonggi woman. There was no response from the Gimcheon woman. I thought that the Gyeonggi woman had a point. Junho's father didn't use to scream at night in the days he went out to earn money every morning, but from the time he had started spending his days at home cooped up in his room looking after the baby, he sometimes had a fit during the night. "You vermin, you don't deserve to live. I'll send you to hell with a single bullet!" "March! Occupy Ridge number fifteen in one stride!" "Where's the nurse? Nurse! Come here at once. Can't you see this blood? Stop the bleeding first!" Junho's father shouted such commands in the middle of the night. The newborn baby woke up crying at her father's fierce screams. "Poor man. What hell he must have gone through for those nightmares to return to him till this day," my mother said in commiseration, heaving a long sigh.

"But did you hear?" the Gyeonggi woman continued. "Junho's father stayed in the military hospital for a few more months after he had his arm cut off. In the mental ward. That's why the police suspected him when the serial murders happened last summer. Because of that record."

"I guess the landlords might be hoping Junho's family would leave. But they are working so hard trying to make a living in this faraway town among total strangers. So, how can it be easy for the landlords to make them leave their room? That's like telling them to freeze to death on the street." the Gimcheon woman said sympathetically.

"Well, we're all among strangers. And life is hard for all refugees. My family also used to be well-to-do in Gaepung city in Hwanghae-do. But the reds took away all our property and we have drifted down this far in the confusion of war. And we're reduced to living three to a room," the Gyeonggi woman said, as if to assert that she deserves as much pity as Junho's father.

"I think Junho's father is truly extraordinary, even for a person from the North," the Gimcheon woman said.

"Didn't you see how formidable Junho's father is, that night of the flood? How he scolded the landlords? I don't think the landlords will have the guts to ask Junho's family to vacate their room. They wouldn't want Junho's father to come at them brandishing his hooks, protesting that he is paying rent for his room just like the other tenants . . ."

I didn't want to listen to the conversation any more, so I stepped into the kitchen of the store. But I had to hold my breath and listen again. The Gyeonggi woman was talking about our family.

"So, I'm saying that it's Gilnam's family who should be leaving. Theirs is the biggest family. So, they cause the most inconvenience to other families, like in the use of the toilet. For me, suffering as I do from stomach trouble, I get so impatient in the morning waiting my turn behind them. But I don't think that point bothers the landlords. The most serious problem is that because of Gilnam's mother, prostitutes come in and out of this house. In the past, *gisaengs* received hard training, so they were intelligent artists good at singing and composing poetry and brushing calligraphy. During the Japanese rule, many *gisaengs* of Gaesong got together and sent a lot of money to the independence fighters fighting the Japanese on the freezing plains of Manchuria. But today, thanks to the American influence, there's no more discipline anywhere, and women who serve as hostesses are just prostitutes and nothing more. The war has turned all young women who aren't positively ugly into shameless prostitutes. They've become so devoid of shame that they take off their blouses regardless of whether anybody's looking or not, and even teenage girls come out to the verandah clad only in their chemise and smoke, sitting with their legs wide apart . . ."

"But how can that hurt this house?" the Gimcheon woman asked.

"Oh, you don't know how it is, because you stay in your store all day and don't know what's going on around the courtyard. The *gisaengs* frequenting this house are a moral hazard to this place. The landlord's family has sons attending college and middle and high schools. And their niece is a high school girl. *Gisaeng* girls coming in and out of the house definitely cause problems. Why, Seongjun, the college student, uses our toilet and steals glances toward Gilnam's room when there's a *gisaeng* visiting. Hoping to catch sight of a *gisaeng*'s face or breast, of course. I heard the old lady chiding him not a few times. How can an old lady of decent lineage put up with such things?"

"Oh, I see what you mean," the Gimcheon woman agreed.

"And that's not all. The other day, I overheard a young dimply *gisaeng* girl asking Gilnam's mother if this is the residence of Chairman Park, who runs a textile factory in Chimsan-dong. I suppose our landlord is a patron of that *gisaeng*'s restaurant. I overheard her describing the drunken behavior of our landlord to Gilnam's mother. Gilnam's mother tried to hush her up, lest the old lady might hear, but that young teenager kept telling her how our landlord got so drunk and danced, stripped stark naked except for his briefs. The old lady happened to be washing mung bean sprouts at the water bin in the courtyard, and she fell into such a fury at those words that she said she'd rather have the room go vacant than have her house become a haunt of vulgar prostitutes. As for the family from Pyongyang . . ." But the Gyeonggi woman's harangue was cut short by something.

After a brief silence, the Gimcheon woman said, "Oh, you seem to have sold everything today. You must be exhausted."

Junho's mother, with her baby strapped to her back and with a bundle of firewood in the fruit basket she was carrying on her head, stepped into the outer yard through the side gate. For about a month now, Junho's mother had been coming home late. Because Junho's father stayed home and cooked dinner, she seemed to be staying late in the market to sell her fruit to the last one. Junho's mother took a good look at the hand cart and the oil drum Junho's father had placed in a corner of the outer yard and stepped into the courtyard through the middle gate. Now, I wanted to leave the scene before the Gyeonggi woman's harangue started up again.

In the dusk, all the shops along Medicine Lane and in the Yommae Market were lit up. I inhaled the smell of medicinal herbs wafting on the chilly evening wind. That smell was always fragrant and pleasant. When I reached the entrance to the market, there were big heaps of cabbages and turnips for making winter kimchi, and in the firewood section there were logs piled in heaps bigger than small houses. I wondered to myself when it would be that our family could buy firewood for the winter in truckloads and make enough winter kimchi to fill many earthen jars. I couldn't believe that such things would be possible within a few years. When I returned home after surveying the firewood market, I found the Pyongyang woman visiting with my mother. The two ladies were in serious conversation about the matter of one of the families having to vacate their room.

"I don't think you need to worry. Even if the landlord's family wanted one of our rooms evacuated, they wouldn't want your room which is farthest from their quarters. If one of their sons uses a room amongst us, we wouldn't be able even to breathe comfortably, the walls are so thin. It's obvious the Gyeonggi family should vacate their room, as theirs is the one closest to the inner quarters. And you know how the old lady loathes the Gyeonggi woman who goes around telling stories and finding faults."

"But the Gyeonggi woman's son has helped the old lady have her dentures made at a cheap price. And you know how good the Gyeonggi woman is at flattering and fawning on the old lady," my mother said sullenly. "This very evening, too, the Gyeonggi woman was making it up to the old lady, asking her if she needed any further dental treatment. She also said her daughter was planning to present her with a can of dried milk, which she said was good for elderly people."

"Oh, the obnoxious creature! Did I tell you what I heard about her? One of the vendors in the market is from Gaeseong. I mentioned to her that I live in the same house with a woman from Gaeseong, and she knew her! She told me that our Gyeonggi woman was not a wife but a mistress. She became the mistress of a rich loan shark who lent money to ginseng merchants. Those children are the offsprings from that union," she whispered, cautiously casting glances at the closed door.

My mother looked at the Pyongyang woman in astonishment. Even her hands had stopped moving. Seonrye, who had been studying with her book spread open on the meal tray, stole an oblique glance at our neighbor.

"Oh, I guess that's why she rarely speaks about her husband. And that's why she is so lazy and so loathes doing any house-keeping, and smokes so much . . ."

"I heard that her loan shark lover and his lawful family were all sent away to work at the Suan Mine in the mountains in North Hwanghae-do, for being reactionaries. I heard that before liberation the Gyeonggi woman, even though she was a mistress, had a housekeeper and never did any work."

"Well, I guess we were all well off before the war, more or less. And we all have many sorrows and regrets to tell. It's no use now to remember the better times. But, anyway, I think the Gyeonggi woman will do anything to go on living in this house. And she'll succeed. Just because her room is the closest to the inner quarters doesn't mean she has to move out. She can just give up her room to the landlord's family and move into one of ours."

My mother, having finished sewing the collar to a blouse, drew out the smoothing iron from the stove and began ironing the collar and lapels of the deep purple silk blouse on the low ironing board.

"Well then it would be Junho's family. I think it must be either Junho's or the Gyeonggi family's. You are working so hard to bring up and educate your four children. How can the landlord ask you to vacate the room, when they are bringing up and educating children of their own?"

"You know, I've managed to win a number of patrons and my business is just becoming established. If I were to move now, I will lose all my patrons. If I moved to the house next door, then the girls would continue to come to me with their business, but they're so lazy they wouldn't come even a few more blocks. If I lose my patrons, then there is nothing to do but for the five of us to become beggars. Moving a few blocks away wouldn't be a matter of life and death for the other families, but *where* we live decides whether we eat or starve. I must stay in Janggwan-dong if my kids and I are to stay alive, but how can we hope to be so lucky as to find a room in Janggwan-dong at this time of the year?"

My mother snuffled. Her face was as anxiety-ridden as her voice, and it seemed that she had no strength in her arms, either, as the iron in her hand was not doing its job properly.

"Aren't you out of material for linings? The fabrics prices are soaring with the onset of cold weather. Why don't you come to the market one of these days?" the Pyongyang woman said, reluctant to agree with my mother's opinion that the other families wouldn't be hit so hard as mine by moving some distance away.

"Thank you. I'll drop by one of these days. Take care," Mother said.

Mother and the Pyongyang woman became close friends, as they had both lost their husbands during the war and were both very independent and hard-working. The Pyongyang woman did my mother the kindness of procuring threads and collar and lining materials for her sewing from the black market she sold her wares in.

"I guess the Pyongyang woman isn't worried at all about having to evacuate the room. With her son tutoring two of the landlord's sons, I don't think the landlords can ask her family to leave. I heard that the landlord's sons' grades are improving, thanks to Jeongmin's tutoring. The landlords ought to invite her family to live in their quarters," Mother muttered to herself after the Pyongyang woman returned to her room. For our benefit, Mother added, "She is a widow, but her youngest son is shielding her from the storms."

Mother couldn't fall asleep for a long time that night, and

she muttered to herself "What if we have to leave this house in this cold winter? How miserable it is, to have no shelter of our own!" "I'll have to consult my sister-in-law tomorrow. I'll have to ask her to visit the landlady and ask her to let us stay on." I could hear Mother saying to herself as I was falling asleep.

The days grew perceptibly shorter day by day, so I could finish delivering the papers only after the sun had set behind Dalseong Park. When I arrived home nursing my empty stomach, it would be dusk. About three days after Mother and the Pyongyang woman had exchanged words about moving out, I entered the courtyard on reaching home and saw a young man piling up firewood against the wall of my room. Mother and Seonrye were handing him the logs strewn on the courtyard one by one.

"Ma'am, why don't you have the logs split tomorrow? I'll do it for four hundred *hwan*, though I normally charge five hundred," said the young man, who was wearing a dog-fur cap and piling the logs as high as his shoulder.

"I told you, I have a son to do it. With four hundred won, we can buy grain for two days," was Mother's response.

"Is that boy your son who's going to split the logs? That skinny boy?" the young man smiled, catching sight of me standing beside Seonrye.

"Didn't you hear me say I'm not going to ask you? Why make me say the same thing over and over? Well, since you've finished piling up the logs, you'd better hurry off. The wood's all been paid for, you know."

"If that kid's to split the logs, half of the wood will simply become useless splinters. You'll lose a thousand *hwan* worth of wood, instead of saving four hundred *hwan*. And he might hurt himself wielding the axe, too. Then, the hospital bill will be more than the price of the wood," the young man kept on saying, continuing to glance at me with his head tilted.

"Stop saying such stupid things and just go," Mother snapped.

The young man lifted his dog-fur cap and headed toward the middle gate, saying, "Well, have a warm winter." His gait, as he walked away with a sack holding an axe and a wedge slung over his shoulder, looked dispirited in the dusk.

Before the days when every household used coal briquet for heating and cooking, as soon as the autumn harvest festival was over and cold wind began to blow in all the streets and alleyways of the city, you could run into chimney sweepers and log splitters. Chimney sweepers had a brush tied to the end of a thin metal band or split bamboo stalk, which they carried curled around their shoulders. They were pitch black from head to foot, so that anybody could tell they were chimney sweepers, even if they didn't go around slowly calling out "Chimneys cleaned." Not only were their faces and dog-fur hats black with soot but their clothes were also encrusted with it, so people gave them wide berth to avoid being smudged. Because the rooms were heated through stone flues under the floor, the flues and the chimneys often got clogged with soot, so that chimney sweepers who had the skill and the tools for clearing the soot out of the flues and chimneys were in great demand.

I wasn't afraid of the chimney sweepers, but log splitters gave me chills. I used to get scared when I ran into log splitters while delivering newspapers. They usually carried sacks holding an axe and a wedge slung from their shoulders. Some of them simply carried wedges stuck into military uniform pockets and carried a sharp axe slung on their shoulders, in the style of outlaws. Some of them had faces covered with whiskers and sunken, starved-looking eyes. When they cast glances into the yards of people's houses as they passed by, trying to see if there were logs needing to be split, they often looked to me like robbers. Many a time had my heart beat wildly when running into them on a quiet back street. I was afraid they might holler at me to hand over all the papers and all my clothes too, down to my very underwear, threatening me with their axe. They called out their trade tunefully, but I couldn't determine the words exactly.

"Gilnam, all this is our firewood," Seonrye whispered joyfully, eyeing the logs piled one third the height of our wall. As she brushed away the perspiration from her forehead with the back of her hand, her eyeteeth showed white in the dusk.

"I feel warm just to look at the logs. Maybe we won't have to heat our room this winter. It may be enough to feast our eyes on the logs to feel warm," Mother said contentedly. "Well, Gilnam, wash your hands and come to eat."

"Looks like we have a real wealthy family among us," Sunhwa said, squatting in front of her improvised kitchen and roasting pork on her portable stove.

The smell of roasting pork made me ravenous. The Pyongyang family always ate well. Of all the families living in the middle quarters, they most often ate meat. Every two or three days, they bought and roasted pork on the stove, or cooked pork soup using minced pork and slices of turnip. The Pyongyang woman would say, "Haven't we seen hordes of refugees dying of cold and hunger? We should eat as best we can, instead of scrimping and saving. After all, we can't live forever. I'm going to eat as well as I can. I hope it will be a consolation to my late husband who died hungry. I'm making it up to him." But Mother told us a different reason for their frequent feast. "Meat is the best medicine for consumptive patients. Do you know how the Pyongyang woman is grieving on account of her first-born? They cook that much pork, but Jeongtae eats most of it. That's his medicine."

I couldn't believe that the delicious roasted pork was medicine. I thought that if I could eat such medicine I'd be happy to have the same disease.

"Oh, how happy you must be! You bought a full sack of rice at the right season, and now you have a high stack of logs, so you need only make kimchi for the winter to have no worry about surviving," Junho's mother observed, carrying their finished dinner tray out of her room. Junho's mother ate dinner with only Junho these days, because from the day before, Junho's father had started going out with the tin drum on his handcart and returning home only around midnight.

"Oh, I know why Gilnam's mother bought up an entire cartful of this firewood. She never used to buy firewood except in small bundles. Yes, I know what she has in mind," the Gyeonggi woman put in.

"Mother, let's buy a cartful of firewood, too. I'll pay for it when I get the year-end bonus," said Miseon, who had changed into her school uniform of black serge with white collars, as she stepped out onto the verandah with her schoolbag.

"Oh, yes, let's do that. Let's buy a whole cartful of logs and have it stacked up high."

"See you later," Miseon said, holding up her wrist to check the time against the electric light, then hurrying across the darkened courtyard, her swaying hips nearly bursting out of her tight trousers.

When Seonrye brought in the dinner tray, we quickly gathered around it and took up our spoons. The side dishes were cabbage soup and kimchi. When I picked up a cabbage leaf and chewed on it, I chewed sand.

"Sister, you didn't wash the cabbage well," I said.

"I did. What's the matter?"

"I chewed sand," I said. But that didn't deter me from eating ravenously. I scooped big spoonfuls of rice into my mouth and transferred as much kimchi from the bowl into my mouth as my chopsticks could hold. Mother often picked up discarded cabbage leaves and turnip stalks on the days she went to the market. It was her belief that even though stealing was a crime, there was no shame in picking up and bringing home discarded vegetable parts that were edible. She said that even though they were soiled and had been trodden on, they could be washed clean and boiled into good soup, so we ought to be grateful for them, thinking of those times that we'd had to skip meals for want of anything edible. Of the four families in the middle quarters it was only mine and Junho's that picked up straw bundles, wood chips, and pieces of vegetables from the market.

When my hunger was somewhat appeased, I noticed that Mother was still outside.

"Mother, come in and eat," I said to my mother who was standing in front of the pile of logs in the dark.

"Don't worry. You go ahead and eat," Mother said, continuing to count the logs, touching each one with her index finger.

"Sister, Mother looks so happy. What made her buy so much wood at one time?" I asked my sister, closing the sliding door.

"Aunt went to see the landlady at her jewellery shop, to ask her to let us stay. The landlady said that she is in a really awkward position because we are all poor folk who can't afford to rent another room easily. So, she told Aunt that maybe if we bought and stored a lot of firewood, then she might be able to tell the others she can't ask us to leave with the load of wood. And of course, we need wood to live through the winter, so . . ."

"But didn't Miseon just now ask her mother to buy a cartful of logs . . . ?"

"Yes, I heard," Seonrye said dejectedly.

The next day, the Gyeonggi woman bought a cartful of fuel wood just like we did. Not only did she buy wood, but she had the young man who delivered it split the logs. Then she piled the split logs along the wall, neatly, with ventilation spaces in between.

As if there were a race for buying firewood, the Pyongyang woman also bought a cartful of logs two days later. So, the entire space between the makeshift toilet beside the middle gate and our room was piled high with fuel wood, as if the house had turned into a wood store. As Junho's family alone did not join the race, we had come to assume that Junho's family was the candidate for evacuating the needed room. Junho's mother continued to return home with a bundle of wood in her empty fruit basket after selling her fruit. She did not remark on the piled firewood of the other families. The old lady of the house made no remark, either. There was no telling whether she knew the intention behind the log-purchasing competition.

One day, as I was going to the newspaper company, Mother asked me to bring home a piece or two of chalk. I asked and got two pieces of chalk from the teachers' room of the Dongin Primary School, after delivering the paper. Mother told me to make chalk marks on our logs. She seemed to be worried that our logs would get mixed up with those of the other families. I drew a vertical chalk line along the middle of the piled logs, so that if anyone took out a log there will be a break in the line. It seemed that Mother would have liked me to inscribe a serial number on all the smooth cuts of each log, as I did on the houses of newspaper subscribers. When I returned to our room after drawing the lines, Mother said disapprovingly, "Is that all you can do? Well, that was easy for you, anyway."

The Daegu basin, located in the center of the Yeongnam area, was the hottest spot in the country in the summer and the coldest in the winter. In the summer it was broiling hot day after day, and in the winter cold wind sliced into your flesh.

One day in late November, there was a surprise attack of cold, and the pond in the courtyard froze. When I put my hands into the water in the wash basin to wash my face, the icy water stung my knuckles and nails. Mother gave me for the first time that morning striped cotton underwear reinforced at the elbows and knees. It was hand-me-down underwear from my elder sister, so the fly had to be cut open with scissors and finished with stitching, and the legs didn't cover my ankles. Underwear should cling to the body, but this one, having conformed to the shape of my sister, had enough space between its seat and my buttocks to hold a gourd on each side. I realized for the first time that Seonrye now had the rounded contours of a young woman.

"Oh, it is biting cold," our landlord muttered, stepping down to the courtyard. He was wearing a thick overcoat and had his felt hat pressed low on his forehead. His breath created a white frost.

Early that afternoon, as we were just finishing lunch, a young man in jacket and a cap stepped into the house and asked to see the old lady. He was an employee of the Oseong Fabric Company who came on errands from time to time.

"I brought the logs the president sent," the young man said.

"I know. He said he'd send logs home. So, have they arrived?"

"Yes, I've got two trucks parked on the main road."

"Well, bring them in and have them piled neatly along the wall in the backyard beside the storage dais," the old lady ordered the young man. She called Mrs. An to clear the yard along the wall of waste and debris.

The three families in the middle quarters were feeling rich for having each bought up a cartful of logs, even though the wood might not be enough to last them through the winter, but the landlord's family had purchased two truckloads of logs, because the landlord's business was thriving. Not only were the tenants of the house impressed beyond words, but up and down the street, all passersby exclaimed and sighed in surprise and envy.

Because the trucks were too high and would have struck the eaves of the houses, they couldn't be brought into the alley, so a handcart was hired to transfer the logs into the alley, and three A-frame carriers carried the logs into the courtyard. When the A-frame men unloaded the logs in the courtyard, two men stacked them up along the wall. The logs were straight red pine, without knobs and twists, and some of them were so thick on one end that one alone would be an armful for me. Of course it is unreasonable to compare the tenants' logs with those of the landlords, but one couldn't help noticing how shabby the tenants' firewood looked in comparison to the landlords'. The Gyeonggi family's logs, as they were already split, looked especially skimpy. Alone among all the inhabitants, Junho's family didn't have any pile of firewood.

Junho's father came out of his room wearing a soot-stained cotton glove on his left hand and carrying a sack of sweet potatoes. He picked his way through the strewn logs with head bent and looking downward to avoid meeting other people's eyes.

"Daddy, I wanna go, too. Take me with you," Junho pleaded, pulling his father's loose right sleeve.

"Dada, Dada, take me, too! I wanna see," My own younger brother Gilsu tagged along with his tottering steps.

"Daddy's not your dada. Daddy's my daddy. You always think he's your daddy," said Junho, snubbing Gilsu.

"Dada! Dada! Take me with Juho," exclaimed Gilsu, tottering after Junho's father hastily, stepping over logs. My brother Gilsu seemed to have an ardent wish to call somebody daddy. He always called Junho's father "Dada."

"It's not a fit place for youngsters like you," Junho's father explained to Junho. "Junho, you play with Gilsu. You play with Gilsu until noon, and then, you copy the letters I wrote out for you on the newspaper. Five times, mind! If you haven't done it by the time I'm home you get caned, okay?"

"But you write letters wobbly, too, daddy!" Junho complained. It seems that Junho's father was practicing penmanship with his left hand.

Without responding, Junho's father turned the two youngsters around and went to the outer yard. His handcart with the tin drum and firewood were parked in a corner to the rear of the

Gimcheon woman's store. Perhaps because of the sudden merciless cold, Junho's father, wearing a dog-fur cap with earflaps and the woolen mufflers his wife had knitted for him, looked shabby and cold.

The porters worked so diligently in spite of the cold that they were soon sweating profusely, and the old lady of the house was looking at them at work with a smile of contentment hovering about her wrinkled mouth. The handcart men and A-frame carriers received their fees and left after dumping all the logs in the courtyard. Two young men, one in a dyed military uniform and one clad in Korean traditional jacket and trousers fitted out with a black vest, were piling up the logs neatly against the wall.

"Ma'am, why don't you split the logs starting tomorrow? If the two of us were to do it, we could finish in three days. We'd do it at a good price, too," said the young man in the black vest, whose face was pockmarked.

"Not yet. Stop pestering us. The logs are still green. They need to dry out to split neatly," the employee of the Oseong Textile Company added. It seemed that the men had been clamoring for the work all the way from the log yard.

"You're right. The logs are still green," the old lady agreed.

"The green logs will make work harder for us. But you win on all counts. If they're split while wet, there'll be no splinters and they'll dry out quicker, for better heat," the young man with the pock-marked face said, lifting a log and handing it to his companion standing on the pile.

"Well, we still have split wood to last us for half a month, so just have them all piled up and go. Don't you know that split wet logs make poor fuel?" the old lady said, and went inside, shivering.

"Look, young men. Pile them up good and neat. If logs come tumbling down, people can get hurt," Mrs. An, the housekeeper, said, looking up at the young man on top of the pile. The young man with a bushy beard, who had been working diligently in silence, responded, looking down at Mrs. An.

"Don't worry, ma'am. I'll do a neat and safe job."

"Well, first the Japanese stripped all our mountains bare, then the bombs scorched all our mountains, and now logging's going on all the time, so how can our mountains not be bald?" muttered Jeongtae, who had been observing the log piling with folded arms.

"In my hometown, if someone was found cutting wood from a mountain, he was taken to the police station and had the daylights beaten out of him," I told Jeongtae.

"Yes, poor folks get the hell beaten out of them if they so much as break off a twig. But there are people who tape off a whole mountain and cut down sturdy pines like those from national forests, and no policeman or forestry officer dares even murmur. There are also wood brokers who cut and sell wood in league with the police and the district office clerks. That's why they say you can do anything with 'pull' these days and nothing without it. You just wait until there's a flood next summer. Whenever there's a flood, the bald mountains send down landslides, and villages and towns get buried in the mud. This corrupt government has its eye only on sucking people's lifeblood out of them, and no interest in forestation and water management." Jeongtae's words were always bitter and sarcastic like that. He rarely smiled. And he never hesitated to use the word 'people', which was taboo because of the Communist connotation.

"Haven't I seen you somewhere?" The young man atop the pile said, observing Jeongtae, tilting his head a little to one side. He wiped the sweat on his face with the soiled towel draped about his neck.

"You look familiar to me, too," Jeongtae replied.

"Yes, I saw you at the laundry site by the Bangcheon Creek. You were asking if there were Teachers' Training School graduates from Pyongyang. You were shouting at the top of your voice."

"Then, you, too went there to look for your family from the North?" Jeongtae asked.

"Yes. I go there often. Not only Bangcheon Creek but anywhere people gather. I always drop by the black market, Chilseong Market, and Seomun Market at least once a day. I will find my family, who I'm told have come down to the South, if I have to search every inch of the land."

"Where in the North are you originally from? From your accent it seems you are more southerly than Pyongan-do."

"I'm from Samjeong-myeon, Suan county of Hwanghae-do. I heard that my parents and all my siblings had fled to the South. Do you know anyone who came from that area?"

"I'm afraid not. I haven't met anyone from Suan, yet."

By the time I left for the newspaper company, the young men had finished piling up the logs and left. Before leaving, they told Mrs. An again and again that they will come by in about ten days, and asked her to please let them do the splitting.

From the pile of pine logs, which were piled up to twice my height, came the fragrant scent of wood, just like from the sawdust mounds in the lumber mills of my hometown.

6

It was the day of first snow. As is the case in most southern provinces, only dry granules of snow fell scattering during the night and ceased before the ground was covered. When the day broke, wind swept the snow to one side of the courtyard. It was slightly windy but the wind was not cutting, and the sunny day was warm.

"They say that on snowy days, lepers do their laundry. Well, wouldn't it be nice if we could make our kimchi for the winter on a warm day like this? Really, with the price of the ingredients soaring day by day, we should make our winter kimchi soon . . ." Mother muttered to herself, sewing fastening ribbons onto a blouse she was finishing for a customer in a rush, having relegated breakfast preparations to Seonrye.

None of the families in the middle quarters had made their winter kimchi. All the families had purchased firewood for the winter, but as the old lady didn't repeat her demand that one of the families vacate their room, all the families assumed that they would be allowed to live out the winter in the house. So, nobody worried about making preserves for winter. In my family's case, Mother was busy all the time with sewing for her customers, and couldn't find the time to plan and make winter kimchi. Mother's customers always wanted their clothes sewn in a hurry. I guess all women like to get their new clothes right away, but since Mother's customers were almost all hostesses who invest most of their earnings on grooming themselves, they didn't have the patience to wait. When Mother told them they'd have to wait a few days, many of them would say, "Well then, this time I'll look for another seamstress," and gather up their fabrics. Then Mother would tell them that she would have their clothes finished by the time they want, in order not to lose a regular customer. So, Mother often sat up until after midnight sewing clothes by the light of the kerosene lamp, because electricity was cut off sharply at midnight. Sometimes her hair got singed from leaning too closely to the lamp. In those days Mother often said, rubbing her eyes, "Oh, my famously keen eyes must be growing dim. I can't even thread a needle right. Gilnam, if you want to be a good son when you grow up, buy me medicine that is good for eyesight. Say 'You ruined your eyes trying to raise us, so take this medicine and recover your good eyesight.'" As a matter of fact, in the mornings Mother's eyes were often swollen and bloodshot.

"Seonrye, there was a big hullabaloo yesterday morning at the commissary. The locks were knocked off and all the goods have disappeared," I heard Miseon saying to my sister as they were both making breakfast.

"Why, was it broken into?"

"Yes, a thief broke in and stole all the valuables. I wonder how he could break in. You know, the shop is guarded by double barbed wire fences that are electrified at night. And the Korean sentinel stands guard all day and all night. The American MP interrogated the Korean guard and even struck him with the gun barrel. And they interrogated all the employees of the commissary, so I had to answer questions all morning, too," Miseon was saying.

I had seen the double barbed wire fences of the American military base in Daegu. At intervals there was a signboard at-tached to them, which warned, "Do Not Approach. Trespassers Will be Shot." I asked Seonrye the meaning of the signboard. I learned then that if you went near the fences you would die. That must have meant that they regarded you as an animal. Even before seeing the signboard, I used to get scared for no reason when I caught sight of a tall, blue-eyed and hairy American soldier in the street. After I understood the meaning of the signboard I would get even more scared.

"So, did they catch the culprit?"

"I guess not. Lieutenant Smith, who is in charge of the commissary, got so mad that he said all Koreans are thieves."

"How can he say such a thing?"

"Well, I guess it's because he was mad. But it's true that Koreans aren't very conscientious. Almost every Korean employee filches this and that from the commissary once in a while. So, they search all the Korean employees at the end of the day. Women employees are searched by women soldiers, but I feel so humiliated when they feel my sanitary pad," Miseon said.

"Do you also filch this and that from time to time?"

"Oh, no. But the others all do."

"I guess it's because of poverty. I guess people wouldn't do such a thing if they weren't so poor," my sister suggested.

"Well, all this makes me want to leave Korea. I don't like Korea and Koreans. And another war might break out at any time," Miseon said, making the smacking sound with her chewing gum. I listened to the conversation between the two girls, sweeping the snow with a bush clover broom.

The landlord's sons and niece soon went out to go to school, and Seonrye and Giljung then also left for school. A little later, Heunggyu, the Gyeonggi woman's son, and Miseon also left for their workplace. Then it was the landlord's turn. The old lady of the house saw her son off. Then I heard her angry voice from the outer yard.

"We're not going to buy anything. We have everything we need. So you'd better try somewhere else," the old lady said.

"Ma'am, we're not trying to sell anything. We're here on a visit," a low voice intoned.

"I know your tactics. You can't fool me. If you're on a visit, who're you looking for? You wait here, and I'll get that person for you. Don't come into the courtyard. Wait out there," the old lady said sharply.

"What's so wrong if we just stepped into your house? Will it tumble down or anything? Damn, what an odious hag," the man with only one leg muttered.

I opened the door of our room. Gilsu trotted out, as if anticipating an exciting spectacle. Two wounded war veterans stepped into the courtyard, pushing aside the old lady.

"Ma'am, these gentlemen came to see Junho's father," Junho's mother, who was spreading washed diapers on the laundry line, said with embarrassment. Then she greeted the wounded veterans with, "How are you? My husband's home."

Of the two veterans, both of whom were wearing worn-out military uniforms and caps minus the insignia, one had his left leg missing, so that the left trouser leg was folded upward at the knee, and was walking on crutches. The other had one side of his face badly burned, so he presented a horrible sight. Even the eye seemed to have disappeared on the burnt side.

The door of Junho's room opened and Junho's father looked out. I came down to the courtyard after Gilsu.

"Hello, Staff Sergeant Han and Sergeant Kim. I asked you not to come to this house. What brings you here so early in the morning?" asked Junho's father in a very disapproving tone, going up to the two men standing beside the middle gate.

"Oh, we didn't expect such a cold welcome from you, Captain. We came to see you early because we missed you," the one-eyed veteran said with a guffaw. Because of his burn scars he looked like he was crying even when he was laughing.

The two soldiers went into Junho's room, and the old lady

stood there for a while like a dog that missed a rooster it had been chasing, then went into the inner quarters muttering something to herself. The Gyeonggi woman also withdrew her face and closed her door, and Sunhwa came out with a bundle of military uniforms to take to the creek to wash.

The wounded veterans stayed for about half an hour in Junho's room. As they were coming out, Jeongtae was sitting on the verandah of his room reading a newspaper and sunning himself in the early winter sun. It was a copy of the *Daegu Daily* I'd brought home the day before. I was also sitting on the verandah with my sister's Atlas book spread open, dreaming of roaming over the Red Sea and the Suez Canal and the Mediterranean Sea. Like Miseon, I, too, wanted to turn my back on the country.

"Captain, you must come. They'll be giving each of us money for lunch and transportation, and a towel, too," the veteran on crutches said, looking back at Junho's father, who had followed them to the entrance to see them off.

"Well, as I said, I have to work for my living, so I don't have the time to attend such rallies," Junho's father said.

"But you must come. All the heroes of the war will be there, so you must come," the one-eyed veteran insisted.

As Junho's father was coming back after seeing them off, Jeongtae lifted his eyes from the newspaper and asked, "Sir, is there a rally of some kind today?"

"Yes, they're having an anti-communist rally at the stadium at noon today in support of the constitutional amendment. I didn't go to a similar rally last spring, so they're insisting that I must come today," Junho's father said.

"That constitutional amendment is a week old, but the newspapers are still full of it. Sir, how can they do such a thing? With one hundred and thirty-five ballots for, sixty ballots against, and seven abstentions out of two hundred and two total, it was declared voted down for a shortage of one ballot, but then two days later they reversed the outcome by saying that it has passed by 'rounding up' the fraction. Are they playing a children's game at the National Assembly? How can they pull such a childish trick?" Jeongtae was fuming, pointing to a corner of the newspaper with his index finger.

"It's a despicable trick. I thought that was disgraceful."

"Is it so they can play such dirty tricks on us that we support the legislature with our tax money?"

"Dr. Syngman Rhee changed the constitution like that because he wants to be the president for a second term. No one who's wielded power wants to let it go. History is full of examples showing that greed for power is the most tenacious kind. Maybe because you can satisfy most of your other greeds with it," Junho's father observed.

"Are you going to attend this rally this afternoon?"

"No, they're not going to give wounded veterans like us employment or anything even if we put ourselves at their beck and call."

"Then, is it only because there won't be any practical advantage that you're not going?"

"Well, there was a time I looked at the whole world critically. But I am mellowed now, if I do say so myself. However, it's true that in this liberal democracy, your worth depends too much on what you own."

"You're right. Money rules this part of the world. This anti-Communist rally, for example. What is the value of a popular rally put together with a hired crowd? And anti-Communism is just a bugbear to scare the people, I mean the citizens, into submitting to threats and bullying. Well, let Syngman Rhee make this divided land his eternal kingdom."

Junho's father, who was returning to his room, paused. Then he went up to Jeongtae and sat down beside him on the verandah.

"You seem to hate anti-Communism. Why do you hate it?"

Junho's father's tone was calm, even though he was obviously ready for an argument.

"I'm only upset that the country's division into pro-Communist and anti-Communist camps makes unification more difficult. To my mind, unification should come before all else."

"To my mind, an anti-Communist rally is something that needs to be held, especially now when we've repelled the Reds at such great cost. Of course, it should be a voluntary rally, and anti-Communism shouldn't be made a pretext for oppressing and torturing innocent people."

"Do you think die-hard anti-Communists will limit themselves to legitimate means?"

"I suppose not. But you must admit that die-hard Communists have murdered countless innocent people."

"Well, because 'anti-Communism' has been so misused the mere mention of the word makes me want to throw up."

"It seems to me idealists like you will have a hard time adjusting to any kind of regime, but I believe that the spirit of anti-Communism is necessary for instilling the value of freedom in the rising generation, and also for young men like you who never fought Communists in combat. What I'm trying to say is that I think those revolutionaries who try to change the world by violent means should be driven out of this land. My fellow soldiers and I have paid a horrendous price to keep freedom alive in this land. Of course, we're still very far from having the right kind of democratic system with freedom for everyone, but even so . . ."

Jeongtae kept his mouth sealed, even though he was staring at Junho's father.

"The reason I'm not going to today's rally is not because I oppose President Syngman Rhee's ambition to prolong his presidency. It's more because I don't have the time to take part in such events, as I am still living hand to mouth, and I'm ashamed to see my former comrades because of my shabbiness."

"You are a good citizen. I know I am still too young and inexperienced to state my convictions before people like you, but the war has divided this nation into those for and those against Communism. Before the war, except for the ideologues, ordinary people didn't hate each other like this."

"You're right. We fought the war as proxies of the United States and the Soviet Union, and it is our people and land that suffered the most damage and paid the highest price. Both sides fought with weapons supplied by foreign powers. And we haven't even achieved unification. After three million casualties, we achieved only an armistice. This has been a war with incalculable loss and no gain, fought for no justifiable reason. I feel so lost, so like a fool . . ." Junho's father said, touching his iron hook with his left hand.

"I heard you're from the North, that you were a schoolteacher before the war. When did you join the Republic's army?"

"Well, I was a teacher for the People's Primary School in Pyeonggang, Kangwon Province. When the war broke out, I was sent to the 'liberated areas' as a cultural propaganda force." Junho's father's voice suddenly gained force as he said, "In July I defected to the Republic's army in the midst of the Mungyeong battle. After a brief investigation I was assigned to the Republic's army as an interrogator of war prisoners. After three months' training in Yeongcheon, I was given a platoon to command the following March. It was made up of soldiers who defected from the People's Army."

"Was there a reason for your defection? Were you perhaps banished from your home after having your property seized by the Communists?"

"Not really. But I just couldn't accept the Communist ways because I was brought up as a Confucian. I feel that a man should be evaluated according to his ability and character. To insist that men are equal just like slices of bean curd from a machine and to organize them into mechanical units was repugnant to my temperament. And I was very unhappy to teach children under an atmosphere of surveillance. Of course, the partisans were only too happy with the system."

"Well, I guess it's a question of what you consider the most important. I came down South to escape the American bombers, but I see many problems this side of the divide. In fact, I think this society has far more problems than the North, because this one is much more complex."

"I heard that after Communist China intervened in October 1950, there was fierce bombing of the North by the Americans."

"'Fierce' doesn't begin to describe it. The entire land is literally in ruins. At first, it was military facilities and big buildings that were targeted, but later on it was simply "carpet bombing." When elementary school kids fled to a back hill to escape the bombing, the Americans blew up the hill. When women and old men ran into rice paddies, frightened by the noise of a bomber, the bomber kept circling over their heads and machine gunned them until every one of those farmers was killed. I don't know what made the Americans hate us Koreans enough to hunt us down to the last one. Haven't you heard that the commander of the Eighth Army reported to his president that the Americans have destroyed North Korea so thoroughly that it is a primitive society now?"

"What did your father do before the war?" Junho's father asked.

"He had his own business in Pyongyang. He ran a small steel mill producing farm implements in Seonkyori."

As Jeongtae was telling this to Junho's father, his mother came out of her room to head for the market with a bundle of washed and mended military uniforms. Wound about her head was a woolen military scarf with the ends tied under her chin, and she was wearing narrow trousers made from a blanket. A money belt was strapped to her waist.

"Son, how many times have I told you not to discuss ideology? Have you ever heard of anyone who fled the North during the war who doesn't claim to have been rich before the war? Have you heard any of them say they'd never been persecuted by the Communists? If you're going to live in the South, you must act and think like those people. If we keep working hard, we'll eventually live comfortably. Don't you know that you can live a good life here if only you work hard? That's the superiority of the South"

"You're right, ma'am," Junho's father said. "The likes of us who have no skills and no capital can't make it rich in this society. But we must work hard and not harbor regrets and bitterness until the day the division is overcome and we can go back to our homes. I will regard my lost arm as having been buried in my hometown. Of course, I won't be able to find it and reconnect it to my shoulder, but I am hoping that I might some day visit my hometown again to dig up my buried arm."

"This war has corrupted everyone," Jeongtae argued. "Everyone has become money-mad and would grovel before the worst of thieves if they had money. Everyone thinks of nothing but making money fast and escaping poverty, and won't stop at anything, even stealing. But under this system only the capitalist thieves can make more and more money, and the honest poor folk remain poor no matter how hard they work."

"Then, you mean to say you despise money? Everyone dreams of being well off, and what dream can be more honest and worthy than that?" the Pyongyang woman admonished, putting on her sneakers.

"What difference would it make if a worm like me has respect for money or not?"

"It's because you have nothing to do all day that you speak nonsense like that. You'd better shut up. Mr. Park, this boy didn't used to be like this before the war. The war has warped him. I should have left him in the North as he wished. Now he blames me for bringing him into this corrupt land. Yes, it's true that children are our retribution for our sins. You'll kill me with your perversity yet!" The Pyongyang woman shouted at her son and, hoisting up the bundle of military uniforms onto her head and picking up a stool with one hand, she strode across the courtyard toward the gate. Jeongtae snatched up the newspaper he had been reading and went back into his room with a scowl on his face.

"That's a very troubled young man," muttered Junho's father to himself, watching the door close after Jeongtae.

Several days later, the sky was overcast from early morning, and a slight drizzle began to fall around noon. Despite the winter season the weather had been rather warm for a few days. I was in my room peeling garlic that Mother had bought the day before to make winter kimchi. Mother listened to the rain tapping the tin roof of our improvised kitchen and then said to me:

"Gilnam, there must be some straw rice sacks in the back yard. Take one and cover our woodstack with it, so the firewood won't get wet."

"Ma'am, when are we going to have the logs split?" I asked, rubbing my smarting eyes with the back of my hands and getting up.

"Why, are you afraid I'll make you do it?"

"Not really, but . . ."

"Watch carefully when the landlord's family have their logs split. I hear there are people who pay to take exercise. So, wouldn't it be a smart thing if you were to split our logs? That way, you exercise yourself, save money, and learn how to split logs."

I had been expecting this sort of thing concerning our logs, so I made no protest when it came.

As I was atop the pile of our logs spreading a straw sack over it, a stranger with an empty A-frame carrier stepped into the courtyard through the open middle gate with diffident steps. I recognized the young man in dyed military uniform and dog-fur cap as the hairy young man from Hwanghae-do, who had done the work of piling up the logs when the landlord's family had purchased their two truckloads of firewood. He quickly ran his eyes over the wood that he had piled up and then rounded the flower bed to head towards the inner quarters.

"Excuse me, anybody home?" the young man said, stepping up to the stepping stone to avoid the rain and peering into the glass door of the living room.

"Who is it?" Mrs. An said, coming out of the kitchen.

"Ma'am, I was here the other day when you had the logs brought in," the young man said, taking off his hat and bowing.

"Oh, yes, I recognize you. You said you'd come back in about ten days, but here you are, before half that time," Mrs. An remarked.

"Oh, I'm not here about splitting logs. I came to protect the logs against the rain. If you give me straw sacks, I'll cover the pile well with them so the logs won't get wet," he said with a smile. Then he added, "Don't worry, ma'am, I won't charge anything for covering the pile."

"Oh, thank you. I was worried how I could climb on top of the pile, and was about to ask that boy to do it for us. Thank you so much. We have straw sacks and straw rope in that barn," Mrs. An said.

The young man took off his A-frame, went into the barn, and came out with several straw sacks and a spool of straw rope. Then he climbed the pile of logs with them. He worked in the rain, but he was so deft that it was soon finished. The old lady of the house stood on the living room floor with her arms folded behind her back and watched him working. As he prepared to leave after coming down from the pile and slinging his A-frame back on, Mrs. An came out of the kitchen with a bowl of steaming rice tea.

"Here. Drink this. You're wet, so you need something to warm you up."

"Thank you," the young man said, and taking the bowl of rice tea in both hands, drank it up standing under the eaves. After emptying the bowl, he wiped his beard and looked up at the streaks of thin drizzle.

"Looks like after this rain we're going to have real winter."

The old lady of the house, who was still in the living room and seemed to want to say something, said at last:

"When the rain stops, you come and split our logs."

"Oh, thank you ma'am. I'll do it for you cheap, and I'll do a good job," the young man took off his dog-fur cap and bowed deeply to the old lady twice. Those must have been the words he had been ardently wishing to hear.

"Although he looks as unkempt as a highway robber, I think he's hard-working and good at heart. A man who fled South from the North with empty hands must work desperately hard to keep his body and soul together. But that young man looks like he could survive even if he were cast away on a field of snow naked," the old lady of the house remarked, her eyes following the young man's back as he walked out through the middle gate.

"That's my opinion, too. He looks rough, but has a good and honest heart," Mrs. An concurred.

I went back into my room and resumed peeling garlic. Mother was hemming by hand the great flared skirt she had sewn. It was made with silk from Hong Kong and had cranes embroidered on the fabric.

"Gilnam, you heard what the old lady said, didn't you? About the young man. He got the job because he is so diligent. In this world, you get work if you're diligent. I guess he was hoping to get the work when he came to offer to cover the pile against the rain purely as a goodwill gesture. That's not a crime. He'd have had to go away without any gain if the old lady hadn't told him to come back and split the logs. But he got the work because he offered his services out of goodwill. His goodwill earned him other people's goodwill. You note that well, Gilnam. If you want people to give you work and help you find what you want, you must first impress them with your honesty and goodwill. You keep that in mind all the time," Mother said. She had been working with the door closed, but she knew as well what went on in the inner courtyard as if she not only heard but even saw everything.

The rain stopped that day as dusk fell. When it ceased, a fierce wind began to blow. The temperature fell sharply with the nightfall, and the wind seeping in through the door was so cutting that Mother draped a blanket over the doorframe. The thin sheet of Korean paper that covered the window quivered pitifully in the wind. But we had not made fire under the floor of our room, even though we had a big pile of firewood. So, our floor was as cold as stone. My brothers and I curled up under one quilt like three shrimp and tried to warm ourselves with the help of each other's body heat and breath. From the next room, we could hear the Pyongyang woman berating Jeongtae. She was accusing him of looking at the world completely negatively, and pointing out that such a negative, cynical attitude was bad for his condition. There was no response from Jeongtae.

"Since he's flanked by you on either side, Gilsu must be warm," Seonrye observed.

"It's true," Giljung said. It was true that Gilsu had the benefit of his older brothers enclosing him on either side.

"I envy you, sister. You sleep between Mother and Giljung. I have to sleep next to this drafty wall, because I moved in last. I have to take the brunt of everything," I complained.

"You're the eldest son in this family. You must endure the most," Mother said from the other end of the room.

"But it's too much," I said weakly. Mother always made me

do the hardest work and always told me I must take it like a man because I was the pillar of the family. Consequently, I had in the back of my mind a sneaking suspicion that I might be a changeling left on my parents' doorstep or a son my father had with a mistress and had brought home for my mother to raise. That suspicion lasted until after I grew up and got married. My mother was always harshest on me with the switch and always made me do the hardest work. Sometimes, I thought that it was because I was not her own son that she left me alone in my hometown for so long, and even after she took me in, didn't send me to school at once but made me sell newspapers for a year. All these things gave me sorrow.

"Giljung, please stop burrowing under our covers like a mole. I get the shudders when I feel your body against mine in the middle of the night," Seonrye said.

"It's because Gilnam pulls the cover off me," Giljung protested.

The five of us in my family slept side by side, with me next to the wall and the drafty window, Gilsu next to me, and Giljung next to Gilsu under a single quilt. Seonrye and Mother shared one quilt, too, with Seonrye sleeping next to Giljung and Mother sleeping against the wall that divided our room and that of the Pyongyang family. I always relished the moments before falling asleep, warming my body against Gilsu's, as if my youngest brother were a stove. Those were the sweetest moments of the day for me. It seems that on that night, Junho's father had one of his nightmares of the battlefield and yelled and screamed. Mother heard him, but I had fallen asleep.

The next morning, we found the drinking water on the tray in our room frozen hard. Perhaps because I had slept curled up so tightly, my whole body felt heavy and all my joints creaked.

Early in the morning, even before the landlord left the house for work, the young man from the day before returned. He had not brought his A-frame carrier but only his axe and wedge in a hemp sack.

"It's so cold today, and the logs must be wet, too. It doesn't seem like a good day for splitting logs," the old lady of the house said, surveying the ground covered with a layer of ice from yesterday's rain.

"It isn't so cold today. Why, in my hometown of Samjeong it often drops to thirty below in mid-winter. And it's not a bad thing to split the logs when they're slightly wet. That way, there are fewer splinters," the young man said confidently.

"Where is this Samjeong that gets so cold?"

"It's in the Suan county of Hwanghae-do. It's deep in the mountains, so we often had snow in April. I worked in the fields and on the lumber yards before the war. I've cut down many huge trees with my own hands," the young man said.

"Well then, splitting logs must be light work for you," Mrs. An said, sticking her head out from the kitchen.

"Sure. You just wait and see. My axe strokes are not like those of your stray workers'."

The young man stripped the straw sacks from the pile and took down some logs from the top, then got ready to begin the job. Having had instructions from Mother, I placed myself on a sunny spot beside the wall, stuck my hands in my trousers pockets, and got ready to watch. The young man selected a log that would serve as the prop. It was a thick log with branches not lopped off.

"Well, I guess I can go right ahead," the young man said, grinning from ear to ear, showing his big yellow front teeth above his beard. It seemed to me not so much a smile of expectation at the thought of earning money as a smile of innocent pride at the prospect of doing work he is good at and showing off his mastery to the old lady and the young housekeeper. The young man first placed a rather thin log upon the prop. After surveying the cut section of the log he seemed to decide which spot to cleave. Then, wetting his palms with his spittle, he raised his axe high into the air and brought it down sharply. With that one stroke, the log was cleft halfway down its length. His second stroke brought the axe right into the middle of the cleft, and the split halves of the log fell to the right and left on the ground, revealing the fair inside. I could see that it was not so much his strength as his skill that split the log so neatly.

"That was splendid!," I exclaimed, and said: "You must have a special method? Which spot on the log do you aim your axe at?"

"Of course you have to have a method. The log doesn't get split because you hit it with an axe, however hard you may bring it down. You must aim the axe where the age rings are densest, and if the log has branches, you must cleave the knot of the branch. Otherwise, the axe can't cut into the log. When the axe has found its proper way into the log, your hands can feel it lightly cleaving through the wood. But if you hit the wrong spot, then your hands feel as if the axe had hit a rock and the rock is sending it back."

"But I guess you need strength, too?" I asked.

"Sure enough. But if you have strength enough to swing the axe, then you can split logs if you simply understand the grain of the log. It's exciting when the logs keep splitting with each stroke of your axe," he said. The young man really worked with enthusiasm. In no time, steam began to rise from his flushed face, and beads of sweat began to form on his forehead. He took off his jacket. His undershirt was soiled dark grey and had holes at both elbows. But the young man didn't seem to mind his shabby appearance and kept swinging his axe with exhilaration. He even chanted a song to himself:

That Jap in sandals
Who came to Suan in Hwanghae-do

Looking for a bonanza,
That Jap in wooden clogs
Who came to Suan in Hwanghae-do
To rob the forest,
He got scared by the totem pole
At the entrance to the village
And, frightened by the tiger,
Pissed in his pants.

He was so absorbed in his work that he looked possessed. Even though still slightly wet, the logs split neatly, so there were very few splinters. The fragrant smell of pine tickled my nostrils as I watched that merry labor. I became absorbed in watching the work, guessing to myself how many axe strokes each log would need, and wondering when he was going to use the wedge. The sweat-soaked young man rolled up the sleeves of his undershirt, revealing his long arms with little flesh on them. In fact, he had little flesh anywhere on his body. He was flat-bellied and flat-chested, and he had little in the way of biceps. So I couldn't help wondering where his strength came from. His skin was gleaming with sweat. At last, he put a thick log on the prop and made use of the wedge. He first placed the wedge on the log and stuck it into the log by hitting it hard with the blunt end of the axehead. When the wedge had made a cleft in the log, he brought the sharp edge of his axe down into the cleft. The thick log was easily split.

The old lady of the house and Mrs. An the housekeeper would come out to watch the young man from time to time and then go back into the room or the kitchen.

"I was not wrong in my judgment. He sure looks rough, but he is an honest and hard-working young man. Give him a hearty lunch," the old lady of the house said to the housekeeper.

My mother also slid open the door of our room from time

to time and noted how attentively I was studying the young man's expertise in log-splitting. If I had been watching any other spectacle, Mother would have bawled me out for loitering and ordered me to come into the room at once and study, but she only seemed glad of my attentiveness.

"Gilnam, why are you standing there in the cold?" Aunt Munja asked. "I brought some dumplings. Come into the room." Aunt Munja was one of my mother's customers who became very close to Mother and sometimes came to see us just to chat with Mother. She was wearing woolen sweaters and her face, without make-up, looked wan, and her voice was weak, too.

"Hello, auntie." I greeted her warmly and followed her into the room. Of course she was not my real aunt, but I knew she liked me to call her "auntie." The mere mention of dumplings made my mouth water. If it hadn't been for Aunt Munja bringing us dumplings now and then, I wouldn't have known that the dumplings that I saw in the shop windows in the Chinese district were such a delicious and nutritious food.

When Aunt Munja unwrapped the package of dumplings, the unfocused eyes of Gilsu, who had been squatting in a corner of the room, brightened up at once. He quickly moved over to the dumplings, which still had warmth in them. I made a quick eye-count of the dumplings. There seemed to be about fifteen to sixteen of them, so I reckoned I could eat about four.

"Gilnam, fetch soy sauce from the kitchen," Mother told me.

It was true there was no one else to do the errand, but I was cross that I should leave the precious food while others stayed with it. When I came back with a bowl of soy sauce, the others had all begun eating the dumplings, just as I had expected.

Aunt Munja was telling Mother, "Sister, I have no joy in life. I go back to my room at night drunk, then fall asleep like a log. But I wake up in the middle of the night from thirst, and I can't get back to sleep. I light up a cigarette to stem my nausea, and I start thinking about myself. All I want to do then is die quickly. I wish I'd died with my parents and siblings while fleeing from Seoul. When I think about that, I feel as if a stone is blocking my food canal," Aunt Munja said. Apparently, she had no appetite, for she ate just one dumpling and took out a cigarette and a lighter from the pocket of her cardigan. Mother pushed her sewing aside quickly, lest sparks from the cigarette fall on the fabric. Aunt Munja slowly exhaled cigarette smoke, and with it a sigh. Her large eyes shaded by thick eyelashes were red with tears.

"There aren't many these days who live because life is fun," Mother said. "Most people go on living just to stay alive. I, too, would have hung myself from the beams a long time ago or eaten the eggs of a blowfish if I didn't have these children to raise. Yes, the last three years and ten months have been longer than ten years to me, and it wasn't just once or twice that I thought of making blowfish soup and eating it with the children to put an end to all these hardships. Those who have had nothing to eat for many days and lived on water know how hard it is even to take one's own life." Mother spoke as if she, too, relished the chance to unfold her bitterness.

"Sister, I couldn't go to work last night," Aunt Munja said, watching me gorging on the dumplings.

"Why, are you ill? You do look much thinner," Mother remarked with concern.

"I stayed in bed all day after coming back from the hospital. I kept bleeding."

"Gilnam, I think you've had enough. Leave the rest for Seonrye and Giljung," Mother said, putting the six remaining dumplings back in the torn wrapping. Then she said, "Gilnam, you go to your aunt and borrow an axe. And split our logs the way that young man is doing the landlord's. That is a man's job, and you are the pillar of this family."

Of the dumplings, Mother and Aunt Munja each had one,

Gilsu had three and I had four, so I was content. As I came out onto the verandah I heard Aunt Munja saying in a lowered voice:

"I had another abortion. It's the second time. I'm so upset and my body feels so limp. I guess I'll skip work again tonight. I don't want to spend the rest of my life fawning on drunken wretches. I miss my life in Seoul before the war, when I had my parents, sisters and brothers, and classmates. I don't even have their photographs any more. But they still loom up in my mind's eye . . ."

My aunt's residence was located at the entrance to Medicine Lane. Aunt asked me to be careful not to get the blade chipped. I promised and returned home with the axe slung on my shoulder. As I was fortified by the unexpected treat of dumplings, I thought I'd go right ahead and begin working on the logs until I left for my newspaper delivery. Returning home, I prepared the ground for the job in the courtyard in front of our room. As I had noted the young man doing, I selected a log with branches still attached to it for a prop. Then I picked a medium-girth log and placed it on the prop. I got ready for the first axe stroke by spitting into my palms and rubbing them together, just as I had observed the young man doing.

"Don't put too much strength in your arms. And be very careful not to hit your feet with the axe. It happens so easily. Don't hoist the axe up too high. Aim right at the center of the log," the young man kindly coached me.

The job wasn't as easy as it looked. It was very hard to hit the middle of the log with the axe. I hoisted the axe up with both hands, and from straight above my forehead I brought it down in a vertically straight line, but it failed to hit the center of the round log, so the log flew up into the air. A bouncing log was just like a wounded animal or fish flopping to and fro if you failed to hit the right spot with a lethal blow. I swung the axe more forcefully, as if I were engaging the log in desperate combat. But my axe often missed the log altogether and hit the prop under it instead. I cast my eyes on the door of my room, hoping Mother would look out and relieve me of the work that was clearly beyond the capacity of a boy my age, saying "I see that's quite beyond you." But the door didn't open, even though Mother couldn't have not heard my sighs and exclamations of "Oh, I can't," and "this isn't going to work."

"Oh, that's too hard-hearted of Mrs. Kim. How can she make that matchstick-thin boy split those thick logs? I'm afraid he'll chop his foot instead," the Gyeonggi woman observed, sliding open her door and leaning out.

I borrowed the wedge from the young woodcutter and wedged it into the center of the log, tapping it with the blunt end of the axe as he had done. When the wedge was securely stuck in, I kept hitting it with the blunt end of the axe and succeeded in cleaving the log in two. The first few logs I had tried to split had so many axe marks that the splinters made a heap around the prop. Of course, as the splinters were going to be used as kindling, it isn't as if I'd made much waste.

The young woodcutter, who had been eyeing me uneasily, came over. I was ardently hoping that he would suggest to Mother that I was too young for the work and that she should let him do it for very cheap, but he never even cast an eye at the door of our room. Instead, as if in league with Mother to make me do the work, he gave me tips, with actual demonstrations:

"Come, let's assume that I have only as much strength as you. Now, look. I'm lifting the axe with only as much strength as yours. Then I just let it fall on the log," he said, and let the axe fall on the log. It was like magic. Even though he hadn't put any strength into the axe, the axe bit into the log and clove it somewhat. He let the axe fall again into the cleft, and when he let it fall the third time, the log split all the way through, as if welcoming the axe with its whole body.

"In this world, there are many things you can't solve with force alone. There are times when a great warrior like Xiang Yu can't kill an ant with a huge rock. It's like that with wood-splitting. The secret is to let the axe come down in a straight line and hit the log right in the center," the young man said, handing the axe back to me and urging me to try for myself. It wasn't easy to lift the axe and bring it down gently, but instead of applying force, I concentrated on having the blade fall exactly on the spot I intended. Then the log didn't bounce any more.

"Oh, it's so hard," I said, wiping the sweat off my forehead.

"You keep on practicing. Then you'll get the knack. In my hometown, boys your age make good woodcutters," the young man said encouragingly.

It was only as a sophomore in high school that I finally understood what he meant by hitting not with force but by following the way of Nature. That was when I tried to hit a ping-pong ball with a ping-pong paddle. Of course ping-pong rackets and ping-pong balls are very different things from axes and logs. However, even if ping-pong balls are almost weightless, it was so hard to propel the ball over the net and onto the other side of the table. The small ping-pong ball would fall somewhere very different from where I aimed, even though the ping-pong paddle was much wider than the blade of an axe. It was because the force I put into the racket made the ball bounce at a different angle from what I intended. When learning billiards, too, I realized that the more forcefully I struck with the cue stick, the less the balls obeyed my will. Then when I taught at a middle school in the countryside years later, I tried my hand at tennis because there was a tennis court at the school. Again I tried to play tennis with brute force, and again the ball flew where it was not supposed to. All these mistakes owe to my not having learned to deploy as little force as possible and to take advantage of the nature of things. Of course, it was a lesson a boy like me couldn't master in one morning.

Giljung came back from school at lunchtime. Mother came out of the room and went into the kitchen to prepare our lunch. But even while we were eating lunch, Mother didn't say a single word about my wood-splitting. In her silence, I could read her determination that if we were to survive the winter without freezing to death, I as the eldest son should do the splitting. When I came out to the courtyard after finishing lunch, Mrs. An came out of the kitchen with the meal tray for the young man.

"Where will you have your lunch?" Mrs. An asked the young man.

"It's fine here. I'll just eat here," the young man said.

"But it's so cold . . ."

"It's all right. When you work, you don't feel the cold."

"Let him have his meal in the yard. You don't take in strangers into the room in the winter," the old lady said from the inner room.

I learned later that the old lady of the house never let stray workers into the rooms during the winter months. Vendors and those workers at the landlord's factory who came on errands had to give their reports and receive instructions below the living room steps. The reason was that they carried in lice. In the fifties, in those days when almost everyone was indigent and sanitation was of secondary concern, before people could change their underwear at regular intervals and before the widespread use of coal briquet helped the extermination of lice with its poisonous fumes, poor folks were harassed by hordes of lice. People scratching themselves anywhere, any time was a common sight. Almost everywhere in the city you could see beggars sitting in the sun and hunting lice in their underwear. At the railway station plaza, workers from American relief agencies sprayed DDT on citizens for free. There were two small covered wagons with red cross marks on the sides parked in the station plaza, and a Western man and woman wearing white gowns sprayed DDT on anyone who asked for it, using a hose with a spout connected to a cylinder. They put the spout anywhere people wanted, on their backs and in their bosom, and even into their crotch. One time, when lice became the topic of conversation, I heard the old lady say, "They say a louse can travel several miles in one night. Of course, a louse can't crawl that far. It rides on people. That's why the wealthy houses of old had guest rooms in the servants' quarters and inner quarters, and had separate bedding for strangers."

The young man spread a straw sack right next to where he was splitting the logs. After taking the tray, he asked Mrs. An to give him a big bowl. Then he put the rice from his rice bowl into the big bowl, put bean sprouts, spinach, and kimchi on top of the rice, and mixed them all together with a spoonful of hot pepper paste. I stopped chopping wood and watched him eating for a while. I always liked watching people eat.

"When did you come down from the North? Where did you part from your family, that you're going around looking for them?" Mrs. An asked the young man, as she perched on a rock beside the pond.

"I didn't come down as a refugee. I was fighting on the battlefield as a soldier of the North's Army and became a prisoner. I was freed from Geoje-do last June when they released war prisoners. I'd heard from a comrade from my hometown who had joined the North's Army later that all my family had fled to the South, so I decided to remain here. I've been roaming all over Pusan, Masan, and Daegu looking for my family but haven't got any news of them yet," he said.

"You must miss your wife and children very much," Mrs. An observed.

"Oh, I'm still a bachelor, even though I'm not so young any more. I'm looking for my parents and siblings," the young man said.

"I'm sorry. Please forgive me," Mrs. An apologized, blushing and laughing. "Would you like some more rice?" she asked.

"Yes, please, if you have some to spare. The soup is so good. It's the first time since I left my hometown that I have tasted cabbage leaf soup mixed with bean powder. And I'd sure appreciate it if you let people in the market know that Ju Eoksul from Samjeong-myeon, Suan county in Hwanghae-do is looking for his kinfolk."

While I was negotiating the logs with my clumsy axe, Mrs. An was enjoying talking to the woodcutter. Mrs. An recounted the story of her life to him. According to Mrs. An, her husband was conscripted into the army in August of 1950, two months after her marriage, and after receiving two letters from him, she received his remains in four months' time. Mrs. An and the young man agreed that the war had ruined their lives. But they told each other that they should survive the difficult years and see better days. If the old lady of the house hadn't come out to the living room and put an end to the budding familiarity between the young man and the young woman, their conversation might have developed further.

After finishing lunch, the young man smoked a cigarette stub and then went right back to wood-splitting. When I returned home later that afternoon after delivering the papers, Mr. Ju was piling up the wood he'd split that day neatly against the wall in a stack. Then he swept the yard clean, and went home after saying he'd come back early the next morning. That night, my arms and shoulders ached so that I couldn't sleep on my side.

The next day, too, Mr. Ju and I split wood. Jeongtae, who had been absent the previous day, saw me struggling with the logs on his way to the outhouse.

"Gilnam, I don't think you can do it. Let's see if I can do it for you," Jeongtae said, taking my axe from me as he stopped on his way to his room from the outhouse. At that, the door of my room opened, and my mother leaned out.

"Young man, you're an invalid. You shouldn't exert yourself. For your illness it's best to rest."

"I don't think a day's exertion would make a significant difference either way," Jeongtae replied. I thought Mother would have no choice but to close the door and let him do the work for me, but she rejected his offer squarely:

"Listen, young man. You shouldn't encourage the boy to look to others to do his work for him. He should learn to finish his work by himself. He shouldn't get in the habit of looking to others to help him, out of commiseration. If he did, he'd never learn to be independent."

Jeongtae seemed rather taken aback by Mother's words, and muttering "Oh, it didn't occur to me to look at it that way," handed the axe back to me.

That day, I got the knack of splitting wood to a measure so it was a lot easier than on the first day, and my arms and shoulders didn't bother me so much at night. I felt my arms and found that my thin limbs were as hard as iron.

Mr. Ju took four days to split the landlords' two truckloads of logs. It would have taken me the whole winter to chop that much wood. But he did a neat job of it in just four days, and on the fourth evening, he left after getting well paid by the old lady, along with generous compliments, after tidying up the yard. Before leaving, he left his advice to his fellow wood-splitter who had no payment to look forward to:

"Listen. If you look at wood-splitting as a chance to show off your strength, you're likely to injure yourself. Wood has its own stubbornness, even dead wood. So, you have to cajole it to let you have your way. I see you have improved vastly. I think you're in a fair way to becoming an expert wood-splitter by next year. Well, see you then. And don't forget to look for the Ju family from Samjeong-myeon, Suan County in Hwanghae-do. I'll drop by from time to time to check for any information."

On the 30th of April of 1975, on the day the United States turned over Saigon to the North Vietnamese regime, putting an end to twenty years of war in Vietnam, I suddenly recalled Mr. Ju's words to me of that day, while watching the amazing scene on television.

7

The old lady's decree that one of the tenant families should vacate their room, which seemed to have been shelved, came up again when December arrived. This time, the landlady, who was famous for her business acumen, took it upon herself to see it through.

"The lady of the house wants all of you to come to the guest room. She has something to say to you," Mrs. An knocked on each of our doors and said. It was around eight o'clock, so it was after dark. She explained that the summons was about vacating one of the rooms.

"Oh, the lightning's going to strike. I wonder which of us she has in mind to throw out?" Mother said, as she pushed her work aside and got up to her feet. Her limbs were shaking. After Mother went out, I saw Junho's mother, the Gyeonggi woman, and the Pyongyang woman, all walking to the inner quarters.

"If the landlady says for us to evacuate, where can we go?" I asked Seonrye, but she had her eyes pasted on the book spread on the meal tray and didn't say anything. I was always sleepy in the evening, what with wood splitting in the morning and newspaper delivery in the afternoon, but the situation left me wide awake. If our family didn't have a room to sleep and eat in, then we were on a shortcut toward becoming beggars. Before the war, I thought beggars were born beggars, but I learned otherwise after the war broke out. If you had no walls to shelter you from the cold glances of the world and had to live on the street, you were surely on your way to becoming a beggar. I had seen many, many families under a bridge or beside a creek who lived on straw sacks and behind straw sack curtains. There were many such under the bridge near the Chilseong Market. They didn't live by begging, actually, but people regarded them as beggars. I didn't think my family could go and live under a bridge, however, because Mother's customers, who were pretty ladies in fancy dresses, wouldn't come there to seek us out and give their business. Downcast by such thoughts, I stole glances towards the brightly lit guest room of the inner quarters and waited for Mother to return. Seonrye and Giljung also seemed unable to concentrate on their books and were listening for movements outside with sullen faces. Seonrye, for whose reading the thirty-watt electric light was too dim, rubbed her eyes often that evening and at last snuffled. Only Gilsu, curled up like a shrimp in the tiny quilt spread on the floor all day long during the winter, was asleep, oblivious to all the worry. I quieted my fears, telling myself that as our room was farthest from the inner quarters, surely ours wouldn't be the one that the landlords wanted.

After about twenty minutes have passed, we heard voices from the inner quarters. I opened the door. The ladies were coming out of the guest room onto the living room.

"I'm sorry. Lottery is fair to everybody, so nobody can complain about its result. I belong to a credit union, and many were the times I needed money desperately but didn't pick the right ticket that month. There was nothing to do but to give up. Then I looked around for people to borrow from, and if I tried hard enough, I found people who had money to lend. It must be the same with finding a room. I'm sure you're feeling like it's the end of the world, but by and by, you'll find a good enough room," the Gyeonggi woman was offering this by way of consolation to Mother who was walking limply.

I blacked out for a moment. A sob escaped from Seonrye.

It was obvious that Mother had drawn the short straw. The Pyongyang woman followed Mother into our room, and Seonrye rushed out of the room to hide her tears.

"Oh, don't be so upset. This was an unlucky day for you. The landlady said she's going to remit one month's rent and pay for your moving expenses, too, so she is not all that inhuman. Us poor folk can do nothing but bow to fortune's turns. I will ask around for a room for you, too. Let's try together," the Pyongyang woman earnestly offered, but Mother didn't seem able to attend to her words. She was staring at the wall like one deprived of willpower. From our kitchen came Seonrye's stifled sobs.

"There can be no room to be had in this Janggwan-dong area in this freezing winter. Maybe I'll have to ask my sister to let us move in with them for the winter. But that won't be easy. My sister has four children, so how can I ask them to live in one room and yield the other to us? I'd be too ashamed to look my brother-in-law in the eye. Maybe when winter vacation begins, I'll send two of my children to my husband's hometown of Jinyeong," Mother rambled on. An idea hit me right then. I had heard the landlady asking the Gimcheon woman to vacate her room.

"Mother, the Gimcheon woman is going to vacate her room. Couldn't we move into her room?"

"What, what did you say?" Mother asked, her eyes brightening up.

"The landlady pressed her to vacate the room soon, and the Gimcheon woman promised her she'll do it within two weeks."

"When did you hear this?"

"About two weeks ago."

Mother stood up instantly and rushed out of the room. The Pyongyang woman and I followed her out. Seonrye and I silently crept toward the middle gate, stole into the Gimcheon woman's kitchen and eavesdropped on the conversation going on in the store.

"Yes, it's true I'm going to move out, but my cousin has a

tenant for this room already," the Gimcheon woman was saying. "Who is it, do you know?"

"It's Mr. Jeong who works in my cousin's jewellery shop. I heard that he is going to move here because from Naedang-dong where he is living in now it takes him an hour to commute to the store by bicycle. He used to work in a jewellery shop in Seoul and came here as a refugee, so he lives in a rented room, too. His wife came by the other day carrying a baby on her back to take a look at this room," the Gimcheon woman explained.

"When did you promise Mr. Jeong to vacate the room, and when are you going to move out?" Mother asked.

"I promised my cousin I'd vacate the room early this month, but the room I'm going to move into isn't free yet. It's been a week they've been saying they're going to move out, and they have their things all packed, too, but they have given loans here and there, so they must collect them before moving to Seoul."

"If that's the case, then maybe I can ask Mr. Jeong to let me live here until the winter's over," Mother said. Her voice was spirited.

"Well, if Mr. Jeong agrees, then I guess my cousin wouldn't object," the Gimcheon woman responded. But she didn't sound hopeful.

Early the next morning, before the landlady left for the store, Mother went to our landlady's jewellery shop with me. Since the shop was located directly opposite Songjuk Cinema in the busiest part of downtown, Mother would have had no difficulty finding the store, but she took me, her eldest son and the pillar of the family, for moral support. There was no one there except an errand girl with bobbed hair cleaning the store. In a little while, Mr. Jeong arrived on his bicycle, his lunch-box tied to the rack.

"Excuse me, sir. You're Mr. Jeong, aren't you? I am a tenant of Mrs. Park, the proprietress of this store," my mother said like a shy girl.

"Oh, yes? What can I do for you, ma'am?"

"Well, as a matter of fact, I heard that you are going to move into the outer quarter of our landlady's house."

"That's true. But the woman hasn't yielded the room, even though it's more than a week from the day she promised to move out. Since she is a kinswoman of my employer, I'm being patient, but this is too much. I'd appreciate it if you'd tell the woman to make good on her promise at once," Mr. Jeong said.

"I . . . I was wondering if you could postpone your move until spring," Mother said cautiously.

"What? Who are you to tell me when to move?" Mr. Jeong's voice grew metallic.

"As a matter of fact, I live with my four children by taking in sewing. So I need to live within easy reach of my customers. Now, the landlady is asking me to vacate the room. I couldn't possibly find a room in the Janggwan-dong area in this freezing weather. And if I move somewhere far from downtown, I'll lose all my customers," Mother was pleading. She was standing there before Mr. Jeong in the attitude of an elementary school pupil being admonished by the teacher. I couldn't stand to see her humbling herself so, and I hated to hear her mention her customers. I left the store quietly. From the tone of Mr. Jeong's voice, I could see that it was not going to be an easy job. With my hands stuck in my trousers pockets, I sauntered the street and waited for Mother to come out of the shop. The wave of students going to school had ceased, so the downtown street was calm. I went up to Songjuk Cinema and surveyed the scenes painted on the signboards. They were showing a Hollywood Western. I couldn't understand why grown-ups would pay to see white people riding on horseback and firing at Indians. While living in Seoul under the Communist rule, flags with red stars on the background were flying from tops of buildings, but in the air there were American planes with white stars on the background. The airplanes dropped bombs on the heart of the city day and night, and sprayed bullets from the sky with machine guns. At the time I'd watched without terror many civilians who failed to flee Seoul get killed or wounded and have their houses burnt by the American bombing and firing. But now, looking back to 1950, four years back, war seemed so terrible. It occurred to me that if there had been airplanes in the days when the Americans conquered Indians, then Americans would have massacred the peaceful Indians with air raids.

Taking my eyes off the signboard and turning them toward the jewellery shop, I saw Mother and Mr. Jeong engaged in dialogue in the street in front of the shop. I suppose they had something to say that they didn't want the errand girl to hear. Mother and Mr. Jeong were standing close together and discussing something earnestly. They seemed to be coming to an understanding, but then Mother seemed to be proposing something and Mr. Jeong made as if to return to the shop, as if to say what Mother was suggesting was completely unreasonable. Then, Mother grabbed Mr. Jeong's arm. That surprised me, even though Mr. Jeong was a married man.

After a long and earnest conversation they seemed to be coming to an agreement at last. Mr. Jeong bowed politely to Mother, like a shopman seeing a customer off. Mother also bowed deeply, with a shy smile. I grew ashamed of the intimacy that I imagined between them and got mad at myself.

On the way back, Mother paid no attention to me walking beside her, and was absorbed in her thoughts all the way. Her face was anxiety-ridden, so I wondered if I was wrong in thinking Mother and Mr. Jeong had come to an agreement. Mother sometimes moved her lips, doing sums internally.

"Ma'am, how did the talk go?" I asked as we crossed the intersection with the Bank of Korea's Daegu Branch, unable to bear the suspense any longer.

"Oh, he's a man from Seoul all right. I never saw anyone so

astute about money. He demands six hundred *hwan* a month. That makes two thousand and four hundred *hwan* for four months. We must pay him the price of forty kilos of rice a month," Mother said.

"Pay him that much for what?"

"For letting us stay in the Gimcheon woman's room until the end of March."

"As much as six hundred *hwan* a month? That aside from our monthly rent to the landlord?"

"Yes. But what choice do we have? We have to stay in the house. If we left Janggwan-dong, then we wouldn't earn enough to feed ourselves," Mother said, and wiped her eyes with the back of her hands. Then Mother said in a hoarse voice. "Gilnam, if your father had been alive, we wouldn't have had to suffer this kind of humiliation. That man thought he could have his way with me because I am a widow living by my sewing. I asked him to let us pay him just one hundred *hwan* less, but he cut me short, saying he'd move in right this week. How can I be a match for that man? It's the same with the drawing straws. I pleaded tearfully that we couldn't possibly move out in this freezing cold, so I wouldn't draw straws, but the landlady must have forgotten her promise to your aunt to let us stay if we had firewood stacked up, and she turned a deaf ear to me. So, I ended up picking the last straw—the short straw. Gilnam, there's only one option for us. You must grow up. You must grow up fast and become a man. That's the only way I can leave behind these humiliations."

I could offer no consolation to Mother. I didn't think that, even if I grew up to be a man, there would be any guarantee that I would win the race for survival. Through newspaper vending and delivery, I had come to realize the harshness of this world and how hard it is to survive in it. I discovered too early how selfish human beings are, and that the race for survival is a rat race indeed. If I were to become the pillar of my family, it would be necessary for me to step on others. For that, honesty and diligence wouldn't be enough. It would also require ability, physical strength, and hard work, and in addition to them greed, cunning, and skill with words as well. I didn't think I would ever be able to make it all up to Mother. From that morning on I thought that I would like to become a woman or an old man overnight. That impossible wish reached its zenith when I was about to join the army. I had no confidence that I could survive three years in the army as a private. So, I wished I were a woman. And when I thought about what came after military service—finding a job, marriage, and supporting a family—I wished I were an old man, past people's expectations and hopes. And I eyed with envy those old men who spent their days wandering the streets and parks.

"Gilnam, you must never let out to anyone that we are paying 600 *hwan* to Mr. Jeong. I promised Mr. Jeong to keep it a secret from our landlady, so it must be kept a secret come what may. A gentleman doesn't let out what he promised to keep secret," Mother said.

That evening, our landlady returned home as dusk was about to fall. The lady, clad in an expensive fur coat, knocked on our door before going up to the inner quarters. She asked Mother to come out to the verandah.

"Mrs. Kim, I heard about your agreement with Mr. Jeong. So you will move into the store after my cousin moves out, and the Gyeonggi family can move into this room, so my son can use the room closest to the inner quarters. But you have to move out at the end of the winter, as you have agreed with Mr. Jeong. I think you'll have to start looking around for a room in February," the landlady said.

"Yes, yes of course. Thank you for your understanding," Mother said and made a deep bow.

"I didn't know Mr. Jeong was so generous-hearted. He said that when he heard you were a widow raising four children by taking in sewing, he couldn't turn a deaf ear to your pleas, being a father of growing children himself. I was so impressed with his generosity that I bought him several pounds of beef to take to his family."

Hearing that, I had an urge to rush to the landlady's shop and plead with Mr. Jeong not to take six hundred *hwan* a month from us, as he'd already earned big points with his employer. But I didn't think I would have the guts to do such a thing even if I grew up fast, like a giant bamboo, and became a man, as Mother wished. The landlady went to the inner quarters, leaving behind the scent of cosmetics. The Pyongyang woman, who had heard the conversation, opened her door and congratulated Mother on having the difficult matter settled so quickly and so satisfactorily. Mother must have been more upset than I was with the way Mr. Jeong turned the matter to his double profit, so she didn't have the presence of mind to even respond to our neighbor's warm congratulations, and gritted her teeth.

The next morning, Junho's mother came to our room and suggested that her family be allowed to move into the store that was to be vacated, and that we move into their room. She said that it would suit them well if Junho's father could sell baked potatoes from the shop. "My husband doesn't like hawking his snacks in the streets, and it would be so nice if one of us could stay home with Junho. We are always so worried about leaving Junho at home all day," she pleaded.

"I know your circumstances only too well, but I must say no. As you know, all my customers are young entertaining women, and the old lady so frowns upon their comings and goings. I feel like I'm sitting on a cushion of needles whenever I have a customer visiting. So, how can we move to your room, which is even closer than this one to the inner quarters? I feel it so fortunate that I won't have to worry about my customers grating on the old lady's nerves, even though it's only for a few months. Even if we have to leave this house for good, come spring, I will spend that interval in the outer quarters," Mother said decisively, and Junho's mother went away without another word.

But Junho's mother came to visit us again that evening, when she came back from the market. She made a present of three flawed apples, which were leftovers from her day's business. Then she said that she had talked it over with her husband, and said that if we let them use just the store part of the outer quarters while we use the room attached to it, then they would pay us one hundred and fifty *hwan* a month. She implored us to put up with the inconvenience since it was only for about four months. She didn't say anything about what they were going to do at the end of the four months when we would have to vacate the outer quarter. Mother responded that she would have to get the landlady's permission, so she would talk it over with the landlady and if the latter agreed, then she would let Junho's father use the store.

"But you must keep it a strict secret that you'll pay me one hundred and fifty *hwan* a month. I'll talk to the landlady if you promise you'll never let it out," Mother said in a stern voice. Mother always emphasized to me that men should value honesty more than his life, but it seemed that she was just a weak woman when it came to the question of money.

"Of course we'll keep it a secret. You know my husband is a man of few words, and I am not a gossip, either," said Junho's mother and returned to her room with a beaming face.

After Junho's mother left, Mother blew her nose and bemoaned how the war had turned her into a cold-blooded monster:

"I'm doing the same thing to Junho's family that that bastard Jeong did to me. To take rent for a store that isn't even mine . . . I must have become a very devil for money. How is it I've become so shameless? It's all because of these dirty times . . ." Mother went on and on. "Dirty times" was an expression Mother was fond of using. It occurred to me that the times were dirty for everyone, not just us tenants. It was at just about that time that two unlucky incidents happened in the landlord's family.

From the time that I first sold newspapers in the busy downtown streets, I often caught sight of Seongjun, the landlord's eldest son, walking with a glamorous woman in luxurious outfit who looked much older than him. I also saw him from time to time escorting a very young woman. The older woman was a war widow in her mid-thirties and a mother of two children, and when the relationship between them grew as hot as baked sweet potatoes the rumor reached his parents' ears. That happened in the fall. He received a terrible scolding from his parents. The landlord's furious threat that if Seongjun ever went out with the woman again he would break his legs could be heard by us in the middle quarters. The Gyeonggi woman picked up from somewhere the information that the woman was a widow of an ROK army lieutenant who died in combat just before the armistice and spread it among the tenants. When it seemed that Seongjun had been brought into line and the parents' anger was beginning to subside, he infuriated them again by ruining a young factory girl working in his father's company.

One evening, the landlord's family was at dinner, after the landlady came back from her shop. The father of the factory girl came to the house and raised an outcry. The landlord and Seongjun had not returned home yet.

"So, you think that because you have money you can do what you like with those of us who have neither money nor connections. You had my daughter quit the factory for fear of rumors, and you promised that you would take care of her if only we gave you a little time, but you disappeared for more than two weeks! Do you know my daughter tried to take her own life? Is her life worth less than a puppy's to you? I learned what was happening after we nearly lost her. Bring this bastard to me, at once! I must find out how he plans to take care of my daughter. Her belly is swelling everyday. I must know what you're going to do with her life and the baby's!"

The man wore shabby clothes and a woolen cap and was visibly drunk. He raised an uproar for more than two hours and even broke the glass door of the living room. The landlady called Mrs. An and gave an instruction in a low voice. In a little while, policeman from the Central Police Station came and hauled the man away. If the officer hadn't taken him away, the whole house would have had to forego sleep that night.

"I will appeal to the law! I will sue him and have him jailed! I won't die until I see him behind bars," the father of the factory girl yelled as he was dragged away by the policeman.

We learned later on that Seongjun had gotten to know her from visiting his father's factory to ask for extra allowance. Seongjun's father must have done something to get Seongjun out of trouble. The father of the factory girl didn't come to our house again. The Gyeonggi woman, who was as good as a detective when it came to scandal, wormed out the information from either the old lady of the house or the young housekeeper, and told the tenants of the middle quarters that the girl's family was bought off with a trifling sum.

"What's fifteen thousand *hwan* to the landlord's family? Why, just the cost of ten dinner parties with *gisaeng* girls would amount to that much. To think that a girl's chastity can be bought with fifteen thousand *hwan*! I guess these days you can even buy God's private parts if you have enough money," the Gyeonggi woman commented.

We heard that Seongjun had to promise his parents, on bended knees, that he will never fool around again and would concentrate only on his studies.

Then, one Sunday afternoon, I overheard this conversation between Miseon, who was reading an English conversation guidebook and Sunhwa, who was knitting.

"The other day we caught three petty thieves who broke into the commissary at night. They were a team of three, and there was a woman of about Junho's Mother's age."

"So, what did the Americans do with them?"

"They kept them in jail for three days and then released them without turning them over to the Korean police."

"Oh, then they were lucky."

"Lucky, my foot! The Americans painted their faces with red paint and wrote 'Goddamn Koreans' on their clothes before letting them go."

"Oh, what bastards! That's too much! You can't get red paint off no matter how hard you scrub with soap. They won't be able to go out until they can get rid of the paint. What can they do to stay alive?" Sunhwa exclaimed indignantly.

I felt my facial muscles stiffen, as if my face were coated with red paint. I rubbed my face with my palms. It would take a month, or even two, to wait for the red paint to come off. I pictured to myself the three people who would be scrubbing their faces with all their might, until their skin itself was scraped off.

"But do you know what the two American MPs did to the woman before letting her go?"

"Oh, I've heard that Americans will go after any woman, no matter how old. I can imagine without your telling me," Sunhwa responded.

Miseon brought up a new topic. "By the way, I ran into Seongjun the other day on the street. He blocked my way in front of the Jeil Church and asked me to go to a bakery shop with him, saying that he had something to say to me."

"So, did you go?"

"I tried to get away from him, saying I was in a hurry to get to my classes, but he grabbed my arm, so to avoid making a scene on the street, I had to follow him. He said he would be going to

America to study next year, so he would like me to teach him English till then."

"What a playboy!"

"And the day before yesterday, he caught me in front of Jeil Church and held out a letter."

"A love letter?"

"Yes, he says in it that I am an oasis in the desert and a pink rose. And he asks me to go to America with him, like two blue birds flying over the blue waters of the Pacific. It was so laughable."

"Oh, such stuff is fit only for high school boys. As a college student he should be able to write a more elegant letter. Obviously, he still hasn't mended his ways. I think he has his eyes set on your glamorous figure. Take care. He may be only in his early twenties, but he is an experienced ladies' man."

"Oh, I'd much rather marry a poor wage-earner than marry into such a household as our landlord's. The ladies' man would make his wife a house slave and keep having one affair after another. It makes me shudder to think of such a life."

"Well, you seem to be a little interested, anyway. Otherwise, you wouldn't be imagining how it would be to be married into that household. You're found out!"

"No. I wouldn't have anything to do with him even if they were to come to take me in a gold palanquin. I don't like such a slick man with a roving eye."

The two girls kept on talking and giggling for a good hour.

It was that night that the landlord and landlady had a big quarrel. It was quite late in the evening when we heard the landlord yelling outside.

"Come in at once! So, you're too ashamed to enter this house?"

I was in the middle of reading a volume of world's classics that I had borrowed from the book lending shop, whose owner happens to be a subscriber to the *Daegu Daily*. Cold wind hit my face as I opened the door a slit to look. I could see, in the near darkness, the landlord dragging the landlady into the house, gripping her by the collar of her fur coat. The landlady tried to resist him, saying something in a low voice, but the landlord didn't relent, and dragged her all the way to their guest room.

We heard violent quarreling from the guest room for quite a while. The landlord's voice was louder, but the landlady seemed to be refuting his charges one by one.

"You'd think that a family like our landlord's, who owns this imposing house and has plenty of money, would have no worry in the world, but it seems everyone has their troubles. You, my children, take care to avoid domestic quarrels when you get married. If you just try to see things from the other person's point of view and be a little understanding, then you won't need to quarrel. You can't be happy unless you have peace at home, and you can't have peace at home if you and your mate are at odds with each other," Mother admonished us, turning the wheel of her sewing machine.

We heard something breaking in the guest room. I opened our door a slit again and eyed the inner quarters. The electric light from the living room of the inner quarters shone bright through the bare branches of trees, and the old lady of the house was crossing the living room to go to the guest room. We heard the landlady protesting between sobs. The Gyeonggi woman came out to her verandah with a sweater draped over her and watched the guest room with arms folded. The other rooms in the middle quarters all had their doors opened ajar, so that there were four horizontal columns of light in the courtyard.

"You should know shame by now. Aren't you ashamed, to be sobbing for all the children to hear?" the old lady of the house scolded her daughter-in-law severely.

"What did I do that's so wrong? I married into this house and bore three sons. And they're growing into sturdy young men.

What great crime have I committed? It's to leave our sons with secure fortune that I started my business. Is that a crime?" the landlady wailed tearfully.

The landlady didn't go out to work the next day and locked herself in the guest room all day. The Gyeonggi woman tried to worm out the reason for the quarrel from Mrs. An, but it seemed that Mrs. An didn't know. Then, the Gyeonggi woman accompanied the old lady and Mrs. An when they went to the mill to have some red pepper pounded for their winter kimchi, carrying a sack of red peppers for them, hoping to satisfy her curiosity, but to no avail.

"The old woman kept her mouth clamped shut out of perversity, so I couldn't draw out anything from her. She kept cursing her daughter-in-law and saying that if it'd been back in her day, the daughter-in-law would have been sent back to her parents. I guess the landlady's got the family into a pretty fix. I don't think she had an affair. My guess is that the credit union that she'd founded has broken up. So she asked for a loan from her husband. Maybe she bought gold and silver with the money entrusted to her and hoarded it up in her store but couldn't turn it back into cash quickly enough. Credit unions are collapsing everywhere these days," the Gyeonggi woman speculated to my mother.

The landlady stayed cooped up in the guest room for three days, and then on the fourth day she went out again as usual. She was wearing heavy make-up, but the bruises around her eyes were perceptible. After the landlady had left for work, the old lady of the house disclosed her daughter-in-law's crime, perhaps judging that she wouldn't be left in peace until she had satisfied the Gyeonggi woman's curiosity. I overheard them as they were talking, sitting in the sun on the edge of the living room.

"You know that place where men and women go around with their bodies pasted together. She was found out by my son dancing with another man in a dance hall," the old lady explained.

"Oh, they closed all the dance halls on the fifteenth of August. But there must be dance halls illegally open. I guess there are secret dance halls doing business on the sly. But, ma'am, how did your son find her in the dance hall? Did he wait in front of her shop and shadow her?"

"I don't know about that. But anyway, he found her in the dance hall and tossed her in his jeep and hauled her home."

"What kind of man was her dancing partner?"

"I heard that he is a police officer. So, she's saying that she wanted to make friends with him so he would help our Seongjun get a passport, in spite of the scrapes he's gotten into. Nowadays, women have become so brazen that even women caught in a lewd act are ready with excuses."

"It's true that dance halls encourage lewd acts and thoughts. This refugee life seems to be fanning the dance craze. Have you heard the rumor? That a gigolo has made dance halls his hunting grounds, and has slept with more than thirty virgins? And many of the girls in his address book are college students who are daughters of good families. Women seem to have no regard for virtue these days. Their charms are at everyone's service, just like a towel in a hotel room. My daughter is a nubile girl, too, and every day I tell her she should guard her chastity more strictly than her life. The world is changing so quickly that old folks like me just can't keep up with it."

"Yes, doomsday seems nearly here. When we were young, a married woman was not allowed to go out except on unavoidable occasions, and when we did go out, we had to hide our face and figure with a long, ankle-length shawl and ride a palanquin. But Western influence has dealt a death-blow to traditional decorum. It's worse in the cities. If I don't want to see such disgraceful sights, I'd have to go back to my hometown or die . . ." The old lady rubbed her back with her fist and went into her room.

The Gimcheon woman vacated her room at last, so on that day, we moved to the outer quarters. As we were moving only from one room to another in the same house, and had little in the way of belongings, the move was not a big job. Still, the whole load fell on me, as Seonrye and Giljung had to go to school. It seemed that they took it for granted that I should do all the work, as I stayed home in the morning, and had no thought of lending their hands even a little. We didn't even have a wardrobe cabinet, so all our property was just insignificant small effects. However, when we gathered them all together in the center of the room they made a big heap, so I didn't know where to begin. Mother had an urgent sewing job to do, so in the midst of the bustle she did her sewing and I was the only one left to shuttle back and forth carrying this and that.

"Gilsu will only upset things or break them. So tell him to play with Junho, and you do the moving. If you just carry them over to the other room, then I will put them in place as soon as I finish this outfit. It looks like it might rain. So why don't you make haste?" Mother said, putting stitches on the blouse.

I complained to myself that Mother must have called me up to Daegu to make me her servant, and looked up at the sky. It was heavily overcast, so the day was gloomy and rather cold, too. If it were to rain, then our shabby belongings would get wet and become even shabbier. I was thinking to myself how wretched it was to be a foundling, when Mother told me that if I didn't want to work I could skip lunch. I told myself that I didn't care whether she gave me lunch or not, as I was going to quit newspaper delivery from that day and leave the house. But my hands were picking up pots and pans and putting them into a big basin.

"Gilnam, you have your work cut out for you, don't you? You'll have to move all that firewood as well," said a compassionate Sunhwa, coming down to the courtyard from her room. She looked very different that day. She had gone out almost at dawn that morning without even cooking breakfast as usual, and now her long braided hair was cut short and permed. She was wearing a Korean traditional outfit, consisting of a white blouse and purple skirt. And she was wearing low-heeled shoes, instead of the rubber shoes she always wore. So, it seemed like it was a special day for her.

"Are you going some place nice?" I said.

"Yes, I am, although it's not to my beloved hometown. When you grow up, Gilnam, someone will introduce you to a nice young woman, too," she responded.

Her mother, the Pyongyang woman, also came out. Apparently she was skipping her business for the day. She, too, was attired in a nice Korean traditional outfit instead of the reformed military uniform she always wore.

"Oh, you must be happy. How delightful it would be to have a daughter married! After Sunhwa gets married, you'll have to have Jeongtae marry soon, so that your daughter-in-law will do the work Sunhwa's doing now," commented the Gyeonggi woman, who had been squatting in front of her kitchen and washing dishes in a basin.

"Yes, and you'd better have your son married. I'm sure he has many willing young women, because he has a secure job," the Pyongyang woman returned.

"Well, as a matter of fact we already have a bride for him," the Gyeonggi woman said, standing up and wiping her hands on her skirt. And she broke wind at the same time, making a fluting noise like a willow pipe.

After I had made several trips transporting our property into the outer yard, the Gimcheon woman came out the side door of the store with a towel wrapped around her head and carrying a bundle.

"Gilnam, the room is all cleared now. And I scrubbed the floor clean, too. You can put your things in the room."

"Are you leaving for good?"

"Yes, we're moving to Chilseong-dong."

"Where is Boksul?"

"He must be outside."

I went into the store through the side door and out into the street. A handcart loaded with household effects was parked there in the alley. Jeongtae, whom I'd thought had gone to his sister's introductory meeting with an eligible young man, was there perched on the handrail of the cart, clad in shabby denim garments. Boksul, who was gorging himself on rolls, looked up at me and said, "Gilnam, we're moving. Mother and I are moving to a nice place."

"Gilnam, I will leave like this without bidding good-bye to everyone, so will you please say good-bye to everyone for me? I am leaving the rolls oven behind like I promised Junho's father," the Gimcheon woman said, running her eyes over the store once more. As usual, her face was as anxiety-ridden as a heavily overcast sky.

Jeongtae began pulling the cart, and the Gimcheon woman pushed it from behind. That made them look like a married couple. They turned into the big street at the end of our alley and disappeared from my view. If Jeongtae's mother, the Pyongyang woman, had caught sight of them, Jeongtae would have had a bawling-out from his mother. The Gimcheon woman should have said good-bye at least to the old lady of the house, as she was the landlady's relative and had been beholden to the family for shelter for a long time. But she left like one fleeing creditors. Partings were very unceremonious things in the city. While I was in my hometown, there were about a dozen refugee families who lived in shelters made up of hung straw sacks at the foot of the train station. When one of the families left to go back to their homes, there was a tearful parting scene. The neighbors saw them off to the station, they held hands, exchanged wishes for reunion some day, and tearfully bade each other good-bye.

When I came back to my room and told Mother that the Gimcheon woman had left with her things piled on a handcart, Mother said, "Why, that's strange. She can have nothing against me, yet she left without saying good-bye." But Mother went on with her sewing.

That made me think that if I left her without bidding good-bye, she would say exactly the same thing. She might say, "Why, how strange. He can have nothing against me, and yet he left without saying good-bye. I guess that's what foundlings are like, the whole lot of them," then go right on with her sewing. But I, unlike the Gimcheon woman, had nowhere to go if I were to leave home. I had never really had childhood pals with whom I played and fought, and the only game I played with my contemporaries was marbles, so I lacked the guts to put my impulses into practice. I only realized much later that it was because Mother knew I lacked the willpower to leave home that she made me sell newspapers and do whatever errands she chose to relegate to me. At that time, I had no one to appeal to for sympathy, and even if I had, I wouldn't have known how to do it coherently.

Mother helped with the moving in the afternoon, and Sunhwa also helped after coming back from her introductory meeting. Mother asked her what the young man did for a living. Blushing, she replied that he was an army captain.

"Then you can get married before the lunar new year's day?"

"Well, he's from Pyongan-do just like we are, and only he and his brother came down to the South. His troop is stationed in Pusan, and his older brother sells relief goods in the black market near my mother's niche, so he acted as the go-between. The meeting went very smoothly, but we have to find the money to rent a room and also for the wedding expenses. So it will be next spring at the earliest," Sunhwa replied.

"Well then, it seems you like the prospective groom."

"He was very much like any other military man. He looked

a bit rough. Neither side has much in the way of kinfolk, so we agreed that it'd be better for the two families to be united soon," Sunhwa said.

"You'll make an excellent wife. You're hard-working and tender-hearted, so you'll take good care of your husband and manage the household well," Mother said.

"But my brother doesn't like my marrying an ROK army officer," Sunhwa said regretfully.

"You're the one who's marrying the officer, not your brother. What does it matter if your brother objects?"

Seonrye and Giljung came back from school and helped as well, so we were able to put our things in order in the outer quarters by the time electric lights were lit. We cooked our dinner on the stove that serves both as a cooking stove and floor heating furnace and ate our dinner two hours later than our habit. Mother gave us more rice than usual, saying that we had all exerted ourselves very much. The room in the outer quarters was a little bigger than our previous room, and had a window facing the house next door. The landlady who returned home late, opened our door ajar and peeped in. Towards midnight Junho's father who returned with his tin drum stove on his handcart coughed in front of our room several times and asked to speak to Mother. When Mother looked out, he said that he would use the store space from the next day.

"Isn't it nice to be living in an independent quarter so we don't have to worry about getting on our neighbors' nerves? Wouldn't it be nice if we could live here until we can buy our own house? Maybe when Gilnam grows up and makes lots of money, we can buy a house of our own. How long are we going to have to wait for that?" Mother said to herself while scrubbing the floor prior to spreading out our bedding.

It would have made sense for the family from Gyeonggi-do to move into our former room, because they had to give up their room, which was closest to the inner quarters, to the landlords.

But the Gyeonggi woman refused, saying that the room stank in the summer because the ditch runs by it, and asked Junho's family to move into that room. Junho's parents complied without a protest. Then the Gyeonggi family moved into Junho's room, and Seongjun moved into the Gyeonggi family's room. That created the situation of Seongjun and Miseon living on either side of a thin wall and facing each other if they both opened their doors. And the Gyeonggi woman was not too happy about the circumstance.

"Oh, I thought they meant to give the room to their second son. I'll be self-conscious about breaking wind, with a young man next door," she complained.

However, since the situation was created owing to her own wish, there was nothing to be done about it. When Miseon came back from work that afternoon, she was really upset and blamed her mother for not having moved into our former room. But apparently the Gyeonggi woman didn't think she could commandeer another shuffle, so she just kept mum.

From the next day, Junho's father baked and sold sweet potatoes and rolls in the store attached to our room. Junho's mother, too, after she came back from the market and cooked dinner, came to the store and helped her husband until around midnight. I moved our pile of firewood into the outer quarters. I had been splitting logs for many days but with such poor results that we were often short of ready fuel.

Five days after we moved into the middle quarters, past mid-December, we made our winter kimchi, after all the other families had made theirs. It was partly because we thought it better to wait until after our move, but we couldn't do it right away even after we moved. Mother said, whenever a fish juice vendor passed by, hawking "pickled shrimp or anchovy," that we should be making our kimchi for the winter, but she had many urgent customers to satisfy, so she couldn't get around to making kimchi.

It was awfully cold and windy on the day we made our kimchi for the winter. Mother rose at dawn and went out to the farmers' market and returned with thirty-five heads of Chinese cabbage and five turnips. Mother was wont to say that in winter, kimchi suffices for the side dish. So she must have been thinking that she'd feed us only rice and kimchi the whole winter. The cabbage was third-rate stuff, with many green leaves, so the heads didn't look good when we split them into four sections, but anyway, our kimchi was twice as much as any of the other families', most of whom made kimchi with only twenty heads of cabbage. Along with the vegetables, Mother picked up a whole bunch of discarded outer leaves of cabbages and turnip stalks from the market ground and brought them home. The rough leaves were to be hung to dry in a spot with good ventilation and used for making soup all through the winter.

In setting out to make kimchi, we couldn't help worrying about the water needed for washing the cabbage, as the city water was hardly enough for cooking and laundry in the winter, being supplied only at set periods and the faucet often freezing into the bargain. Not only the landlord's family but the families from Gyeonggi-do and from Pyongyang bought water from the water-vendor, and Junho's mother washed her cabbages in the creek before bringing them home to make into kimchi. So, it was almost a matter of course that we should buy water to wash the cabbages.

But you couldn't expect my mother to buy water. "I heard that this family produced high officials for three generations. So I wonder how they could have not dug a well? Well, it can't be helped now. Gilnam, you go to your aunt and borrow a water pail yoke. And go to the Chinese school and get water from their well. They say you can get their underground water from the water pump. Two full buckets would be too heavy for you to carry, so bring half-buckets. I think you'd have to make at least three trips for us to have enough water for making winter kimchi," Mother said to me after breakfast.

In the middle of Jongro street, which ran from the end of our alley, there was the famous Chinese restaurant, Gumbanggak. From my house to the Chinese school, situated across the street from Gumbanggak, it was more than three hundred meters. But there was no disobeying Mother, unless I was prepared to go without meals. So, I had no choice but to head for my aunt's. Mother never took back her words. If she said I'd have to skip a meal, she never relented and fed me. If she said she'd whip me after she finished her sewing, she always picked switches from the charcoal sack and flogged me. Before she began to flog me, she always said, "This will hurt, but don't yell and scream, or you'll wake people in the next room. If you make a noise, I'll throw you out, whether you have somewhere to sleep or not," and whipped me mercilessly.

I flattered the janitor of the Chinese school and succeeded in getting two bucketfuls of water. But it was obvious that he wouldn't let me draw water a second time, so I didn't know how I could go about it. Then I thought of the extra copies of the newspaper from the day before, the copies I should have used to canvass for new subscribers. I took two days' copies of old newspapers to the old janitor and was able to draw water from the school two more times. While I was carrying the water, cold wind slashed my ears, my shoulders felt like caving in, and my legs shook. But the most painful to bear was my wet hands freezing. At first, my fingers got swollen red, then they turned dark blue, and it felt as if they were going to fall off. While delivering newspapers I could have my hands stuck in the trouser pockets, but to walk with a yoke with water pails hanging from either end, I had to hold the strings hanging the buckets to the yoke. Otherwise, the buckets swung wildly and water splashed out, so I could hardly walk a step. I stopped in the middle several times and tried to warm my hands with my breath, but they continued to hurt. I wondered if my fingers would turn into icicles. Among all the possessions of the landlord's youngest son, the thing I envied most was his soft leather gloves. I wished that day that I had at least cotton gloves. The memory of my freezing hands on that day remained with me for a long time. The pain was comparable to the cold that froze my nose and my whole face later in my life as I was standing sentinel before the iron fence on Daeam-san Mountain near the DMZ during my years of military service.

Our winter kimchi of that year was a heavily salted affair with only red pepper powder and pounded garlic for flavoring, but it tasted heavenly. Even though, with the passing of years I have tasted many exquisite dishes, my favorite dish always tends to be kimchi. The unfermented kimchi of those days was the most delicious food I've ever eaten in my life, and my mouth still waters when I recall that kimchi of that year. For many days, I ate my rice with only cabbage leaves torn to strips for a side dish. Or rather, they were meals of kimchi strips with rice as a side dish. Naturally, my rectum got torn and ached whenever I went to the toilet. Strips of undigested kimchi came out mixed in my feces, and I had great difficulty squeezing them out. I was the first to visit the outhouse in the morning, as my stomach ached violently from early dawn. That morning, after several days of hard stool I decided that from then I wouldn't even eat one piece of kimchi and just mix rice with water and eat it. I was groaning in the outhouse, pressing my belly and straining myself. The Gyeonggi woman said I should hurry up and come out quickly.

"So, he didn't come home last night, either?" I heard the Gyeonggi woman ask someone.

"I asked everywhere, but nobody knows where he is. I heard that they are nabbing military service dodgers these days, so I even asked the police, wondering if he may have been nabbed by an MP," Sunhwa's voice replied.

"Have you searched the refuge camp in Yeongcheon? He may have gone there looking for people from his hometown," the Gyeonggi woman suggested.

"I'm going there today," Sunhwa replied.

I figured that Jeongtae must have been absent from home for two days. Since I had come to this house I have never known Jeongtae to stay out at night. So, his absence made me worry. Knowing how he criticizes the South Korean society, I worried that he might have been arrested for speaking against the government.

After breakfast, I came out to the store, because it was uncomfortable sitting in my room with only Mother. Junho's father, wearing a hat resembling a chef's, was baking sweet potatoes in one tin drum and rolls in another.

"Is it better for you to ply your trade in the store, rather than in the streets?"

"Yes, it is. By selling two kinds of snack I can make a little profit. I wish I had a store like this of my own. I wonder when I can return to my hometown. Of course if the country is unified by the North, I suppose a defector to the South like me will have to pay dearly for it . . ."

"At what time of the day do you have the most customers?"

"There's no definite time. But many neighbors come around to buy snacks in the evening. Some drop by and pick up a bag of baked sweet potatoes or rolls on their way home from work."

Because he had been right-handed, Junho's father was awkward with his left hand. So it was taxing work for him to attend to two tin drum ovens with his left hand. He had his cotton glove only on his left hand, so I thought to myself that maybe a pair of gloves would last him twice as long as they would ordinary people. I recalled hearing that because of his strong eye glare and his iron hook, small children who came to buy snacks took to their heels. I could imagine the despair on Junho's father's face at such times. So, his wife came to his rescue. A few days before, Junho's mother knocked on every house in the Janggwan-dong alley. She asked the neighbors that her husband, who had the misfortune to be a wounded veteran, was selling baked sweet potatoes and rolls, so please to let their children buy those for snack instead of candies and cookies which are bad for the teeth. She didn't forget to mention that her husband had been a schoolteacher before the war but now has lost a limb and can't go back home. She was persuasive. Her freckled and wan face and calm tone gave the impression of a good woman under harsh fortune, and naturally her husband's business was much more brisk after that.

"Which of the two sells better, *yaki-imo* or rolls?" I asked.

"Baked sweet potatoes," Junho's father said and turned to look at me. "You must have been born in the last years of the Japanese occupation. And it's nearly ten years since we were liberated. So, you mustn't use Japanese words like *yaki-imo* and *bento*. It's hard for grown-ups to shake off ingrained vocabulary, but you who have gone to school under the independent republic must not use such Japanese words. Do you understand what I mean?"

I hung my head guiltily. For a while I watched Junho's father baking rolls in silence with my head bent low. Then I recalled the conversation I had heard earlier that morning.

"Sir, do you know that Jeongtae hasn't been home for two days?"

"No, I didn't. Why hasn't he?"

"Nobody seems to know."

"Has he been arrested?" Junho's father said, as if to himself. It seems that that was what everyone thought of in connection with Jeongtae.

"He's a bright guy, but he'll come to harm if he persists in that negative attitude. If he does, he's bound to get in trouble in such times as these," Junho's father continued, more to himself than to me.

Jeongtae still was not back after four days, and nobody had any clue to where he might be. The Gyeonggi woman, when she visited Junho's father's shop, speculated that as Jeongtae had been especially considerate of the Gimcheon woman, they might be living together as man and wife now. The Pyongyang woman also seemed to harbor such suspicions when Jeongtae's absence became prolonged, but nobody in the house knew where the Gimcheon woman had moved to. Nobody had asked her the exact location of her new home, and the Gimcheon woman had only said vaguely that she was moving to Chilseong-dong. I had witnessed for myself Jeongtae transporting the Gimcheon woman's belongings on the day she moved, so I, too, suspected that Jeongtae might be staying with her, but I didn't know where the Gimcheon woman had moved to. In Chilseong-dong there were thousands of poor people's houses, and almost every one of them had one or two refugee families as tenants, even though the war was over by now. There were so many plank huts of refugees leaning against the dike of Sincheon Creek, which flowed through Chilseong-dong from Bangcheon, so it would be almost impossible to search all the houses there, but Sunhwa combed the huts in between her trips to Bangcheon to wash old military uniforms. "It's so awful to lose a family member after getting nearly killed to come down this far," she would say when she came back dead tired and without gaining any information. Jeongmin, who stayed up almost all night these days preparing for the college entrance exam, went around looking for clues of his older brother's whereabouts after school. He was going to apply to the College of Law at Seoul National University. Everyone believed that he would have no difficulty passing the most competitive entrance exam.

8

Christmas carols began blaring from loudspeakers in the radio shops, and the boughs of Himalayan cedar standing in the courtyard of Jeil church were spread with cotton snow and strips of color papers, and a painted cardboard Santa Claus hung suspended. When I finished my newspaper delivery, shivering in the cold and wending my way home past Songjuk Cinema, I could feast my eyes on well-clad passersby jostling each other as they walked. One could see that business was thriving that year. But the bustle and luxury was limited to that area only.

"Family of Five Commit Suicide Eating Blowfish"

"Many Found Frozen to Death: Four in Daegu Yesterday"

"Father Arrested for Selling Offspring to Employment Agency after Days Without Food"

"Orphans in an Orphanage Rebel and Escape over One-Meal-a-Day"

Such headlines adorned the newspaper every day. But I could still see Seongjun walking arm-in-arm with a stylishly dressed young woman, and Donghi frequenting bakeries with her friends, none of whom were in school uniform. I always averted my eyes and avoided them when our paths crossed. I wasn't looking for them, but two other people. Jeongtae and the Gimcheon woman were not to be found in any of the areas I delivered newspapers to. The man with the knife scar on his face had not crossed my path since that autumn day, either.

Every fourth Sunday of the month, jewellery shops and clock and watch shops closed. But late that morning, our landlady went out, attired in her fur coat and fox-fur shawl. That day, there was no newspaper delivery, so I was sitting on the sunny verandah and reading a detective novel by Kim Nae-song, which I'd borrowed from one of the subscribers, who ran a book-lending shop. In a little while the landlady came back with a girl who had her hair cut short and who looked about ten. The girl was wearing a loose checkered coat that was obviously from relief goods, and her calves were bare. Her sneakers were torn, her hair was matted with nits, and her face was eaten up by ringworms, so she was very much like the orphans I ran into every day on my delivery route. But her glittering eyes and firmly shut mouth made her look like a girl of strong will.

In a little while, I heard someone crying out, "Logs split!" so I looked out and saw an A-frame carrier in overalls. When he approached closer, he turned out to be the hairy Mr. Ju.

"How are you, Captain, Sir," he greeted Junho's father thus, with a military salute, even though he had served in the North's Army and Junho's father in the South's.

"It seems like almost a week since I saw you. So, have you been doing well?"

"Fairly well, sir. Have you run into anyone from Samjeong-myeon, Suan county in Hwanghae-do in the meantime?" Mr. Ju asked, just as he asked anyone by way of greeting.

"No, young man, I'm afraid not; and stop calling me Captain. It makes me ashamed. And if I'd got news of anyone from your hometown, I'd have brought it up as soon as I laid eyes on you. You said you'd take a trip to Pohang to look for your kinsfolk. Was it to no avail?"

"I ran into someone from Goksan, in the depth of the mountains. It was nice to meet someone from near my hometown, but I met no hometowners or kinfolk," Mr. Ju said regretfully and then, turning his eyes on me, said, "So, have you split all the logs?"

"No, it's such hard work that I only split a couple a day," I replied. One day, on one of his tours of the Janggwan-dong area, Mr. Ju suggested to me that he'd split our logs for free, as he could do it in only a couple of hours. But I knew my mother would never allow that, as she'd only snubbed Jeongtae when he offered to help me. If he'd broached the topic, Mother would have snubbed him with, "Have you got nothing to do? Why are you trying to take away from my son work that will build up his muscles, foster a spirit of independence, and fulfill his part as the pillar of the family?" I didn't carry his words to Mother, and had been working on the logs one or two at a time.

"Oh, I've carried freight four times this morning, so I think I'll snack on some rolls," Mr. Ju said, took off his A-frame, sat down on the doorsill of the store, picked up a roll and sank his teeth into it. As Mr. Ju had no room of his own and slept in the refugee shelter in front of the station building with all kinds of homeless people, it wasn't likely that he would treat me, who has shelter and a family, to a roll, but I couldn't help swallowing. Feeling my eyes on him, Mr. Ju picked up a second roll and offered me half of it.

"Will you eat this and go to the inner quarters and ask Mrs. An to come out to see me for a second?" Mr. Ju said and smiled shyly, wrinkling his nose. I threw a quick glance at the door of my room. It was dark inside the glass panel, and I could hear the noise of the sewing machine. Mother had told me, over and over again, not to eat other people's food without paying, but my fingers closed on the roll of their own accord. I ate up the roll in the outer yard before stepping into the courtyard. When I approached the inner quarters the door of the kitchen was closed. The kitchen door was almost always open, so I thought it very strange.

"Are you in there, Mrs. An?" I said.

"A young lady's taking a bath, so a bachelor shouldn't look in," Mrs. An said from the inside.

There was even a sound of water being poured over a body, so I thought Mrs. An was taking a bath. And I heard her merry laughter. Because Mrs. An had the sunniest disposition of anyone in the house, I thought she was having fun even while washing herself. Then I recalled her plump white flesh, which I had glimpsed the previous summer when she splashed water on herself in the kitchen.

"Mrs. An, come out for a minute. There's somebody wanting to see you," I stammered, with a flushed face.

"Who?"

"It's someone you know," I said and came back to the outer quarters. In a little while Mrs. An appeared, wiping her wet hands on her apron. Mrs. An didn't look like she'd just had a bath, so I felt like a fool for having imagined such things.

"Oh, it's you, Mr. Ju. Do you have any good news? You're grinning from ear to ear," Mrs. An observed.

"How can anything good have happened to the likes of me who's blown by the wind here and there like a fallen leaf? I just asked you out to share this snack. You treated me to delicious food for four days while I was chopping logs for your employers. It was the first time since I came South that I was treated to such good food, so even now I think of the meals you served me. I will be grateful forever. So, I guess there's nothing wrong if I treated you to a roll or some baked sweet potatoes. Why don't you have your fill, and let me pay? I have enough in my pocket for that," Mr. Ju said, brushing his beard to shake off flour.

"Well, you may have picked up some money off the street, or you may be using your emergency fund mouldering in your money belt, but a treat is a treat, and I'll feast myself. Thank you, Mr. Ju," said Mrs. An, taking up a baked sweet potato. Peeling the skin, she broke it in half and offered me one half. Again, I quickly took the proferred food and bit into the flesh of the sweet potato, from which a delicious pale green mist was rising. It was sweet. I must have had luck with food in my stars that day, as I was offered a snack no less than twice. Mr. Ju hoisted up the water kettle and let the spout pour water into his mouth.

"I always ask people in the market to let me know if they ever see anyone from Samjeong-myeon, Suan County in Hwanghae-do, but without result. If it's so hard to find someone in this small country, how can anyone find their families in a huge country like America, once they lost them?" Mrs. An said.

"When I walk the streets peering at faces, I imagine my mother rushing up to me from somewhere and shouting, 'Oh, you're here! Not dead as I was afraid!' but that hasn't happened yet. They say Korea is a small country, but it's much too big for me. It's so hard to find someone in the wide, wide land of South Korea," Mr. Ju said, getting to his feet and rubbing his hands together.

"We have an orphan girl in this house now. The mistress brought an orphan from the orphanage, and my, was she dirty. So I heated water and gave her a bath. Dirt peeled off her like thick noodles, endlessly. After I scrubbed off the dirt, her rail-thin body was just skin and bones. So, I told the girl that I'll look after her like my own younger sister and make her plump and fair before a year's out."

"Oh, yes, that's a worthy thought. They say heaven remembers your good deeds to the sick and the aged and the orphaned," Mr. Ju said, paying Junho's father for the snacks, and shouldering his A-frame back on. All the while, Junho's father remained totally silent, and tended to his stoves and rolls with an embarrassed and grateful smile. Mr. Ju looked up at the bright winter sky, and muttered to himself "Which road shall I explore now?"

"Ma'am, the old lady wants you," the orphan girl, who had just joined the household, came to the store and said to Mrs. An. The girl, who in the morning looked like a spindly chestnut rolling on the ground, looked a totally different person now. She had changed into a traditional style blouse and skirt, and her face was so fair that blue veins could be seen on her forehead.

"Oh, it's time to go to the market. I have to buy a lot of food today," Mrs. An said and called to Mr. Ju, who was stepping out of the store. "Mr. Ju, come by in the morning the day after tomorrow. I'll give you a rich breakfast. So filling that you won't feel hungry even if you skip several meals," she said and smiled.

"Why, is there a feast in the family, or a commemoration service?" Mr. Ju asked.

"Well, the day after tomorrow is Christmas, and there's going to be a Christmas Eve banquet at the house tomorrow night. Oh, no, it's not a banquet but a "party." I hear there's going to be more than a dozen guests. So the living room will be full. And they're going to have catering service from Gumbanggak. Two famous chefs are coming to prepare special party food."

I opened my eyes wide. I didn't know what a "party" was, but my heart throbbed just to hear of such an event taking place. There would be bright lights, and many dishes of delicious food, and soft music, and well-dressed people and their laughter. Such luxurious pastimes of the rich could not but make the heart of a rustic boy like me throb. I thought to myself that I would have fun on the night of the twenty-fourth, peeking at the party in the inner quarters.

It was after dusk fell and electric lights were lit when Sunhwa and Jeongmin came home with tired steps. They were coming back after making inquiries of Jeongtae all day that Sunday. Not only were their steps tired, but their faces were clouded, too.

"So, it was to no avail today, either?" Junho's father asked.

"In Seomun Market we met a former classmate of our brother who attended Pyongyang Teacher Training School with him. He had no recent news of him, but said that another classmate by the name of Gibok, who was a close friend of our brother, is a teacher in Seoul, so maybe he went to see this friend. He said our brother missed that friend very much," Jeongmin said.

"And any news of the Gimcheon woman?"

"None. Captain, what should we do, now?" Sunhwa asked, with a tearful face.

"Your brother's a grown man. He'll come home when he feels like it. I wouldn't go around looking for him," Junho's father said.

"But he's ill, and it's so cold . . ."

"Oh, that police detective was here today. Asking for news of the Gimcheon woman," Junho's father said, as if he'd just remembered. I had come out to the store after having my dinner and was basking in the warmth of the tin-drum oven. I recalled the face of the police detective with the sharp chin. He, too, must be ransacking the city looking for the Gimcheon woman, just as the Pyongyang family was doing in search of their first son. Well, to be precise, the police detective was looking for the Gimcheon woman to find the man with a knife scar on his face.

The next day, I went to the *Daegu Daily* building as usual. It was a cold day, so I had my hands tucked into my pockets and walked with my shoulders hunched. The street was overflowing with Christmas songs. Students returning to their homes, dismissed from school early, were filling the streets. When passing boys my age and older who were wearing school uniforms and caps, I clung to the wall and yielded the street to them, like one guilty. The students were rejoicing that winter vacation had begun. All the schools broke up for the winter vacation from the twenty-fourth. The bookstores selling New Year's calendars and Christmas cards were bustling with schoolgirls. I gazed at the schoolgirls choosing beautiful Christmas cards, thinking that I had no one to send cards to nor anyone to send me cards. I felt very lonely. I walked on, with my eyes fixed to the ground. My sneakers, which Mother had bought me when I began newspaper delivery, now had the soles partly separated from the upper part, so that the toes were gaping, even though they'd had the services of the shoe repairman twice.

In the backyard of the newspaper building, delivery boys were playing at soccer, with a ball that had too little air in it. Hanju was not there yet. As winter came and the weather got cold, his mother had taken to her bed and couldn't sell salted fish any more, so twelve-year-old Hanju, as the pillar of his family, was supporting his whole family with his earnings. He was now selling not just chewing gum but candy drops, chocolate, pencils, fingernail clippers, and earwax removers. Only when Mr. Son came out and distributed papers to be delivered in the Jungbu area did Hanju rush in with a flushed face, panting for breath. Just as Junho's father did before he began selling baked sweet potatoes, he was carrying a small bag.

"You, you're always late! And you've gained no new subscribers in the past month," scolded Mr. Son.

"But none of the subscribers on my route stopped subscribing. Isn't that something? It's so hard to gain new subscribers in these hard times," Hanju returned, undaunted.

"How is your mother?" I asked Hanju.

"We took her to the hospital for the first time yesterday. They said it's a heart ailment. Mother had difficulty walking up hills even before the war. And she's been eating so poorly, has had too much shock and worked too hard since the war began. So there's nothing for me to do but to try to earn money every minute. My shoulders are heavy," Hanju said. Even though the winter wind was cold, Hanju had beads of perspiration all over his face and his breath was hot.

"Does she have medicine?" I asked.

"Yes, we got several days' medicine, but . . . the doctor said the best medicine is to rest well and eat well. It's so painful to watch her panting for breath," Hanju said.

"I'm sorry I can't help you in any way," I said.

"How can you? You have your own load," Hanju said, grinning. "This is the best business season for me. With Christmas and the New Year. So I have to go and sell hard. So, Gilnam, so long! Take care!" Hanju bounded off to the street, after patting me on the shoulder. He would be selling his wares until midnight, wending his way through the downtown streets.

I returned home through the residential area, avoiding the busy downtown. While delivering the papers, I didn't feel the cold so much because I almost ran from start to finish, but on my way back home, I felt the cold evening wind slicing into my skin and stinging my bones. The cold on the way home made me sad and lonely, no less than hungry, so like my mother who complained of "dirty times" I also muttered to myself that I had no joy in life and no joy to look forward to. I wished I could disappear into the cold darkness, dispersing into a trillion particles smaller than dust.

When I turned into the Medicine Lane, many of the herbal clinics and medicine dealers were lighting up, and there were many people traversing the street. At the entrance to the long alley leading to my house I saw Seongjun and Miseon. Miseon was in school uniform as she was on her way to her night school, and was carrying a school bag. Seongjun seems to have followed her out of the house, as he was wearing wooden clogs. They were standing facing each other and were saying something with a very serious expression.

"As I said, I'm not asking you to be my partner. I'm just asking you to interpret for the captain. I'm taking private lessons in English, but my English isn't good enough yet for me to serve as an interpreter, so I'm asking you for help," Seongjun was pleading.

"Well, as I told you, I'm not going to your party tomorrow. We have an event at our church tomorrow evening which I have to attend," Miseon was saying.

"Miss Park. I have applied for a passport, and I will be flying to America in about a month. This is my last request before leaving this land. So, please do me this favor. I won't bother you any more with my confessions of love. I do have willpower, when I choose to exert it," Seongjun said, shrugging his shoulders and upturning his palms in imitation of the American gesture.

"Oh, you're as sticky as pine resin, aren't you?" Miseon said, and looked at her watch.

"Well then, I'll expect you to help at the party and won't look for an interpreter," Seongjun declared and strode off into the lane before me.

On the evening of the next day, I was to witness a "party" for the first time in my life. The first thing that amazed me was that Miseon, whom I didn't think would be at the party, was there. As a matter of fact, what was so amazing was not so much her presence there as her transformation. Miseon was wearing heavy eye-makeup, had blush on her cheeks, and had her lips painted bright red. It made her look a couple of years older than she was. She looked as ravishing as a Western movie actress seen on the billboards of cinema houses. Ordinarily, she went to work lightly made up, and then came back home to wash her face clean of any trace of make-up, and went to school with her hair tied together at the back and wearing a school uniform, so that she looked like any innocent schoolgirl. But tonight, not only did her make-up make her look mature, but her dress, which I heard later that she'd borrowed from the commissary, made her look sexy as no woman had ever appeared to me. That black satin dress was cut low over her breasts, in the shape of the letter Y. On her breasts, scores of transparent beads sparkled. And her dress was so voluminous that I imagined an urchin as big as my younger brother Gilsu could hide in there while playing hide-and-seek. That she didn't seem shy or embarrassed at all while exposing more than half of her breasts was beyond my belief. I knew Miseon had ample breasts, as they shook beneath her blouse when she walked. But to see her white breasts thus exposed and to glimpse the deep cleavage in between made my heart throb. Even to a twelve-year-old boy, it seemed natural that any grown-up man, to say nothing of a playboy like Seongjun, would yearn to squeeze those breasts.

The guests at the party included our landlord's cousin who headed the company that had a monopoly on selling office supplies to the Second Army and his wife, my landlord's relative who was the president of the Yeongnam Fertilizer Company and his wife, another relative of my landlord who was an army captain in military uniform, the head of the anti-communism section of the Daegu Police Station and his wife, a young American army captain who had a big nose and brown hair, and a bureau chief in the provincial government and his wife. Of course our landlord and landlady and Seongjun were present as hosts. "I heard that this is a party to help smooth the way for Seongjun to go to America to study. That's why the American soldier who got him an admission to an American university and the high-ranking police officer who gave him personal reference were invited," Mrs. An explained to the Gyeonggi woman, identifying all the participants.

The Gyeonggi woman and myself were the two onlookers from the middle quarters. Junho's family were all in the store, trying to make the most of the Christmas Eve rush of customers, and the Pyongyang woman had gone to the gathering of her hometown people in the hope of obtaining information about her son. Sunhwa and Jeongmin seemed to be in their room but apparently weren't paying any attention to the party going on in the inner quarters. Heunggyu, the Gyeonggi woman's son, was dating the only daughter of a dried fish dealer in Seomun Market, so he must have been spending a blissful time with his sweetheart. "He got to know her while treating her cavities. Her family has been famously rich since her grandfather's time. Her father has no less than three stores in Seomun Market, and has an eight-hundred-cubic-meter mansion in Gongpyeong-dong. The bride's family says that a dentist son-in-law can marry into their family empty-handed, so we won't need to spend any money for the marriage," the Gyeonggi woman bragged. I had hoped that Heunggyu and Sunhwa would marry each other, as they were both refugees from the North, but perhaps the fact that each family knew the other's poverty too well made it difficult for them to get united.

I sat there on the verandah of the Gyeonggi woman's room shivering in the cold, and kept my eyes on what was going on in the brightly-lit living room of the inner quarters. The Gyeonggi woman, fortified against the cold with a blanket draped over her and smoking one cigarette after another, was watching her daughter in the midst of fantastically well-dressed people, like one watching over a lamb in a den of wolves. In the living room, the huge stove was burning with a red glow, and the stereo was belching out American popular songs. On one side of the living room was a long-legged table spread with a white tablecloth, on which lay many dishes of food and bottles of wine and spirits. Each guest went around the table with a plate in hand and filled the plate with as much food as they wanted. It aroused my envy that people could eat as much as they liked of the mountainous heaps of food at their disposal. The waiters from the Gumbanggak Chinese restaurant in swallow-tail tuxedo and bow tie were waiting on the guests.

"What a barbaric way of eating! To eat standing up and talking and giggling! I wouldn't know what any of the food tasted like," the Gyeonggi woman said sullenly.

"Oh, I think that's a swell way of eating. Wouldn't it be nice to eat as much as you want?" I countered her.

"Gilnam, when do you think you'll be able to have so much

food heaped up on your plate and eat your fill?" the Gyeonggi woman said, sneeringly. I felt the sting of her sarcasm, but I couldn't make any response, partly because of the cold but more because of the despair that I would never be able to eat food that way.

It was more than twenty years later that I learned that such a manner of eating food is called buffet-style. I'm sure the Gyeonggi woman who always pretended to know everything didn't know what it was called and had never seen it taking place with her own eyes. The Korean style feast is to have food prepared on a table and for the guests to sit around it and eat. But the Western way of eating, walking around carrying a dish or perching on a chair looked very natural and refined, even though unfamiliar to my eyes. The guests talked and laughed, eating good food to the accompaniment of sweet music. To me, the scene inside the glass door of the living room was like a clip from a movie.

"I shuddered to see the dress when she first put it on. But it blends so well in a party like that. My daughter certainly has a sense of style. You think her beautiful, too, don't you?"

"She's just like an actress in a Western movie. Any grown man would fall in love with her," I said.

"Well, even though you're young, you sure have a good eye," the Gyeonggi woman remarked.

It was true that Miseon, who was the only nubile woman in the party, looked conspicuous. The other women were all in Korean traditional dresses, so her dress made her stand out. But more than that, one could see that she was leading the American officer around the room and making him acquainted with all the guests. Seongjun was following her around like a puppy. Or rather, he was a wolf casting voracious glances into the cleft between her breasts. The Gyeonggi woman kept her watch over the wolf from a distance. There were other observers of the party, too. Seongjun's two younger brothers, high school and middle school students, were watching the party scene from the guest room of the inner quarters. Their private tutor, Jeongmin, wasn't giving them lessons because it was Christmas Eve. Donghi was nowhere in sight. She seemed to be spending the night outside.

In the brightly-lit kitchen of the main quarters, cooks dispatched from Gumbanggak were continually making more dishes. Mrs. An carried the cooked food on large plates into the living room. The orphan girl, whose name was Oggi, was helping, and I saw her licking the plate in the dark like a puppy whenever she was carrying the empty plates into the kitchen. I was hoping that I, too, for keeping a keen watch over the glamorous scene, would be offered the privilege of licking some empty dishes, like Oggi. I cast glances at the kitchen trying to decide whether I should approach the kitchen on my part, as it didn't seem like anyone would come over to where I was sitting to offer me such a privilege, when the Gyeonggi woman exclaimed, "That's what I was afraid would happen!" I quickly turned my eyes toward the living room. A dance was just beginning. Men and women formed dancing partners and were floating around the living room floor in tune to slow music.

"My, when did the bad girl learn to dance like that!" the Gyeonggi woman exclaimed, breathlessly.

My landlord and landlady made one couple, of course, and Miseon was dancing with the big-nosed American army officer. The Korean army colonel and Seongjun had no partners and were watching the others dance, sitting on easy chairs. When one dance was finished, everyone laughed and clapped their hands, and Seongjun quickly changed the disk on the gramophone. The new music was a quick and brisk waltz tune. Seongjun quickly snatched up Miseon and led the dance, and the others also changed partners.

"Oh, that bastard and that bitch! I hope their legs collapse under them. I was wondering how long that playboy would keep his ass on a seat while a dance was going on. And that bitch! She could have refused, and he couldn't have forced her. She must be out of her mind to allow him to hold her like that. She might get seduced by him," the Gyeonggi woman fretted and fumed. She looked ready to throw off the blanket and rush up to the inner quarters, but apparently changed her mind and lit a cigarette.

While I was watching the dancing scene rapturously, Giljung came up to me with silent steps, crossing the courtyard. He told me Mother wanted me. I came back to reality at that, and it hit me that if I went back to our room I would be whipped. Mother had sewn all night long the night before, because there was a big Christmas and year-end rush of customers, and she had been sewing all day long that day, too.

"Is Mom angry?" I asked my younger brother.

"Yes." Giljung said, nodding.

"Very angry?"

"I think so."

When I went into our room, Mother began yelling at me at once. Mother had a powerful voice, which she tried to restrain while we were living in the middle quarters because of so many other tenants beyond the thin wall and the proximity of the inner quarters, but since we began living in the outer quarters and out of hearing of the other inhabitants she seemed to feel no need to subdue her voice. So, her voice was as loud as became her powerful build.

"You, good-for-nothing! Do you think there will be questions on rich people's parties in the middle school entrance exam? Is that why you were watching it like an enchanted idiot? What good can it possibly do you to watch rich people flaunting their money? Oh, poor me! To pin my hopes on such an idiot for my eldest son, and raise him by working until my eyes are ready to give out!" Mother's voice was tearful.

"I am sorry," I said, guilty and fearful.

"You idiot! If you like to watch rich bastards gorging on rich food, you might as well be their servant all your life and wipe their bottoms for them! You worthless imbecile!" Mother yelled at me, glaring at me with her bloodshot eyes while going on with her sewing.

"I won't watch such sights again," I offered.

"Leave this house at once! I don't care even if you die of hunger and cold! If you don't want to leave, bring half a dozen switches!" Mother yelled furiously, but it was followed by a piercing scream. The sewing machine needle had stitched her left index finger, boring a hole into her nail. While Mother was frozen in panic, blood gushed out of her finger and began staining red the aqua-blue silk blouse that she was sewing.

"Mother, reverse the wheel, quickly!" "Mother, you're bleeding!" broke from Seonrye's and Giljung's lips simultaneously.

When Mother lifted the needle out of her finger by reversing the sewing machine wheel, blood gushed out and more dripped on the fabric.

"Oh, what am I going to do about this brocade blouse? What if she says I should make her a new one?" Mother sobbed, grabbing her injured finger but with her whole attention on the spoiled silk blouse. "Seonrye, you go out to the kitchen and bring water and soap," she said.

Seonrye went to the kitchen and came back with a basin of water and a cake of soap. In the meantime Mother took out a handkerchief from the drawer of the sewing machine and tied her hurt finger. Then she wetted the section of the cloth with the blood on it and carefully rubbed soap on it. I stood beside the door and watched her scrubbing like mad. My heart throbbed wildly and my legs shook.

"Mrs. Kim, is something the matter?" Junho's mother, who must have heard her scream from the store, asked outside our door, but it seemed that Mother could attend to nothing except getting the stain out.

"What if I can't get the stain out! What if she asks me to make it whole? Where can I get the same fabric?" Mother kept wailing tearfully.

I decided that I should leave home and family there and then. Mother had threatened to throw me out, and if I bowed to her threat and offered her half a dozen switches, she'd beat me savagely as never before. "Why don't you disappear from my sight! You'll just consume rice and will never be worth your feed! I'll just think that I lost a child in the confusion of the war. I won't be missing you or anything!" Mother would berate me with such words and stop whipping me only when I fell in a swoon foaming at the mouth. Even after that, for days and days she would blame me for causing her fingernail to be pierced and having a silk brocade fabric stained with blood. And she would beat me afresh, as if to revenge her "dirty times" on me.

I came out of the room silently. I put on my sneakers and came out to the lane through the store. The wind was cutting.

"Where are you going, Gilnam, at this time of the night?" Junho's mother, who was baking rolls with her baby daughter strapped to her back asked, but I returned no answer. However, I looked back, thinking that it was the last time I was seeing Junho's family. Junho's father was handing over a bag of baked sweet potatoes to the little daughter of our district chief. There was another customer waiting to buy baked sweet potatoes. Santa's blessings extended over such small shops, too, apparently.

I stuck both my hands in my pockets, which were empty of any money. I walked the lane toward Jongro, rather than toward Medicine Lane. I tried to brace myself, telling myself that I was an orphan without parents and siblings. I told myself that from that night nobody was going to tell me what to do, but at the same time I had to survive without anybody's help. I was not going to go back to any of my kinfolk, whether Mother, sister, or younger brothers. I was never going to seek family and kin even if I were to freeze to death on the street. When I made up my mind like that and clamped my molars together, two streaks of tears flowed out of my eyes. I wiped them off with my balled-up fists.

Jongro Street was brightly lit and there were many pedestrians. Carols resounded through the street. All the passersby looked happy in spite of the cold, and I was the only loner. I had nowhere to go. The face that loomed up before me at that juncture was Hanju's. He must be plying his trade all night long, as it was a night without curfew. I decided to look for Hanju. I ran toward the busy section of the city around Songjuk Cinema as fast as I could.

I combed Jungang Road until around midnight, ransacking the Songjuk Cinema area, Dongseong-ro, and Hyangchon-dong, looking for Hanju. I even stuck my head into restaurants and tea rooms. While peering into a beer hall I was grabbed by the scruff of my neck and thrown out. Whenever I saw the back of a boy who was Hanju's height and bulk, I shouted "Hanju!" but none turned out to be Hanju. I thought that if I told Hanju my plight, he would surely find a way for me to survive, but he was nowhere to be found. I even had the feeling that he was hiding somewhere to avoid me. I felt tired out, after thus searching the downtown streets for several hours.

Only after midnight, when the streets began to grow deserted, did I realize I wouldn't be able to find Hanju. The shops began to turn off their lights and close their shutters. Only drunken men wending their way home with wobbly steps and shouting drunken messages remained on the street. In great disappointment I headed toward the train station. I needed shelter from the cutting wind.

There was some warmth remaining in the waiting room of the station. People like me, who had no place to sleep, were sitting hunched up on the wooden benches. Or maybe they were passengers waiting for early morning trains. I saw some beggars with begging bowls. But Hanju was not there. I squeezed myself between two people on a bench, hoping to get warmth from them. I was not crying but my heart was broken and I had no idea what I could do to keep alive. I realized to the marrow of my bones how essential four walls around one and a roof over one's head are for survival. That realization was to serve me well later in my life. I regretted that I did not beg forgiveness from Mother and let her whip me all she liked, but it was too late. Tired of keeping my eyes on the door of the waiting room hoping for the appearance of Hanju, I pulled both my feet up on the bench and buried my head between my bent knees. And I fell asleep.

I had a most painful and terrible dream. Mother ordered me to put both my hands on the sewing machine, flat with fingers close together. Then she pressed my hands down and forced my nails under the needle. The needle of the sewing machine sewed up my fingers together, boring holes in all ten of my nails. My fingers were spouting blood like a water fountain. "This will teach you a lesson. I sewed up my finger because I was too tired after working all night for you, so you must learn how hard it is to keep away hunger," Mother said in an embittered voice while I was screaming desperately. Mother's face looked like a witch's, with eyes slanting upward, and the whites of her eyes were red with blood.

I woke up feeling an awful pain in my nails. The day was dawning. The plaza outside was dimly lit. The garbage man was sweeping the floor of the waiting room. I hurried out of the waiting room, afraid that thugs would harass me, or that Mother would come looking for me with switches.

I walked along Jungang Road. The sun was about to rise. A bean curd vendor's bell could be heard, and a morning paper delivery boy passed me, making my heart glad. But I was so hungry it was difficult even to walk, and I could feel a great emptiness in my stomach. I had eaten dinner the night before, and it was not time for breakfast yet, so normally I should not have been racked by hunger, but I felt as hungry as if I'd starved a whole day. It could be because I had run around too much the previous night looking for Hanju, or it could be my stomach was howling for food, knowing that there was no prospect of a meal that morning. When I turned into the back street of Hyangchon-dong I realized what it was I had been looking for. There was a big trash can beside the back door of a restaurant. I sniffed the trash can like a puppy, peering into the can. I was no different from a beggar. In fact, I was a beggar now, trying to find something to eat among the trash. When I picked up frozen noodles with trembling fingers from the can, I was ashamed even though there was no one around. Hot tears ran down my cheeks. I told myself that I couldn't live unless I ate something, anything, so I'd better brace myself to eat food thrown away by others.

I met Hanju between the Mangyeong-gwan Cinema and the Daegu Police Station, a little after the noon siren sounded. I was sitting hunched up in a sunny corner of the street, because I had no strength left for walking. It was Christmas day, and Hanju was a veritable Christ to me.

"Hanju!" I called.

"Oh, it's you, Gilnam. Why are you sitting there? Have you been crying?"

"No, not crying," I mumbled and told him how desperately I'd looked for him the night before and why I decided to leave home.

"Oh, how stupid of you to leave home and family for something like that! If one were to leave home for such trifles the whole city would be overflowing with homeless children. Listen, Gilnam. Why don't you go back home? I'm sure your mother's waiting for you and worrying about you."

It made me angry that Hanju did not sympathize with me and mouthed platitudes. I recalled the phrase "to have one's foot struck by a trusted axe," and regretted that I'd yearned to see Hanju so desperately.

"No, you don't know how hard-hearted and pitiless my Mother is. I'll never go back home. Mother wouldn't wait for an idiot like me. To tell you the truth, my mother's not my real mother. Father had me by another woman and brought me home. So I don't even know who my mother is, though I hope to find her some day."

"Is that so?" Hanju said, his eyes dilating. My conscience hurt me, so I couldn't say 'Yes.' Instead, I nodded.

"If you haven't eaten since last night, you must be hungry. Come. I earned some money last night while you were looking for me, so I'll buy you some rolls. Come along," Hanju said and grabbed my arm. He led me to a covered wagon selling rolls. I ate two rolls, and Hanju ate one. Hanju looked at me gorging on rolls like someone who hadn't eaten for a week, and gave me advice, as if he had been an older brother to me.

"You know, your mother may not be your real mother, but your siblings are the same blood as you, aren't they? You have no way to stay alive by yourself. That's simply foolishness. You must keep a tight rein over yourself and have courage. For boys like us without fathers, the only way we can survive is to work hard with a stout heart. They say that there is a blessing for the patient," Hanju said. I could not contradict him. But I didn't want to go back to my home. Hanju paid for the rolls. When we came out of the wagon he took hold of my hand affectionately and tried to make me promise that I would go back to my home. I didn't make that promise.

"Well, I must go. I have to sell these things and earn money. You, too, you must earn money and go to middle school next year. So, you must go back to your family. There's no way a homeless boy can go to middle school. Well, see you at the newspaper company. Newspaper delivery is about the best job boys like us can have," Hanju said and grinned, exposing both his eyeteeth, and bounded away in the direction of the Army cinema.

I delivered newspapers for the *Daegu Daily*, the *Yeongnam Daily*, and the *Dong-a Daily* until I was a sophomore in high school, but Hanju stopped delivering newspapers after delivering for the *Daegu Daily* for two years. Because of his mother's long illness, he couldn't go to middle school in the evening as he had yearned to, and got employment as a printer's assistant instead. So, we were 'colleagues' for only the two years we both delivered the *Daegu Daily*.

"You can go to school but I can't," Hanju said. "If I don't earn money, my mother and my sister and I can't live, and we can't buy Mother's medicine. Newspaper delivery doesn't add up to anything, and you don't acquire any skill from it. And they don't want you when you're older. So, I decided to take the job at the printer's. And I'll be a printer when I grow up."

So, I stopped seeing him every afternoon, but I often visited him at his printing office located in the back street of Bukseong-ro after I finished my delivery. The office was a small one specializing in printing name cards and legal and business transaction forms. He was working diligently as a young assistant, his face and clothes smeared here and there with printing oil. His mother passed away that summer. "Mother said she couldn't rest easy even in the other world, leaving me and my young sister in this one, and grabbed my hand so hard. I didn't know Mother, who'd been ill for so long, had that much strength left," Hanju told me and brushed away tears from his cheeks. That was the only time in my knowledge that Hanju's bright, smiling face clouded over.

Hanju's mother passed away from an illness four years after the armistice, but the ultimate cause of her death was certainly the war. The poison of war lurked in our bodies for a long time and at last claimed our lives. The root cause of my youngest brother

Gilsu's death was the war, too. So, the number of war victims far exceeds those who died on battlefields, in bombings, and while seeking refuge.

Here's what happened to Hanju: when I visited Daegu while on leave from military service, he had become a foreman in the printing company, which had grown several times in scale. I was fulfilling my military duty while attending a night college. He had ink stains on his face and overalls and grinned at me just like in the days we delivered newspapers. Then he said, imitating my Southern dialect, "You're a private. I earn money, so I will buy you rice wine." At the time he was already married, and even had a son because he "yearned so much to have close kin." While sharing rice wine with him, I asked what became of his sister Myeonghi. I knew her well because while attending middle and high schools I went to see him at the rented room he lived in with his sister. Myeonghi had begun working as an errand girl in a restaurant as soon as she finished primary school. She was not a very pretty girl but she had as much will for survival as her brother. After working in the restaurant for a while, she got employment as a factory girl in a socks factory, and then was going to middle school in the evenings at the same time. That was before I joined the army.

"She is now working for a textile factory in Chimsan-dong. Well, to tell you the truth, in the days we delivered newspapers together I rather wished you would marry Myeonghi. I thought you'd make an ideal pair, as a man from the south and a woman from the north are said to suit each other ideally. But it's impossible now. There's too great a discrepancy between you and Myeonghi. I guess everyone has his allotted lot and suitable spouse," Hanju said and smiled sadly. That was my last meeting with him. After I finished my military service and was working as the editor-in-chief of the university paper, the printer's shop that printed the school paper was located in Bukseong-ro. So while the paper was in the press, I went over to Hanju's printing company. But he wasn't working there any more. His former employer said that he had accepted a job offer from a printer in Seoul for the reason that Seoul is closer to his hometown.

When looking back on my life in Daegu, I recall Hanju as the person most responsible for giving me courage, by living and working so stoutly and honestly through those "dirty times." I recall with special gratitude his recommending me as a delivery boy, saying to Mr. Son "You can trust Gilnam," and his quoting the Bible passage "Blessed are the patient" to me the night I left home. I think I owe my patience and honesty to his principles and his example more than to anyone else's.

I checked the time through the windows of the clock and watch shops, and went to the newspaper building before it was two o'clock in the afternoon. As I stepped in through the back gate, I saw Seonrye standing beside the janitor's booth. She was in her school uniform and had several books in one hand and her lunch-box in the other. I was awfully glad to see her, like I was seeing her after a long absence, but I felt embarrassed, too, so I dropped my eyes to the ground and kicked the dust with my sneakers that had the gaping toes.

"Gilnam, how can you leave home for such a trifle? Where did you sleep last night?" Seonrye scolded. I returned no answer.

"Mother put aside her sewing and cried for a long time last night. She said that she was working so hard to raise her children, so if her children don't want to live with her, there was no reason for her to work any more. As I was leaving for the library this morning Mother told me to look for you at the newspaper building in the afternoon."

Seonrye had the entrance exam for high school coming up very shortly, so she studied in the school library all day. The Daegu Teachers' Training High School had its entrance exam earlier than all the other high schools, and only the best middle school graduates dared apply. Even so, the odds of success were four to one.

There were many things I would have liked to ask her. Questions like, didn't Mother say that she's glad she doesn't have to feed me any more, or if she hadn't vowed she would beat me till I was half dead if I ever dared to come back home, and whether she could get the blood stain out of the blue silk fabric, and if Mother's finger was healing. But I couldn't bring the words out, so I glumly cast glances towards the printing room. I could hear the rotary press spinning. Several of the delivery boys were practicing football kicks, and Mr. Son was giving Myeong-su a bawling-out. Apparently he was scolding him for not having gained any new subscribers.

"Come home after you finish delivering the papers. Mother will be waiting for you with beef soup. You must be hungry. Here. I brought you my lunch-box. Eat it somewhere sheltered," Seonrye said and held out the box.

"No. You eat it. I'm not going back home. And this is the last day I'm delivering the papers. I will leave this city altogether. And I'll be going far, far away. I won't go to Jinyeong. Tell Mother I'm going far away. You'll all be fine without me." I was saying things that were the opposite of what I yearned to say. I felt my throat tighten, and tears welled up.

"What on earth are you saying? Where can you go? And why should you go anywhere? You have a home. You're not an orphan," Seonrye said.

"Tell Mother not to look for me. She took me in just to make me deliver newspapers, and she won't even send me to school. All I had from her were whippings. I'm not such an idiot as to keep clinging to her just to get beaten and to split firewood for her. I'm going to fend for myself from now on. Not all those who fend for themselves are orphans. I can live by myself. I made plans on how to, last night in the station lounge," I kept on my desperate soliloquy. Then, I began walking toward the backyard of the building where the other delivery boys were practicing football. My sister grabbed me by the arm.

"Gilnam, you're wrong. Mother promised you she'd send you to middle school next year. Don't be perverse like that. Come home after delivering the papers today. I heard that the station lounge teems with hoodlums who kidnap children to sell off to criminal gangs."

I didn't want to stand there quarrelling with my sister in plain sight of the other delivery boys and Mr. Son. So I cried out, nearly screaming, "Go away, I tell you!" Seonrye, visibly offended, left me then, but again said that I must come home that evening.

An idea occurred to me, and I asked Mr. Son for an advance of two hundred *hwan*. I told him that my sister came to see me because she had run up her tuition for some time, so unless she paid up, she couldn't get her diploma. Mr. Son gave me the two hundred *hwan* without hesitation, and wrote in his notebook the amount and the date.

Hanju hadn't arrived by the time I left the newspaper building with the papers stuck under my arms. Hanju was sure to have a scolding from Mr. Son when he rushed in late.

When the delivery was finished I turned into Janggwan-dong Lane, went as far as where I could see Junho's father's store, and loitered for a long time. I wondered whether I should go to Mother and ask forgiveness. I wondered if it might be true that Mother would be waiting for me with beef soup. I thought Seonrye's words might be just a decoy, and instead of beef soup, Mother would meet me with a hail of abuse and merciless whipping. She would accompany her shower of switches with words like "So, you thought you could fend for yourself? How did you like it? At that rate, you'd have become nothing but a hoodlum, so I'd better kill you right off." I loitered there hoping my sister or brother Giljung would come out of the room to look for me. Then if they saw me and persuaded me to come home, I'd follow them. But none of my family members came out. I imagined my family would be eating dinner, sharing their worries about me, but as I had told Seonrye that I could fend for myself, I didn't have the courage to show up among them.

I turned around. Slowly emerging from the lane now sunk in ink-black darkness, I told myself that there was only one place I could go. Cold and hunger gripped my body like a vise. I thought that I would buy myself some baked sweet potatoes for dinner out of the two hundred *hwan* advance I'd gotten, and store the rest of the money somewhere safe in my undergarments. I thought that the best place would be the cuffs of my trousers legs, if I undid the hem and placed the money inside. I knew that Hanju stored his money there to safeguard it from ruffians.

"Cool acorn jellies or sweet and glutinous rice cakes for snacks! And steaming hot red bean porridge, too!" The night snacks vendor wove in and out of the street, hawking his goods. As he passed me, I saw that he had on his A-frame carrier a red bean porridge pot wrapped in an old blanket, an acorn jelly pot and a hamper for rice cakes. He was wearing a dog-fur hat, and a military coat dyed black. When I recalled the taste of the red bean paste that I'd tasted while living in the pub in the market street of Jinyeong, my stomach growled, and my mouth watered. But I couldn't use the money on snacks.

"Steaming hot red bean porridge and sweet and glutinous rice cakes!" the vendor wailed behind my back. I looked back at him. He would be shivering in the cold as he weaved the streets hawking his merchandise until the curfew fell. When I thought how hard it is for so many people to survive each day, I felt something hot pressing up my throat. It was bitter bile.

Walking Jungang Road with my hands stuck in my pockets, I did not look for Hanju any more. I thought it certain that he was not on my side but on my mother's.

I went to the train station lounge as I had the day before. The chairs were already filled with jobless people, vagabonds, and people waiting for the early morning train, so there were no vacant chairs for me. I squatted down on the cement floor, buried my face between my knees, and fell asleep.

I had a sequel to the dream of the day before. It had to do with the story of Howe, the lame inventor of the modern sewing machine. Seonrye had told me his story. In my dream, Howe was dreaming of being led to an execution ground, and I was dreaming his dream.

Howe's wife earned a living for herself and her husband by working as a seamstress. Howe, who was lame and had no job, always felt awfully sorry for his wife who had to work late into the night. He racked his brain, trying to think of a way to save his wife labor. Sewing is simple, repetitive work, so Howe thought it should be possible to mechanize sewing. Howe thought and thought, trying to imagine a way to mechanize sewing, but it wasn't easy. But one day, he had a strange dream. In that dream, he was led before an Indian chief, and the chief told him that he would be put to death if he couldn't invent a sewing machine inside of an hour. But he couldn't think of a way even then, so he was led to the execution ground. The executioner approached him with a poised spear. The spear glinted in the sun, and at that moment, Howe saw that the flattened end of the spear had a hole in it. That instant, Howe shouted "That's it!" And he woke up. Ordinary needles had their eyes at the rear end, but the Indian's lance had a hole in the front end. Howe hit upon the idea that if you had a needle with a hole for the thread in the front end and let the thread twine with the thread underneath, you would have a machine that could sew fabrics. A Frenchman named Simon and an American named Hunter also invented sewing machines that sewed on a similar principle, but their machines didn't get wide usage. Howe invented the machine independently of them, inspired by his dream. He had to have his idea patented, and as he didn't have the money to materialize his idea, he had to go around in search of capital. An Englishman expressed interest in funding his idea, so he crossed the Atlantic but came back disappointed. In the meantime, sweatshops in England and America criticized Howe's invention virulently, because if a sewing machine were invented, they would lose customers. There were so many demonstrations in front of his house that his neighbors had their sleep disturbed. At that juncture a businessman named Singer appeared before him. Singer, who was a shrewd businessman, stole the blueprint sketch of Howe's sewing machine, added foot pedals and the fabric pushing device and quickly applied for patents in many states. He named the machine Singer Sewing Machine, and sold it everywhere. He held "Singer Sewing Machine Exhibitions" and "Singer Sewing Machine Operating Competitions," and aggressively marketed the machine with the advertising slogan, "A Machine in Every Home." And he thought of the revolutionary marketing strategy of payment by installment. He made bales of money overnight. Now, the Singer machine was synonymous with the sewing machine. Mr. Howe was greatly disappointed. He continued to live in poverty. When the Civil War broke out soon afterwards, he joined the Union army even though he was not young any more.

Just like Howe did the moment before being pierced to death by the Indian's lance, I also woke up, with a vivid sense of the hole at the tip of the Indian's lance. I looked around. It was dark outside, and the lounge looked deserted. I was shivering so violently that my teeth rattled, making a noise like the sewing machine, and the cold stung me to the marrow. On my right, a young beggar boy had fallen asleep with his head leaning against my side, hugging his beggar's can. Because I thought that the beggar boy and I were in the same situation, I didn't mind his dirt-stained face pressing my side but was more glad than not that he fell asleep leaning on me. I scratched myself for a while and fell asleep again.

While I was sunk in sleep, shivering even as I slept, I heard someone calling my name. At first, I thought poor Howe, who had been beaten out by the capitalist Singer, was calling to me, a fellow failure.

"Gilnam, Gilnam."

I opened my eyes. The beggar boy had disappeared, and I saw the folds of a black cotton skirt in front of me. I looked up. When my eyes met those of my Mother's, which were moist and looking down at me sadly, I became ashamed and dropped my face back between my knees. Tears welled up.

"Come. Let's go home," Mother said and began walking ahead of me. She blew her nose into her handkerchief and wiped her eyes. I followed Mother and stepped down into the station plaza. The sky above the station building was beginning to brighten. I felt like a pony being led to the market for sale. It was just what I felt when I followed Seonrye to Daegu. To be more exact, I felt like a fugitive from the law being arrested and led to the police station. Mother didn't say one word to me until we reached the house. She just kept walking and didn't even look back to make sure I was following.

When the breakfast tray was brought in, I could see that only my soup bowl had slices of beef in it. At that moment I was convinced that I was Mother's own flesh and blood. Even after that, there were many occasions when I thought that surely I couldn't be Mother's own son or she wouldn't treat me like that. But that morning, I was certain that I was Mother's own son. Because of the hot feeling welling up from my heart, I couldn't eat much, and Mother never said a word.

As if in atonement for my guilt, from the next morning on, I split firewood diligently. I wielded the axe with all my strength, as though I were splitting up the dirty times and the poverty that caused me such humiliation and pain. I was not interested in the news the Gyeonggi woman brought that Donghi, the landlord's niece, was going to be expelled from school for spending the night out on Christmas Eve. She was among a group of three boys and three girls who spent the evening together. It seems that a neighbor informed on them to the police for disorderly behavior, and the police informed her school. Such a way of spending Christmas Eve might not draw much attention now, but such behavior back in 1954 could cause a girl of marriageable age to receive no marriage offer altogether. I didn't care if she got expelled or not, or if Jeongtae was found or not. I was only intent on making it up to Mother who never said a word about my leaving home and thereby deepened my guilt. I thought the only way I could cancel out my criminal act even partially was to split firewood diligently and deliver newspapers without a mistake.

My wood-splitting skill improved as I put heart and soul into it. When I lay down to sleep, I could feel that I had hard muscles on my arms and chest.

9

New Year's Day came. It is a time for gladness, but there was no particular cause for joy in my family. Everyone turned a year older by the Korean calendar, and because restaurants closed for a few days around New Year's, Mother also had a few day's rest, after the year-end rush of business. The newspapers didn't publish during the three-day official New Year's holiday, so I was able to rest for three days as well, but because I'd promised my mother that I'd finish splitting firewood during those three days, I had to work on it diligently.

On the fourth of January, when the newspaper came out again, there were two news reports that remained foremost in my memory for a long, long time. The first item was reported with banner headlines on the society page, but as I'd started delivering the paper without reading it, I didn't know about the report and only discovered the fact by myself when I reached the spot reported on.

The Hope Orphanage was one of my two subscriber orphanages. It was the one that was not a model orphanage, having a very unkempt appearance with malnourished-looking orphans in rags. When I reached the orphanage to deliver the paper, the small yard was filled with spectators and the police were trying to stave off the spectators from approaching the quonset hut. According to what I overheard from the spectators, the director and his family had absconded with all the relief money and goods that had poured in for Christmas and winter from around the world. And that was not all. They also found buried in the hill to the rear of the building five small bodies of orphans. The corpses had died of starvation. The spectators were fuming with fury against the unscrupulous director and his family. In the window frame to one side of the quonset hut the pale, emaciated faces of surviving orphans hung like gourds, eyeing the spectators. That meant the loss of one subscriber for me.

When I returned home after delivering the papers, I found Seonrye making dinner and Mother absent. It was rather late for grocery shopping, so I asked Seonrye where Mother was.

"Aunt Munja killed herself. So she's gone there," Seonrye replied gloomily.

"Killed herself? Is she dead?"

The first thought that occurred to me was that there's going to be no more delicious dumplings.

We waited for Mother without eating dinner, but Mother didn't come home until it was quite dark. I'd heard that Aunt Munja lived in Gyesan-dong, just off Janggwan-dong street, but I didn't know exactly where. Giljung and I went out to the end of the lane to wait for Mother. The street was brightly lit with lights from the herbal clinics and medicinal herb shops, and a cold evening wind swept down the street. Children who must have had good dinners were playing hide-and-seek in the streets. I did not envy the children and just hoped Mother would appear quickly. Giljung's feet must have been freezing, because he kept hopping up and down.

An American military jeep that had been rushing towards us with brightly lit headlights stopped at the lane's entrance. The driver was a black soldier. Miseon, who was wearing a red muffler and had a shoulder bag dangling from her shoulder, got out of the jeep from the rear seat, and an American officer who had been sitting beside her on the rear seat also got off. It was the same American officer who had been a guest at the Christmas Eve party. The couple stood face to face at the entrance of the lane and exchanged a few words in English. The American officer draped his arm around Miseon's slender waist. The children who had been playing hide-and-seek hurled insults at the American officer and Miseon before running off giggling.

"Swala Swala. Chewing gum give me."

"Americans big nose. Americans big ass."

"It's an American whore. American whores suck American cocks."

Miseon threw poisonous glances at the children and turned into the lane, the heels of her shoes clicking as she strode away. The American officer waved at her and got onto the front passenger seat of the jeep. The jeep started up, spewing blue smoke from its tail pipe. Usually, I liked the smell of that smoke, but it made me dizzy today, perhaps because I was hungry.

We saw someone walking from the direction of Gyesan Cathedral, carrying a big piece of furniture hoisted onto her head. It was Mother. She was walking with a mirror stand with drawers that was far too heavy for a woman to carry. Whenever the mirror shook, Mother's feet also wavered, like one drunken. When Mother saw us, she set the mirror stand carefully down on the ground. Giljung and I then held one side and Mother held the other, and in that way, we carried the mirror stand home.

"Where did you get this, Mother?" Seonrye said excitedly, brightening up at the sight of the lustrous mother-of-pearl-inlaid mirror stand.

"Because Munja had no kin there is no one to claim her belongings. Her landlady said Munja often spoke of her seamstress, who was like an elder sister to her, and said I should take the mirror stand as a keepsake. I said, now that she's dead, nothing can fill her place for me, but the landlady said many of her entertaining women friends envied that stand, so I'd better take it away quickly."

"It's a real stylish stand," I said.

Mother, who had been sitting on the verandah, took down the towel which she had been using as a pad on her head and wiped her eyes. She was casting vacant glances at the bare tree in the outer yard.

"What's the use of trying so hard to live? Life and death are separated by only a thin line. Munja must have felt all the more lonely, with the new year coming and all. She must have decided to go and look for her kinfolk early. She always said she hated to live, but I didn't know she would take her own life. How sad she must have been, when she took the poison. Life is a vale of sorrow indeed! Oh, these dirty times! For a young woman in the bloom of youth to take her own life! And there are only a few fellow whores to mourn her death! I think I'll just have a bite to eat and go back and weep for the poor girl some more," Mother said.

The next morning, a policeman came to our house with a *gisaeng* woman to show the way. As Mother had experienced policemen visiting her in Seoul and Jinyeong, thanks to my father's activities, she was visibly shaken at the appearance of the policeman. He stuck his head in and checked the mirror stand first of all.

"Why, I brought that home because the landlady insisted that I take it. I didn't just pick it up and carry it home," Mother explained hurriedly.

"Ma'am, I didn't come here because you did anything wrong. The mirror stand is rightfully yours," the policeman said, smiling.

"Why, then, what do you want?"

"I don't want anything."

"Then why are you here?"

"We looked up the dead person's domicile registration, and found that she has no close kin. At least none we can contact. So, we looked into the cause of her death and found out from the landlady that the dead woman had left a will. In the will, the young lady says that you, ma'am, are to take anything among her belongings that might be useful to you. So, you must come to the police station some time and take away her property that we are holding there."

"Oh, I don't want any. Please take that mirror stand with you, too. I don't care whether you take it to the police station or sell it and give it away to poor people. Please take it off my hands," Mother said, waving toward the mirror stand, as though she found its presence distasteful.

"There's one thing more, ma'am. As the dead lady was a popular *gisaeng* in a high-class restaurant, she must have made a good sum of money. But we didn't find even a ten-*hwan* note. So, we're interrogating the landlords, but do you happen to know if the dead woman belonged to any credit union? Or do you know which bank she had an account with?"

"No. I don't. Munja sometimes brought snacks for my children but she never spoke about her finances," Mother said, somewhat flustered. "And I tell you, I won't take any of Munja's property. It's true I live from hand to mouth with my children, by taking in sewing, but I never coveted anyone's property. So, you can give away Munja's belongings to any orphanage or nursing home. I brought that mirror stand home as Munja's keepsake, but I wish you'd take that away, too."

"Well, it's nice to find someone so much above greed, at a time like this. If you don't want the mirror stand, you can dispose of it in whatever way you like," the policeman said. After a few more questions the policeman went away, saying that he would come again later. Even after the policeman left, mother pressed her bosom with her hand and tried to calm her breath. Her face was drained of blood. I was suddenly reminded of Hanju's mother, who was ill in bed with a heart ailment.

Two days later, no less than four police detectives descended on the house at dawn. That night, my youngest brother Gilsu had coughed all night and into the dawn. We were sleeping with his cough in our consciousness when there was a knock on the store door and the main gate simultaneously. It sounded very urgent. Mother sat up and smoothed the bosom of the sweater she had slept in, and I also woke up, because I had been feeling the urge to relieve myself. Our paper-paneled window, which overlooked the courtyard of the house next door, loomed up in pale ink color.

"Who, who is it?" Mother asked in a panic-stricken voice.

"Open the door, at once!" A strong voice answered from outside.

"My God! At this hour! What can it be?" Mother mumbled, putting on her skirt. My whole family was wide awake now. Seonrye turned on the electric switch but light didn't come on. Mother went out to the store and opened the side gate to the alley. A policeman in full uniform and carrying a gun, a detective in plainclothes and two uniformed soldiers without the insignia trooped into the store. They combed the store with their flashlights.

"It's the second room from the middle gate in the middle quarters. Raid that room and take everyone to the station!" ordered the plainclothes detective. He was thickly built and had close-cropped hair.

"Oh, it's not us," Mother muttered, sighing with relief. "I'm too frightened to go see what it's about. Gilnam, you go and find out," Mother said.

With Mother's permission, I followed them silently into the courtyard as they trooped noisily in. Once inside the courtyard, one of them rounded the middle quarters to guard the back wall, and the plainclothes detective pulled at the door of the Pyongyang family's room roughly. But the door was locked from inside. The detective kicked the door and yelled they should open it. From the room came Sunhwa's scream. I suddenly realized that the figure kicking the door was not a stranger to me. It was the sharp-jawed Detective Kang, who had been to our house a few times to interrogate the Gimcheon woman about the man with a knife scar.

When the door was unlocked, Detective Kang kicked it open and stomped in without bothering to take off his shoes. Soon, the Pyongyang family's room was in ruins and the occupants were trying to pull their clothes on in a great panic.

Everyone in the middle quarters woke up and poured out of their rooms. Junho's little baby sister cried like she had been burned. Doors of the rooms in the inner quarters were also pushed open and people poured into the living room.

"You bitches and bastards, come out with your hands on your head! Hurry up or I'll shoot you all," Detective Kang shouted roughly.

The three members of the Pyongyang family stepped down to the courtyard, in clothes hurriedly thrown on and without shoes. Jeongmin, who was feeling for his shoes, was hit hard on the shoulder by the policeman with the butt of his gun. They were made to kneel on the ground, with their hands folded on top of their heads. Three of the intruders, including the soldier who returned from the back yard, went into the room with their shoes on and began turning over the family possessions. Flashlights licked the room madly.

"What is it? Why're you doing this to us? You must give us the reason," the Pyongyang woman protested, albeit in a fear-strained voice.

"You dare ask why? You commies! Jabber any more, and I'll break open your skull, all of you!" the detective threatened, running the flashlight over the faces of the Pyongyang family from inside the room.

The three men in the room turned over everything in it until the dawn broke, and the policeman kept watch over the kneeling Pyongyang family in the yard. The search team even turned over the makeshift kitchen. They ripped off the sown-on duvet cover of the comforter and wrapped the things they'd sorted out for evidence in it. Most of them were books Jeongtae had been reading, and there were some notebooks, too. The policeman put handcuffs on the Pyongyang family.

"Now, stand up and come along," the uniformed soldier said to the family.

"We'll come, but why should you put handcuffs on us? You should at least tell us why," Jeongmin said.

"What, you brat! You dare ask why, as if you don't know? Let me kick some sense into you," the soldier said, kicking Jeongmin on the knee.

"Sir, the owner of the house is a VIP, so you'd better not treat them too roughly," Detective Kang said to the man with the crew cut, pointing toward the inner quarters with his chin, and led the Pyongyang family out through the middle gate. The soldier slung the bundle of evidence to his shoulders. Seonrye and Giljung, who had been watching the scene in front of the middle gate, quickly stepped aside to make way.

The man with the crew-cut hair and the policeman then strode up to the inner quarters where the landlord's family was lined up along the edge of the living room and the guest room, and looking down at the middle quarters.

"Are you the master of this house?" the man with the crew-cut asked our landlord, who was standing on the verandah of their living room.

"Yes."

"I'm afraid you'll have to accompany us to the CIC. Not only you but your wife as well."

"The CIC? The intelligence agency? Why, what for?" our

landlord asked blinking his eyes, his face growing rigid at the mention of the CIC.

"There's something we have to investigate. You'd better come along at once."

"Show us the arrest warrant signed by a judge. I won't move without a warrant," the landlord declared and said to his eldest son, "Seongjun, hurry to your uncle in Samdeok-dong and ask him to come immediately."

"Uncle or no uncle, you must come with us at once. Go get your coat. We're not like the police. You'd better not provoke us. God only knows what'll happen if you provoke us," the crew-cut took out a pistol from his trenchcoat and stepped up to the platform of the inner quarters.

"All right. We'll go with you. But let me change first," our landlady, who was in her nightgown, said quickly and disappeared into the guest room.

The old lady of the house stepped up to the crew-cut. "What do you want from my son and daughter-in-law? We have army officers and a police commissioner among our relatives. This is totally unseemly in a respectable house."

"I've already said we need to investigate. Do you know what an investigation is, old lady?"

"Investigate what?"

"Get out of the way. They'll find out soon enough."

Seongjun ran out through the middle gate, and in a little while our landlord and landlady followed the officer out.

The people standing in the courtyard were so stunned by what had happened in the matter of half an hour that they all stood there dumb. It was drawing near the time to cook breakfast, but no one made a move. When the policemen and military officer all left the house, my mother came into the courtyard and stopped in front of the outhouse. The first to break the silence was the Gyeonggi woman.

"It's Jeongtae. He must have caused big trouble. I always thought he'd make trouble some day. He must be in the CIC prison in connection with some ideological crime. That's why the police treated the Pyongyang family as communists," the Gyeonggi woman said and looked around. But none of the tenants dared utter a word in response. The Gyeonggi woman then turned to Junho's father and addressed herself to him: "What do you think, Mr. Park? Don't you think I guessed right?"

"Well, that's quite likely. I suppose it has something to do with his ideology. But I didn't think Jeongtae would do anything so extreme . . ." Junho's father said, frowning heavily.

"Maybe Jeongtae was in contact with a spy from the North? Or even engaged in espionage himself?" Heunggyu ventured.

"There's no way to know. There's such a big ideological rift between North and South, and the two sides hate each other so much, so if Jeongtae violated the ideological line, it's a grave matter indeed."

"Heunggyu, you see how dangerous it is to step over the ideological divide? You must pick your way carefully, like one treading on thin ice. The most important thing is to keep your mouth closed. You must never discuss ideology, no matter what. The likes of us who came down from the North should be a hundred times more careful not to draw suspicion on any point of ideology," the Gyeonggi woman warned, shuddering with fear, trying to wrest a promise from her son.

"Don't worry, Mother. I have no interest in such matters. I prefer the free world, so you needn't worry about me becoming involved in such things."

"Miseon, please go to the States quickly and invite me there. Heunggyu will have to live in Daegu because he's going to marry that girl from here, but I don't want to live here. Who knows when another war might break out? I'm dying to leave this country altogether." The Gyeonggi woman was hanging onto her daughter's hand and appealing to her like a child pestering for sweets.

"Calm down, Mother. Nobody's going to touch you. There's no reason," Miseon said, trying to reassure her.

The old lady of the house, who had been listening to the exchange in the courtyard, walked toward the Gyeonggi family.

"Hey, do any of you know why the police took away my son and daughter-in-law? They didn't put handcuffs on them, but it was terrifying. Is it just because we are their landlords?" the old lady asked.

"Oh, ma'am, can't you guess? There was something between the Gimcheon woman and Jeongtae, and they must be in this together. I saw the sharp-jawed police detective visiting the Gimcheon woman's store from time to time. The Gimcheon woman is a relative of yours, isn't she?"

"Oh, yes! I forgot!" the old lady looked up at the dim sky and sighed.

"Jeongtae must be the Gimcheon woman's lover, or they must be in league together in some ideological plot. And the Gimcheon woman's a cousin of your daughter-in-law. I suppose the intelligence agency needs to find out some things."

"Yes, I objected to my son's match with this daughter-in-law. I had a bad premonition. But the go-between insisted that she was good-looking and came from one of the best families. What's so great about a family of independence fighters? Independence fighters all ended up bankrupt and in jail. I told them that our families don't suit each other!" the old lady almost wailed.

"Ma'am, whose family are you talking about now? The Gimcheon woman's?"

"My own in-laws. The Gimcheon woman is my daughter-in-law's first cousin. In our family, there was no one who did such dangerous things. Members of my family all had comfortable and prosperous careers as officials of the Governor General's Office."

The old lady stopped short and cast uneasy glances towards the middle gate, fearing someone might be eavesdropping.

"I heard that your daughter-in-law finished high school during the Japanese occupation years. Why, that's like a Ph.D. these days. In my time, only brilliant girls from good families could go to high school," the Gyeonggi woman said pompously, as if to remind everyone of her own educational background.

"What's the good of a high school education for a woman who's to keep house? It only makes her arrogant and disobedient to her mother-in-law," the old lady countered.

Mrs. An looked into the Pyongyang family's room. The whole room was a mess of scattered clothes, papers, and torn books. The wardrobe chest and drawers were all wide open and the chest was toppled to one side, with the lid open and its entrails hanging over the edge.

"How could they leave things in this state? I guess I'll tidy up the room a bit," Mrs. An said and stepped into the room, taking off her shoes at the verandah.

"Hey! Don't you dare go in there. If you do, you'll be summoned for investigation next. Go and make breakfast," the old lady ordered her housekeeper.

"Gilnam, come into the room. Seonrye, you'd better wash the rice," Mother called.

When I stepped into the outer yard, Seongjun rushed in through the wide-open main gate panting wildly, followed by a middle-aged man in police officer's uniform and a police hat with a gold band. The officer was a police commissioner in charge of Communist activities at Daegu Police Headquarters, who had been a guest at the Christmas party.

None of the five people who had been taken to the police station came back before I left for newspaper delivery that afternoon. On my way back from paper delivery, I passed by the black market and looked for the Pyongyang woman, but her place was empty. I also peered into the glass wall of the landlady's jewellery shop, but the landlady was not there. I came home, and none of the Pyongyang family was back. Their room remained a chaos, as it had been in the morning. It was a bleak sight.

It was well into the night when we heard Junho's mother greeting our landlord and landlady with "Oh, you're home at last. We were so worried." Giljung, who had been looking outside through the palm-size glass panel in the door between our room and the store, said "It's our landlord and landlady." The landlord couple entered the house through the store, before Seonrye had time to run out and open the main gate for them.

"Seonrye, Gilnam, if anybody asks about anything, just say we don't know anything. Say you don't know anything about Jeongtae or the Gimcheon woman. Anything you might say, however trifling, can get us into big trouble," Mother tried to drill the point into us.

"Unk, I don't know. I don't know anything," Gilsu said, like one talking in sleep. Gilsu had been running a fever for two days and often raved. He also couldn't get anything down, except watery gruel. It was a pitiful sight, the fragile child rolling his crossed eyes and raving in his husky voice. We couldn't take him to the hospital, but his fever subsided of its own accord in the morning. His cough, however, persisted. Gilsu had grown even thinner and paler, so that he looked like a deformed child with a giant head.

"Poor Gilsu. My poor child," Mother muttered, pulling up the coverlet to cover his shoulders. I recalled the incident Mother repeated to us now and then. It happened while I was in Jinyeong, so I can only imagine how it must have been. The year after Mother settled in Daegu, Mother had a hard time feeding her children but managed to feed them two meals a day. But one day she ran out of grain altogether, so the whole family had to go hungry for a whole day. The next morning, Mother borrowed a bowl of cooked barley from her sister, made that into gruel, and gave it to her three children, going without food herself. My brother Giljung must have swallowed the hot gruel in too great a hurry, so he vomited all he ate. Then he ate his vomit. Mother scrubbed the remaining vomit with a rag. Later she found Gilsu sucking the rag. "Gilsu has brain damage. But his hunger must have made him sharp," Mother said. I also believed that Gilsu's hunger must have made him sharp for that moment. But by and by, I came to think differently. I suppose it was not because Gilsu thought that the rag must have particles of gruel, but because like other children he sucked anything that he could grab hold of. Whichever theory might be correct, our hearts ached for Gilsu after his early death, when we recalled how he spent his short life in hunger and illness.

Early the next morning, when I went into the courtyard to relieve myself after washing my face, I found the outhouse already occupied. And I saw Sunhwa cooking breakfast on the lit stove of her kitchen. The verandahs of the rooms in the middle quarters had several removable floor panels that could be lifted off when cooking on the stove that also served as the furnace for heating the rooms. I was so glad to see Sunhwa that I was going to rush up to her, but the Gyeonggi woman squatting beside her with a cigarette in her mouth and talking to her made me halt.

"I heard that the CIC is very hard on ideological suspects. Did they torture you? Did they strip-search you?" the Gyeonggi woman asked Sunhwa.

"Ma'am, please stop fanning my fury. Would I be here making breakfast if I'd been tortured?" Sunhwa sullenly retorted.

"Did you see your brother? Did they bring him to you and try to verify his statements?"

"No, we didn't see him. I suppose he's somewhere in custody. I'm relieved we don't have to go around looking for him any more."

"But didn't you see the Gimcheon woman? She didn't move

to Chilseong-dong, did she? She lied to us and disappeared with your brother, I bet."

Sunhwa made no response.

"If you're going to visit your mother in her cell, you'll have to take her a lunch-box. In the basement interrogation room, they feed you rice with beans and interrogate you without letting you sleep. So your mother needs to eat well to survive that. You must buy chicken and beef and cook them and take them to your mother."

"Never mind about that. Keep your advice to yourself." Sunhwa, her patience exhausted, snapped at the nosy woman.

"Is that any way to talk to your elder? I was worried about your family, now that your mother can't ply her trade, so I gave you friendly advice. How dare you, a mere teenager, talk back like that? If you had been my daughter-in-law I'd have taught you manners even if I had to drill it into you with a stick," the Gyeonggi woman said and stood up, throwing her cigarette butt into the stove.

"Don't worry, ma'am. I'm not going to be your daughter-in-law. What a provoking, interfering woman!"

"You dare call me 'woman,' you impertinent slut! I'll teach you manners! I'll have you put in jail for a hundred days and let them torture you!"

The air was rife with war clouds. Heunggyu opened his door and tried to soothe his mother, and Jeongmin also opened his door and looked out. Junho's mother ran in from the store in the outer quarters and tried to make peace.

"Calm down, both of you. Both of you have come far, far away from your hometowns to survive. So, you shouldn't let yourselves be upset. Sunhwa has had a hard day and night at the CIC so she's naturally on edge. You shouldn't mind what she says."

"How can I not, when I am snubbed by such a young thing?" the Gyeonggi woman said, then turned to me and asked, "Is there someone in the outhouse?"

"Yes, there is," I replied.

"We ought to move to somewhere else. As the ancient sage said, you should pick your neighbors wisely. I can't stand this any more. And we might get into trouble because of bad neighbors," she said, and shouted towards her daughter in the room. "Miseon, get up and make breakfast. Grill the mackerel. You come home so late these days even though the school is out, so you get up late."

Junho's father came out of the outhouse. Knowing how the Gyeonggi woman unscrupulously breaks into the queue, I stepped into the toilet quickly. The Gyeonggi woman kept complaining. She was obviously referring to Jeongtae, and her words were akin to a curse, so my heart sank.

"To try crossing the armistice line to go North is sheer idiocy! Doesn't he know how closely the border is guarded? And what does he think he can do in the North? The man and the woman must be stark mad to try to go back to that hell! Aren't they sick and tired of the Communists? Such idiots deserve to be shot to death on the spot! Three million people have died on account of the war, and the whole country is haunted by their ghosts. How can they think of going to live among the red fiends?"

"Ma'am, you shouldn't speak such malevolent words, even in anger," Jeongmin protested. Heunggyu and Junho's father also tried to stop the Gyeonggi woman's ill-tempered tirade. Amazingly, the Gyeonggi woman had already obtained detailed information concerning Jeongtae.

Could it be true that Jeongtae had been arrested trying to cross the armistice line to go North? Could such a thing really have happened? Is the North a better place to live in than the South, enough to risk your life to reach? And what happened to the Gimcheon woman and her son Boksul? Did they also try to go North? Then, could it be that Boksul's father is alive in the North? The questions tumbled through my mind as I strained to relieve myself. Had the Gyeonggi woman not urged me to come out quickly, I would have kept squatting there trying to take a shit and gone on dreaming up mental puzzles.

It was three days later that the Pyongyang woman returned home, looking like someone out of her wits. From the next day, she went out to the black market again to sell dyed and mended military uniforms. The CIC soldier and Detective Kang visited our house to question her further. Around that time, the incident that Jeongtae had been involved in came to be known in the house. The source of information was the Gyeonggi woman. "Maybe the Gyeonggi woman has bored a hole in the wall between her room and the Pyongyang family's and keeps eavesdropping day and night, just like a rat. That woman can't rest easy unless she has ferreted out everybody's secrets, right down to the tiniest detail," Mother remarked. In any case, the Gyeonggi woman's report was so plausible that the inhabitants of the house could not help listening to her, albeit allowing for some exaggeration and embellishment.

One day, I overheard the Gyeonggi woman talking to Junho's father in his store as she snacked on baked sweet potatoes.

"Jeongtae tried to defect to the North with the Gimcheon woman and Boksul. I understand that there are many stragglers of the People's Army and the Communist partisans defecting to the north even now, in the mountainous areas of the Taebaek Range. So they have their established routes and guides. Anyway, the Gimcheon woman and her son crossed the border safely, but Jeongtae was arrested by the Korean soldiers. Isn't it strange that a woman could cross the border with a child but a young man failed to? I think we can make two guesses. There are crossings along railroads, you know. We hear on the news of railroad officers dying at those crossings while trying to save women and children walking over the tracks. So, it could be that Jeongtae helped the Gimcheon woman and Boksul over the border and was arrested while trying to climb over the barbed wire fence. Another possibility is that Jeongtae helped the Gimcheon woman and her son go North and was coming back to Daegu himself. That's my guess. What do you think?" the Gyeonggi woman asked.

Mrs. An, the housekeeper, also obtained information from somewhere and told my mother. Mr. Ju, the wood-splitter, often passed through Janggwan-dong Alley and stopped at Junho's father's store, where Mrs. An would come out to talk with him. Afterwards, she often opened the door between our room and the store and tipped my mother as to what was going on.

The landlady's own family had been famous in the Gimcheon area as a *yangban* family that produced cabinet ministers over many generations. But from the last years of the Joseon Dynasty, the men of that house had engaged in resistance activities against foreign powers, especially the Japanese, so inevitably, the house had suffered decline in worldly terms. The Gimcheon woman's husband was an intellectual who attended college during the Japanese occupation years, but owing to his Communist activities, he met national liberation in a Gimcheon jail. With the outbreak of the Korean War, when the Communists occupied most of the South, he was made the vice chairman of the Gimcheon City People's Committee, and when the Communists were beaten back by the UN forces he fled North to avoid retaliation by the Republic. The family that lived in the outer quarters before the Gimcheon woman was a second cousin of the landlady who came back from Japan after national liberation and defected to the North when the Korean War broke out. With so many communists in the maternal family, Seongjun had difficulty getting clearance for his passport, and that was why the landlord's family took the trouble of holding a party inviting VIPs connected to security offices. They also seemed to be seeking ways to bribe people in really high places.

As the days passed, more sad news circulated concerning the Pyongyang family. Jeongmin, who was going to apply to the

Seoul National University College of Law, suddenly decided to apply to the College of Medicine of Gyeongbuk University instead. It was because, having an elder brother who was known to be a communist, Jeongmin could not become a judge or a prosecutor even if he passed the National Bar Exam. But because he switched to the science track just a couple of months before the entrance exam, and there was a wide discrepancy between the exam subjects for the humanities and science majors, success in the exam was no longer a sure thing as before. It was also rumored that Sunhwa's engagement to the army captain from the same hometown would have to be broken because an army captain with a communist for a brother-in-law cannot remain a commander of the ROK army. In a word, what Jeongtae did wrought havoc on the entire family. In contrast, the marriage talks of the son and daughter of the Gyeonggi woman seemed to be going smoothly.

One evening, while I was sitting in Junho's father's store, Heunggyu came into the store with his sweetheart. "Would you like to taste baked sweet potatoes?" Heunggyu asked his girlfriend.

"But I already had two creamed rolls," the young lady said shyly.

"Oh, I just wanted to give our good neighbor a little bit of business," Heunggyu said awkwardly and asked, "Won't you come in and say hello to my mother?"

"Oh, I'm afraid it's rather late to just pop in to say hello. And I haven't brought any present, either. I guess I'll say good-bye for today. See you in the bakery the day after tomorrow," the girl said.

"Let me walk you to your house," Heunggyu said. The two sweethearts walked toward Jongro Street. The young lady wasn't at all pretentious like most daughters of rich families. She was wearing a brown sweater over dark trousers and wasn't wearing any make-up. And she wasn't slim like fashionable ladies, either. She looked more innocent and good-natured than refined. When Heungyu appeared in the store again, whistling, Junho's mother complimented him with, "You have chosen a really nice girl." Junho's mother must have noted similar points about the girl as I had.

Miseon's romance with the American army captain named James seemed to be going on well, too. The Gyeonggi woman bragged that Miseon would be leaving for America with Captain James, who was being ordered back home in the spring. Captain James now acted like a prospective son-in-law, and sometimes strode into the house to present his mother-in-law with a military duffle bag filled with American goods. The Gyeonggi woman exhibited the goods throughout the neighborhood and sold some of them to the landlady's family and other neighbors. Heunggyu treated me and my siblings to delicious cookies and chocolates. When the Gyeonggi woman bragged about Captain James, Seongjun looked out of his room with a furious face. After listening for a while, he closed his door with a loud clatter and played American pop songs on his radio at full volume. But he had no one save himself to blame for his loss, as it was he who had begged Miseon to attend the party.

According to Mrs. An's report to my mother, Seongjun had said to his grandmother over a dinner table, "I can't tell the age of Americans very well, but I don't think Captain James is a bachelor. I think he must be at least thirty. He must have a wife and children waiting for him in America. Miseon is sure to be discarded after the captain has made a plaything of her."

According to the Pyongyang woman's report to my mother, the Gyeonggi woman advised her daughter in this way: "I know it was to win the heart of Captain James that you went to the party in that scandalous dress. I know what's in my own daughter's mind. But you mustn't sleep with him until you are in America as his wife. And you mustn't board the plane until you see his divorce papers with your own eyes. If you take one false step, you'll ruin your whole life. You must be level-headed and prudent. That's the only way to become a winner. A woman has only one chance in life, you know that." The Pyongyang woman had overheard this advice through the wall between her room and the Gyeonggi family's. The Pyongyang woman had dropped in on Mother after visiting Jeongtae, who had been transferred to the police jail from the intelligence agency.

"He was so haggard he was mere skin and bones. He stated at the investigation that he loved Communism enough to risk his life, so he was going to go North because he found an underground partisan to go with him. I guess it'll be hard for him to come out of jail alive. He was arrested because he broke into a cough the moment he began scaling the barbed wire fence. I guess that disease will kill him. We survived that furnace of American bombing only to lose him like this," the Pyongyang woman lamented, sobbing.

It occurred to me that the underground partisan Jeongtae is said to have referred to might be the mysterious man with the knife scar on his face. It seems that the man and the Gimcheon woman and Boksul were able to cross the border but Jeongtae's cough gave him away just as he was climbing the barbed wire fence, and he was arrested by the military patrol.

10

From the middle of February, the days grew noticeably longer. At night, the temperature continued to drop to below twenty degrees Celsius, and the papered door, whipped by the night wind, wailed pitifully. So, I always went to sleep with my youngest brother Gilsu in my arms, as if he were a stove to keep me warm, even though he coughed in his sleep. But towards noon when the sunshine spread, the day grew warm and bright.

The influenza that year was so severe that Gilsu stayed in bed for over a month, but he survived the cold and began to play outside. As Mother said, it was a miracle that Gilsu survived the winter without the benefit of any medicine. But Gilsu was not a lively and playful child any more. His hair had all fallen out, and his legs, none too sturdy to begin with, had thinned like a bird's. He could not walk normally and shuffled along, holding on to walls.

"Brodo, let's go see Unk," Gilsu often said to me, meaning for me to take him out to Junho's father's store. When I carried Gilsu, who was as light as new cottonwool, to Junho's father's store, Junho's father greeted him with, "How are you, my dear?" and picked out a small baked sweet potato to give him. Gilsu could no longer follow Junho around to play with him, so he sat on the doorsill of the store and ate the small baked sweet potato for more than an hour, tearing it in tiny, tiny morsels and holding the morsels in his mouth until the flesh was quite melted.

I still recall vividly Gilsu as he sat on the doorsill under the February sun watching the people passing down the lane and taking a tiny morsel off the baked sweet potato with his spider-like fingers. In fact, when I recall that cold winter with the wailing of the doorpaper, my life in that house with the sunken courtyard looms up before me like a lonely lamp hung in a windy, wintry sky.

Gilsu, who had warmed up my winter nights like a puppy or a kitten survived the cruel influenza of that winter to live three more years, but died with the "dirty times," before our family was able to shake off poverty. Because of his uncertain gait and pronunciation, he was refused admission to primary school and died one cold winter night of meningitis, at age eight, without ever having had the benefit of hospital care. At the time, we were renting a room in the boarding quarters of the Deokje Oriental Clinic on Medicine Lane, at about a hundred yard's distance from the house with the sunken courtyard. Gilsu's body was put in an empty rice sack made of straw and was carried on an A-frame to a nameless valley behind the lake on the western edge of Daegu to be buried there.

The year after Gilsu's death, I was to realize how unfair even death was in this world. I was a high school sophomore at the time. In the late fall of that year, I saw a funeral procession that made Janggwan-dong Lane overflow with scores of funeral banners and filled Medicine Lane with dozens of automobile sedans. It was the funeral of the old lady of the house with the sunken courtyard. She died at over eighty years of age. Her son, our former landlord, who had grown by then to be one of the foremost figures in the textile industry of Daegu, was marching in the procession clad in hemp mourning garments. He had grown quite pot-bellied. The limousine carrying her coffin and heading toward the family burial ground in Seonsan county was covered all over with white chrysanthemums, except for the windows.

Gilsu had died after living less than one eighth the lifespan of the old lady and without ever having eaten his fill of pure white rice. His pitiful death made me wonder if it was in retribution for some crime he'd committed in a former life, for which he had earned the wrath of the Creator. Mother often repeated, with tears running down her cheeks, "Gilsu was as guileless as anyone who ever lived. He craved food a little, but he had no other greed. He never lied, nor deceived anyone. So whenever he dies, he'll go straight to Heaven. And he'll live a blissful life there. It makes my heart a little lighter to think he'll have his reward in Heaven." When Gilsu heard this, his haggard face would light up with a smile and he would say, as if Heaven was just next door, "I'll play with Fada in Heven." It looks now like it had been a prophecy. I still believe that his illness that deprived him of all flesh and hair and left him mere skin and bones was caused by undernourishment. Lack of nutrition made it impossible for his brain and internal organs to develop and function as they ought. It sears my heart even today to recall emaciated Gilsu reiterating throughout the day that his head "hut" and continually yearning for food. I try to erase my memory of Gilsu by replacing it with the image of the Ethiopian child haggard with undernourishment. I recall Gilsu more often as he was during the months in the house with the sunken courtyard, drawing quick breaths in my arms in the cold room, like a puppy sleeping under the verandah. Now, my other brother Giljung and I each have a classy apartment and sleep in the winter in a well-heated room, kicking off our coverlets. Could Gilsu be looking down at his older brothers as an angel on winter nights, or as a lonely and warm lamp lighting up the winter sky? Maybe Gilsu's Heaven is an abode where there is no hunger and no cold. Has Gilsu found our father in Heaven and is he playing with him there, or is he searching for him, peering into all corners of this country with his crossed eyes, muttering 'Fada,' to find the father whose face he can't remember and whom he doesn't know whether he's alive or dead? Not knowing the ways of Heaven, I search the sky for an especially lonely star, one that twinkles all alone, and dimly shines and fades, and try to discern in it my unfortunate brother's face.

Jeongtae's trial began in March of that year, after Seongjun had left for the U.S. to study and forsythias were in bloom in the flowerbed of the house with the sunken courtyard. To leave for study in the States was at that time as rare and glorious an event as becoming a cabinet minister. We tenants of the house had all imagined that the Gimcheon woman's defection to the North had quashed her close relative Seongjun's dream of going to the States once and for all. But it seems that his father's money and connections could smooth out even that fatal obstacle. Seongjun must have felt a lingering attachment for Miseon. Before leaving, while bidding good-bye to the tenants of the middle quarters, he told Miseon that he would write when he arrived in the States and said he hoped to see her there. But as America was a vast country, it didn't seem likely that he could find her in it.

In Jeongtae's trial at the district court, the prosecutor demanded life imprisonment, and he was sentenced to twenty years. The Pyongyang woman said, with a heavy sigh, that if Jeongtae had stated that he regretted his communist sympathies, the recommended sentence would have been fifteen years and he would have been given ten years. The inquisitive Gyeonggi woman tagged along with her neighbor to the trial and reported that Jeongtae gave a forty-minute speech on the need for the North Korea to liberate the South and the need for the realization of a Communist republic on the entire peninsula.

"He was a man of spirit all right. Though he kept coughing fitfully, he asserted that the United States was responsible for the division of Korea and that South Korea is a colony of the United

States. And whenever he referred to America, he always called it the U.S. imperialists. And he said that the whole of South Korea, being in the grip of former pro-Japanese individuals in political, economic, military, and police sectors, was proof that it was a colony of the U.S., which was trying to rule South Korea just as the Japanese had in the old days. The judge put a stop to his tirade. Because he kept saying words like oligarchical capitalism, imperialistic colonial economic system, class conflict, and war for liberation, the judge asked him why he had fled to the South. Jeongtae answered that he and his father believed that due to the intervention of Communist China, the liberation of South Korea was a certainty, so he fled South to escape the carpet bombing by the United States and wait for liberation by the Communists." The Gyeonggi woman gave such a vivid report that it was as if we were present at the trial.

Jeongtae refused the services of the defence lawyers provided by the government, refused to appeal, and chose to spend his days in prison "until the day South Korea is united with North Korea."

I graduated from a provincial college and immediately got a job in Seoul with a publishing company. But I married a girl from Daegu, recommended to me by my aunt who lived till then in Janggwan-dong. My wife's family still lives on the hill in Bongdeok-dong in Daegu. So, I used to spend my summer holidays in Daegu, the hottest town in the country, staying with my wife's family and roaming that city of many memories. Now, my children are preparing for the university entrance exam and have no time for vacationing, and I also quit my editorial job quite a few years back to devote myself to writing, so we don't vacation as a family any more. But until a few years ago, when I was still a salaried worker, I vacationed in Daegu with my family. I met a former college classmate that day, shared a drink with him even though it was broad daylight, and walked along the Jungangtong

Road. It was approaching six o'clock but the sun was still high. Walking along, I noted a signboard outside a new five-story building with a terribly familiar name on it. It said "Dr. Jeongmin Choi's Internal Clinic." I thought it could be no other than my very next door neighbor in the house with the sunken courtyard. Jeongmin had applied and gotten admitted to medical school at the time. After a slight hesitation, I walked up the staircase to the clinic, which was using the second and the third floors. Jeongmin, who was then in his late forties, had already turned half grey. Naturally, he didn't recognize me at first. His face, now bespectacled and no longer famished-looking, seemed strange to me, too. I introduced myself and we grasped hands tightly. Since it was closing time for the clinic, he and I went to the tearoom in the basement of the building. We each ordered a glass of iced coffee. Naturally our talk turned to the days we spent in the house with the sunken courtyard and our fellow tenants of those days.

"You remember Junho's father, don't you?" Jeongmin asked. Of course, I remembered Junho's father.

"He is running a bookstore on the road from the Chilseong Market to Gyeongbuk National University. I ran into him a while ago while passing that street. And his wife was running a small convenience store right next to the bookstore. The two-story building with the stores on the first floor and the living space for the family on the second floor belonged to them. I shared a glass of beer with Junho's father in the beer hall nearby. He had grown much older."

I asked how Jeongmin's own mother, the Pyongyang woman, was faring. "She is living with me. My sister married an engineer, and her son has just started working for a company after graduating from college this spring. Oh, your mother must be not too many years younger than mine?"

"She passed away three years ago, because of high blood pressure," I said, and hesitantly asked about Jeongtae.

"Oh, my brother. Well, you remember it was at the beginning of 1955 that that incident happened. He lived out his twenty years' prison sentence with only one lung, and was released in January of 1975. But in July of that year, the thing called the "national security law" was enacted, so he was jailed again after only seven months of liberty, for declining to convert to capitalism. In name, it was 'protective custody,' but that's the same thing as imprisonment, of course. To harbor that ideology through all these bitter years . . . it's nothing short of amazing. He's spent 28 years in prison now, just as many years in prison as out of it. His one remaining lung has also deteriorated, so the other day I went to see him in Cheongju Protective Detention Center and pleaded with him to sign the 'conversion' papers and be released, as it is Mother's last wish to eat and sleep with her first-born if only for one day before she passes away. But my brother made no response. My mother is old, but it's not wholly due to her age that she has almost lost her eyesight. It's from crying continuously." Jeongmin couldn't go on, and took a handkerchief out of his pocket and removed his spectacles to dry his eyes.

Two months ago, I read from the newspaper and magazine articles about Mr. Seo Jun-shik. A Korean resident in Japan, he came to study in the College of Law at Seoul National University, was arrested in 1971 by the Security Headquarters of the Korean Army as a member of the espionage circle of students from abroad, and was sentenced to seven years in prison. But due to the enactment in July 1975 of the "national security law," he was incarcerated for ten more years, after thrice refusing to convert. He was finally released last May with the "restricted domicile" proviso. I had recalled Jeongtae while reading the article on Mr Seo in the monthly magazine *Well with a Deep Source*. His words, reported on page eighty-eight of volume eighty-eight of that magazine, speak for all the Jeongtaes of this country:

What is most cruel to me is that old communists who have only a limited lifespan left due to fatal illnesses are not released to enable them to spend the remainder of their lives with their families, but are kept in prison until they are in critical condition and are continually pressured to sign 'conversion' papers, with promises that they will be instantly released upon making an oath of 'conversion.' This obviously is not "imprisonment on account of clear and evident danger of re-commission of crime." I have lived here for a long time, but have only seen one man who signed 'conversion' papers so that he could spend the remainder of his life with his family. All the rest kept their human dignity and right of conscience in the very face of death and struggled with their illnesses until they were released just before death. These are Song Suneui, who died of the cancer of the liver, Choi Jeomsu, who also died of liver cancer, Gong Indu, who died of a brain tumor, Mun Gap-su, who died of stomach cancer, and Yi Sangryul, who died of an invasion of parasites in his brain. I can never forget these old men . . .

Most of these men were arrested and sentenced in the early 1950s before or after the armistice, either for helping the Communists or for spying for them. They had served their long prison sentences but were imprisoned again on account of the "national security law." If Jeongtae is still alive, as an unconverted Communist, he must be about fifty-five.

After Seonrye passed the entrance examination to Deaegu Teacher Training School, I submitted my application for entrance to Gyeongsang Middle School. Gyeongsang Middle School was not a first-rate school in Daegu, but it was not a third-rate school, either. It was a middle school that middle-range students applied to, and had in its favor low tuition, being a publicly funded school. I began studying only two weeks before the entrance exam, with my sister, who was now freed from her own entrance exam, as my tutor.

"Oh, I didn't know you were so poor in math. You can't even do fifth grade math, so how can you solve the math problems on the middle school entrance exam?" Seonrye often fretted while teaching me. As a matter of fact, while attending primary school in Jinyeong working at the same time as a kitchen boy in a tavern, I had few textbooks and notebooks and did little in the way of preparatory study and review, being under nobody's supervision. And as it was a very rural primary school, what they taught was very elementary, too. During the year in Daegu, also, I only pretended to study before Mother's eyes and in fact gorged myself on children's story books and novels, so I had forgotten almost everything I learned at primary school.

"If you fail in the entrance exam, you can forget about going to middle school. It's a waste of time for a person without brains to try to study. You can keep delivering newspapers and do street vending for the rest of the day, like your friend Hanju," Mother told me, to my greater discouragement.

It was around that time that Miseon finally obtained marriage papers with Captain James and left for the States as his spouse. Miseon was extremely sorry to be leaving without being able to attend her brother's wedding. Captain James promised again and again that he would invite his mother-in-law over to the States. Even so, the Gyeonggi woman asked her daughter tearfully to take her to the States as soon as possible. But as the tenants of the house with the sunken courtyard all had to disperse in mid-April of that year, I don't know if the Gyeonggi woman realized her dream of going to America.

It was because the landlord's business prospered so well that we tenants had to be thrown out. The fiat to vacate the rooms came from the landlord himself late in March, right after I failed the entrance exam to Gyeongsang Middle School. One Sunday morning, we had just finished breakfast when Mrs. An came over to our rooms and told us that the landlord wanted to see all the tenants.

"He's going to tell us to vacate the room," Mother said sullenly, but without showing much surprise. From a few days previously, surveyors had been striding all over the middle and outer courtyards, referring to a land map and measuring this width and that length. So, the tenants guessed that something was going to happen. As we had promised to vacate our room for Mr. Jeong of the jewellery shop, we had already secured a room to move into. The new room was the side wing of a tiled-roof house at the end of Janggwan-dong lane almost at the entrance of Jongro Street. We were to move there on the eighth of April. We had to deposit fifty thousand *hwan* for security and pay a monthly rent of thirty-five hundred *hwan*. When I heard that, I was astonished that Mother had saved enough money for the security deposit, making us go hungry throughout the previous summer. I admired her for it a little, but in fact, I resented her fortitude more.

"I heard that the whole middle quarters, and this room and the store, and even the main gate will be torn down. And a new Western-style house is going to be built," Mrs. An said.

"Yes, I heard that from the Gyeonggi woman," Mother said.

Mrs. An turned to go, but turned again and said hesitantly, "Mrs. Kim, I'm going to leave this house, too." She was blushing all over like a teenager.

"Why? Are you going back to your hometown of Seongju?"

"No . . . You know that Mr. Ju, who split firewood last winter? Well, he and I decided to go to the country and farm together. My family is going to give us a small patch of land, so we are going to till the land, raise pigs, and clear some more land. He said he would like to spend his life tilling the land in some quiet countryside, and I thought that would be nice, too."

"Oh, congratulations! I'm sure Mr. Ju is a born farmer. He's diligent and kind-hearted, so you'll have an easy life with him. He's lonely, so look after him well and give him plenty of affection. I wish you lots of children and a long and prosperous life together," Mother said, sniffling from emotion. Mrs. An left before the middle quarters were demolished, saying that she must not miss sowing time.

A few years ago, KBS, the national television network, had a marathon campaign of "Find Your Lost Family," in which those people who had lost their family and kin during the Korean War came forward with the names and descriptions of their missing family, posted them on the walls all along the KBS building, and tried to find or be found by their family. I turned on the television whenever I had the time and looked for the figure of Mr. Ju. I still remember that he was from Samjeong-myeon in Suan County of Hwanghae-do Province, from his having repeated the name again and again. But I never spotted Mr. Ju among all those people looking for their families. Of course, it could be that he had already found his family and therefore had no business in the campaign, or that he was there to look for his family while I was not watching. In any case, I did not see him then, but I saw a middle-aged woman's tearful face which had a faint resemblance to that of the little orphan girl brought to the house to serve as Mrs. An's assistant. The woman was identified as Okkeum, who used to live in a certain orphanage in Daegu. I can't be sure that she was that little girl Oggi, but I think it's a reasonable guess that they were the same person.

Aside from that, I saw in a newspaper a person who had some relation to the house with the sunken courtyard. It was in the year that I finished my military service, so it was in the fall of

1966. I was working on the campus newspaper in the Gyeongbuk Printing Company when I took up a daily paper to skim through. Then I saw a tiny photo of a person who looked very much like the suspicious man who came to visit the Gimcheon woman from time to time. His longish face resembled the man's, but the photograph was too small for me to tell whether he had a knife scar or not. The article that went with the photo said: "Undercover Spy Arrested. The spy has been working in the Daegu area as a North Korean agent from immediately after the armistice. Between 1954 and 1963 he went to North Korea three times to hand over various military secrets of the South. He has also been active in winning over converts to expand the Communist network."

My guess could have been wrong, but I decided that the man was the very same man who had the long knife scar running from his left cheek to his chin. I imagined that it was he who led the Gimcheon woman and Jeongtae to the armistice line to guide them over to the North. Whenever I imagined the breathless moment in which Jeongtae's party climbed over the wire fence, I always called up the face of the man with the knife scar on his face as the pathfinder.

When I followed Mother into the inner courtyard, all the tenants were gathered along the platform of the inner quarters. The landlord was standing on the verandah, with his arms folded.

"I am sorry to be announcing unwelcome news so early in the morning, but I must ask you to vacate all your rooms before the tenth of next month. As all of you were witnesses last summer, this house always suffers flooding in the summer because of the sunken courtyard. So, we're going to demolish the whole of the middle quarters and raise the courtyard to be level with the street. And we're going to build a two-story Western-style residence. As we have to put the roof on before the rainy season begins, the earlier you vacate your rooms, the better for us. The store and the servants' room need to be torn down to build a chauffeur's room and an overseer's room. As you know, we installed a telephone line last month, and I bought a new jeep, so we need a chauffeur's room."

When the landlord stopped speaking, Junho's mother stepped up to my mother and whispered into her ear: "Isn't that Mr. Jeong a thief? How could he exact from you the six hundred *hwan* compensation, when he must have known that the room and the store were going to be torn down, so he can't have any claim to the room?"

Mother just smiled. I had already called on Mr. Jeong at the jewellery shop to hand over to him the six hundred *hwan* for March. And Junho's mother knew the arrangement between my mother and Mr. Jeong.

All the tenants of the house with the sunken courtyard vacated their rooms on the 10th of April. The Pyongyang family moved to Dongin-dong, at the other end of the black market; Junho's family moved to the refugee town in Bokhyeon-dong, near the apple orchards. The Gyeonggi family was lucky in that Heunggyu's bride's family rented a whole house for the newlyweds, so the groom and the mother-in-law both relocated to their pleasant new house. My family moved to our newly rented room, which was only about a hundred yards from the house with the sunken courtyard.

One day in mid-April of that year, on my way to deliver the newspapers, I witnessed the four rooms of the middle quarters of the house with the sunken courtyard, the room in the outer quarter with the attached store, and the lofty gate all being torn down. To me, every particle of those structures was saturated with the sorrows and tears and anger of the sixteen poor people who once regarded them as their precious nests. I felt a pain akin to the pain of a corner of my heart being hacked out. I was depressed the whole day.

My life in the ensuing years was gloomy. Only in mid-April of that year was I able to get admission to a middle school and able to wear the school uniform and student cap that I had so longed for during the whole preceding year. I was able to get into a middle school because I one day caught sight of an ad leaflet pasted on an electric pole about a newly inaugurated middle school looking for students. The name, Suseong Middle School, came from the Suseong Bridge on Bangcheon Creek. When it opened it had no building of its own, so it began teaching in borrowed classrooms on the campus of the high school affiliated with the Gyeongbuk University Teachers' College. The faculty consisted of five people including the principal, and the pupils numbered barely forty, consisting mainly of those whose school life had been interrupted because of the war, like myself. Quite a few of them were young adults, who had carbuncles all over their faces and showed traces of beards. Some of them went to the toilet to smoke during recesses, and some of them, nominally middle school freshmen, bullied high school students and exacted money out of them. Even those students who were not outright delinquents had no interest in studying, so many of them just sat in the classes doing something else or clamored for the teacher to tell them "anecdotes." Most of the teachers also went about their job half-heartedly, perhaps because of the lack of any school tradition or because they were depressed by having been transferred to such a low-prestige school. I was severely disappointed with middle school life, but as I had failed the entrance exam to Gyeongsang Middle School, I had no choice but to attend the school which after all offered the advantage of low tuition.

Then one time late in April of that year, during a day of my listless trips to school and my newspaper delivery routine, I was to witness the sunken courtyard of my old residence being filled with the new earth brought over by dump trucks. I stood there watching the scene, thinking to myself that my first year in Daegu was being buried under that earth. It filled my heart with sorrow. At the same time, I was glad that my frequent hunger and sorrow would be buried under earth, too, never to reveal any trace. And a new two-story Western house was going to stand on it, as if to press my wretched memories into the earth for good.

Kim Won-il was born in 1942 in Chinyong, Korea. He published his first collection of stories, *Soul of Darkness*, in 1973 and it won the Hyundai Munhak Literary Prize in 1974. His first full-length novel, *Twilight*, was published in 1978. A novelist with more than two dozen books to his credit, Kim's primary subject is the tragic circumstances surrounding the division of Korea.

Suh Ji-moon was born in 1948 and grew up mostly in Seoul. She has translated numerous classics of Korean fiction and poetry into English.

THE LIBRARY OF KOREAN LITERATURE

The Library of Korean Literature, published by Dalkey Archive Press in collaboration with the Literature Translation Institute of Korea, presents modern classics of Korean literature in translation, featuring the best Korean authors from the late modern period through to the present day. The Library aims to introduce the intellectual and aesthetic diversity of contemporary Korean writing to English-language readers. The Library of Korean Literature is unprecedented in its scope, with Dalkey Archive Press publishing 25 Korean novels and short story collections in a single year.

The series is published in cooperation with the Literature Translation Institute of Korea, a center that promotes the cultural translation and worldwide dissemination of Korean language and culture.

MICHAL AJVAZ, *The Golden Age.*
The Other City.
PIERRE ALBERT-BIROT, *Grabinoulor.*
YUZ ALESHKOVSKY, *Kangaroo.*
FELIPE ALFAU, *Chromos.*
Locos.
IVAN ÂNGELO, *The Celebration.*
The Tower of Glass.
ANTÓNIO LOBO ANTUNES, *Knowledge of Hell.*
The Splendor of Portugal.
ALAIN ARIAS-MISSON, *Theatre of Incest.*
JOHN ASHBERY AND JAMES SCHUYLER, *A Nest of Ninnies.*
ROBERT ASHLEY, *Perfect Lives.*
GABRIELA AVIGUR-ROTEM, *Heatwave and Crazy Birds.*
DJUNA BARNES, *Ladies Almanack.*
Ryder.
JOHN BARTH, *LETTERS.*
Sabbatical.
DONALD BARTHELME, *The King.*
Paradise.
SVETISLAV BASARA, *Chinese Letter.*
MIQUEL BAUÇÀ, *The Siege in the Room.*
RENÉ BELLETTO, *Dying.*
MAREK BIEŃCZYK, *Transparency.*
ANDREI BITOV, *Pushkin House.*
ANDREJ BLATNIK, *You Do Understand.*
LOUIS PAUL BOON, *Chapel Road.*
My Little War.
Summer in Termuren.
ROGER BOYLAN, *Killoyle.*
IGNÁCIO DE LOYOLA BRANDÃO,
Anonymous Celebrity.
Zero.
BONNIE BREMSER, *Troia: Mexican Memoirs.*
CHRISTINE BROOKE-ROSE, *Amalgamemnon.*
BRIGID BROPHY, *In Transit.*
GERALD L. BRUNS, *Modern Poetry and the Idea of Language.*
GABRIELLE BURTON, *Heartbreak Hotel.*
MICHEL BUTOR, *Degrees.*
Mobile.
G. CABRERA INFANTE, *Infante's Inferno.*
Three Trapped Tigers.
JULIETA CAMPOS,
The Fear of Losing Eurydice.
ANNE CARSON, *Eros the Bittersweet.*
ORLY CASTEL-BLOOM, *Dolly City.*
LOUIS-FERDINAND CÉLINE, *Castle to Castle.*
Conversations with Professor Y.
London Bridge.
Normance.
North.
Rigadoon.
MARIE CHAIX, *The Laurels of Lake Constance.*
HUGO CHARTERIS, *The Tide Is Right.*
ERIC CHEVILLARD, *Demolishing Nisard.*

MARC CHOLODENKO, *Mordechai Schamz.*
JOSHUA COHEN, *Witz.*
EMILY HOLMES COLEMAN, *The Shutter of Snow.*
ROBERT COOVER, *A Night at the Movies.*
STANLEY CRAWFORD, *Log of the S.S. The Mrs Unguentine.*
Some Instructions to My Wife.
RENÉ CREVEL, *Putting My Foot in It.*
RALPH CUSACK, *Cadenza.*
NICHOLAS DELBANCO, *The Count of Concord.*
Sherbrookes.
NIGEL DENNIS, *Cards of Identity.*
PETER DIMOCK, *A Short Rhetoric for Leaving the Family.*
ARIEL DORFMAN, *Konfidenz.*
COLEMAN DOWELL,
Island People.
Too Much Flesh and Jabez.
ARKADII DRAGOMOSHCHENKO, *Dust.*
RIKKI DUCORNET, *The Complete Butcher's Tales.*
The Fountains of Neptune.
The Jade Cabinet.
Phosphor in Dreamland.
WILLIAM EASTLAKE, *The Bamboo Bed.*
Castle Keep.
Lyric of the Circle Heart.
JEAN ECHENOZ, *Chopin's Move.*
STANLEY ELKIN, *A Bad Man.*
Criers and Kibitzers, Kibitzers and Criers.
The Dick Gibson Show.
The Franchiser.
The Living End.
Mrs. Ted Bliss.
FRANÇOIS EMMANUEL, *Invitation to a Voyage.*
SALVADOR ESPRIU, *Ariadne in the Grotesque Labyrinth.*
LESLIE A. FIEDLER, *Love and Death in the American Novel.*
JUAN FILLOY, *Op Oloop.*
ANDY FITCH, *Pop Poetics.*
GUSTAVE FLAUBERT, *Bouvard and Pécuchet.*
KASS FLEISHER, *Talking out of School.*
FORD MADOX FORD,
The March of Literature.
JON FOSSE, *Aliss at the Fire.*
Melancholy.
MAX FRISCH, *I'm Not Stiller.*
Man in the Holocene.
CARLOS FUENTES, *Christopher Unborn.*
Distant Relations.
Terra Nostra.
Where the Air Is Clear.
TAKEHIKO FUKUNAGA, *Flowers of Grass.*
WILLIAM GADDIS, *J R.*
The Recognitions.

SELECTED DALKEY ARCHIVE TITLES